In the
SPACE
left BEHIND

In the SPACE left BEHIND

By Joan Ackermann

Laura Geringer Books
HARPER TEEN
An Imprint of HarperCollins Publishers

I want to thank Laura Geringer for inviting me to write a
novel and for having faith in the outcome. Without her
invitation, I never would have embarked on this journey
and I never would have met Colm or Lloyd Henry. Thank
you so much, Laura, for your steadfast support.
—J.A.

HarperTeen is an imprint of HarperCollins Publishers.

In the Space Left behind
Copyright © 2007 by Joan Ackermann
All rights reserved. Printed in the United States of America.
No part of this book may be used or reproduced in any manner
whatsoever without written permission except in the case of brief
quotations embodied in critical articles and reviews. For information address
HarperCollins Children's Books, a division of HarperCollins Publishers, 1350
Avenue of the Americas, New York, NY 10019.
www.harperteen.com

Library of Congress Cataloging-in-Publication Data
Ackermann, Joan.
    In the space left behind / by Joan Ackermann.—1st ed.
        p.   cm.
    Summary: Fifteen-year-old Colm embarks on a cross-country journey with the
father who abandoned him as a child.
        ISBN-10: 0-06-072255-X (trade bdg.)—ISBN-13: 978-0-06-072255-5 (trade bdg.)
        ISBN-10: 0-06-072256-8 (lib. bdg.) — ISBN-13: 978-0-06-072256-2 (lib. bdg.)
        [1. Fathers and sons—Fiction. 2. Abandoned children—Fiction. 3. Travel—
Fiction.] I. Title.
PZ7.A1828In 2007   2006022172
[Fic]—dc22   CIP
                                                                     AC

Typography by Neil Swaab   1 2 3 4 5 6 7 8 9 10   ❖   First Edition

For Kirven with LOVE

 Chapter One

The night that Colm Drucker's mother got married for the third time, an old paint-encrusted screw gave way outside the house and snapped in half, letting fly a second-story window box jam-packed with sand and artificial flowers. It was a wonder the screw had lasted as long as it had, for it was the only screw in one of the pair of wrought-iron brackets that had supported the heavy window box for more than a decade, offering faint floral cheer to motorists heading north on Palmer Street.

Colm discovered the window box, completely intact, the faded flowers sticking up in the same haphazard arrangement they had held through several winters, in the yard the next morning. Unfortunately, although the window box had survived its steep headlong dive, the family dog had not. The weighty box had landed squarely on

Chester's head. Chester, part Rottweiler, part spaniel, liked to sleep alongside the cool concrete foundation below the dining room on hot summer nights, and the night of Fiona Drucker's wedding was a scorcher.

Holding the dish that contained Chester's breakfast, a few bits of kibble mixed in carefully with a third of a can of wet food, Colm stared down at the dog. Nearly fourteen—a year younger than Colm—Chester had lost the majority of his teeth and couldn't really chew.

Now the dog was still, his head buried under the window box. It must have been an instantaneous death; his rounded brown body and comfortably outstretched legs suggested deep sleep.

Dog dish in hand, Colm looked up at the side of the house and quickly caught a glimpse of the lone remaining bracket protruding beneath his mother's bedroom window. He blinked a few times.

Who would he tell?

No one was home. Fiona was on her honeymoon with Don Schroeder, an old classmate from high school who had just a few months ago showed up on their doorstep after Fiona had mistakenly dialed his number instead of the druggist's. Colm's older sister, Cameron, didn't live with them anymore. She'd moved out a year ago, at age sixteen, after a fight with Fiona. His younger sister—well, *half* sister, though he didn't think of her that way—Bunny, just fourteen months old, was with Fiona and Don en route to Las Vegas.

They were supposed to call that evening and give him the name and number of the hotel where they were staying. It was July Fourth weekend. Colm had expressed concern they might have trouble finding a hotel room on such a popular holiday weekend, but Don, sitting stiffly at their kitchen table, had unflinchingly swigged down a cup of Fiona's slightly burnt black coffee and told Colm he wasn't worried.

"But what will you do if you can't find a room?" Colm had pressed, picturing his mother and Bunny out on a sidewalk in Las Vegas with their new suitcases and no place to stay.

"No prob," Don had answered simply, his focus completely consumed by the sight of Fiona walking away down the hallway and turning to go up the stairs.

Fiona had been a knockout in high school, and her beauty had only deepened with age and strife. Don, a little on the portly side, could not believe his good luck in having won her hand in marriage, and he was drifting these days in somewhat of a stupor.

"Las Vegas is a very popular vacation destination. I bet the hotels book up months in advance."

"Could you pass me a toothpick, sport?"

Colm didn't relish being called sport, but he'd passed Don the shot glass that contained the cinnamon-flavored toothpicks.

Don was a nurse—*a male nurse*, as Fiona enjoyed relating at any opportunity.

"Very nurturing. A caregiver," she'd say longingly, as if she had yearned since childhood for nothing more than for someone to come along and give her care.

Fiona had wanted to get married on the Friday of July Fourth weekend because she said her wedding day was *her* independence day—independence from a shabbily constructed life, much of it spent in other people's homes, cleaning. Cleaning houses was Fiona's primary means of support ever since Colm's father, an inveterate gambler and a liar, had left them years ago.

Would he tell them about Chester when they called? He was concerned the news might ruin their honeymoon. Well, not ruin it, but maybe put a damper on it. Perhaps better not to mention it. But would they be more upset to come home and find out it had happened and he hadn't told them?

He could hear cars speeding by the house, ignoring the rusted SLOW CHILDREN PLAYING sign, the motorists' view of the tragedy blocked by the neatly trimmed hedge. All

4

these years, Colm had worried that Chester would run out on the road and be hit by a car, and look what had happened to him, safely chained up by the house.

A bead of sweat dripped down his face. It was eight in the morning and all signs pointed to another day of stifling humidity and record heat.

Maybe he'd call Cameron and tell her, though his sister had never been particularly fond of Chester. And she was probably still asleep, hung over from the wedding.

For a while they'd doubted that Cameron would even show up—she and Fiona hadn't been speaking for over a month—but she and her boyfriend, Todd, appeared at the Pittsfield City Hall an astonishing half hour early. Fiona had burst into tears at the sight of her daughter sitting on the granite steps out front, Cameron's toothy, cockeyed grin greeting her in a friendly undeclared temporary truce.

They'd all had a surprisingly good time at the event, and everyone seemed to go the extra mile to get along. After the signing of the marriage certificate, Don had taken everyone—all eight of them—out to dinner at the Emerald Room atop the Hilton Hotel.

Compared to his predecessors—husbands and suitors—Don stacked up pretty well. He wasn't a felon, or twenty years younger than Fiona, and he spoke fluent

English. (Bunny's father, a Portuguese sailor who had picked Fiona up in the parking lot of a Dunkin' Donuts, never mastered much English.)

Up in the Emerald Room, aided by the champagne and giddy from the event, Don had stepped up to the plate in his role as groom, regaling the wedding party with the one joke he knew and a few carefully rehearsed anecdotes. He had told the story well of how he'd answered the phone and been curiously charmed when some woman had asked sweetly whether she could get another refill on an expired prescription.

Don also managed to smoothly interject how he'd been elected class treasurer for both their sophomore and junior years. Although Fiona distinctly remembered not voting for him, now the title of "class treasurer" made her catch her breath slightly as she reached under the table and proudly clasped his hand.

She'd been off by one digit, dialing 2748 instead of the number for Brooks Pharmacy, 2758.

"Thank God for that lazy pinky," Don said, leaning over and nuzzling his nose into Fiona's neck. Which was ridiculous, Colm thought, because Fiona didn't dial with her pinky and laziness had nothing to do with it.

Colm, holding Bunny, whose tiny arms were clasped tightly around his neck, had studied his mother's smile as she tilted her head toward Don's, closing her eyes and melting into him. Normally Colm loved to stare at her smile and lose himself in it, but now it seemed curiously removed from him. It seemed to stretch far, far away—far from the Emerald Room, far from Massachusetts. It was already on its way across the country to Las Vegas, already on its way to a distant world where his mother would never have to vacuum another person's living room, never have to scrub someone else's stove top, never have to drive across town to buy rubber gloves in quantity on sale.

Colm noticed, standing in the yard, that his right foot had fallen asleep.

He noticed, too, a large horsefly walking around on Chester's back, and it took him a second to remember why the sunlit brown flesh hadn't quivered to eject the fly the way it always did.

He wiped his brow with his free hand.

After breakfast he would jump on his bike and head over to Larmon's Hardware to pick up some wood screws to reattach the bracket. On his way home he'd stop by Mr. Hafferty's, their neighbor, to borrow his ladder. Colm mowed Mr. Hafferty's lawn and often did little odd jobs around the house for him. They had a heavy retractable ladder, but it was a pain in the neck to use and needed a new rope.

It occurred to Colm that he could dump the ancient hardened sand and artificial flowers, buy a bag of potting soil, and plant some real flowers in the window box for Fiona's return. She would love that. Geraniums, maybe. Or begonias. She liked begonias.

Inside the house, the phone rang.

Colm stayed put.

His mind moved toward the back door, toward going inside and answering the phone, but he couldn't quite ride his body over there. Something inside him was jammed.

Maybe it was his mother calling, giving him an update on their travels. With this thought, he firmly stepped sideways onto his left foot and hurried across the yard toward the back door, ignoring the pins and needles in his numbed right foot. He raced through the back hall, through the kitchen, down the front hall, and into the living room to the phone.

Still holding the dog dish, he reached for the receiver.

"Hello?"

There was silence.

"Hello? Mom?"

Someone on the other end cleared his throat.

"Um . . ."

"Who is this?"

". . . Uh . . . Lloyd . . ."

Colm, disappointed, turned toward the window.

"Lloyd who?"

More silence.

"Lloyd Henry."

Colm didn't say anything. The name was familiar, but at that particular moment Colm was unable to remember why.

"Is this Colm?"

"*Who* is this?"

"Your father." He cleared his throat again. "It's your father."

Colm held the receiver for a few moments with no change of expression whatsoever. He might have been standing in an outfield, glove in hand, waiting for a high pop-up to drop. Something inside him landed, and he hung up.

His attention turned to the dog dish in his other hand.

A deepening bruise in his chest caught at his breath as he slowly walked up the hall and into the kitchen. After turning the dish over in the sink, he ran some cold water, turned on the garbage disposal, and watched Chester's uneaten food disappear.

Chapter Two

"**M**etal fatigue."

That was the diagnosis Pete Wartella had given Colm at Larmon's Hardware when he'd showed him the broken nub of screw later that morning.

Although Colm was unfamiliar with that particular phrase, he knew Pete well. In fact, Pete, the manager, had on numerous occasions offered Colm a job as salesman since he knew the inventory so well. Colm had an uncanny knack for fixing things and spent a lot of time at the store buying parts and hardware.

As the man of the Drucker household, Colm had taken it upon himself to learn plumbing, electricity, and other mechanical skills useful for the upkeep and maintenance of a house. He enjoyed these pursuits and considered working for Pete, but at fifteen he was legally too young to drive the forklift out back, or handle any of the power tools in the lumberyard. Being a salesman didn't hold much appeal for him.

"Really? You're only fifteen?" Pete would say, and Colm would nod.

It was hard to believe because Colm was not only tall and sturdily built for his age, but he projected the earnest, steady focus of someone much older. Colm had inherited Fiona's striking good looks—penetrating brown eyes and a head of thick curly hair. Sometimes strange women would come up and ask him if they could touch it. His response was usually to aim for the nearest barbershop and get a haircut.

"You could use the forklift when no one was around," Pete hinted once when Colm was helping him locate a box of rubber doorstops. "And I could pay you under the table."

Colm gave the offer serious thought. He was tempted.

"I don't think I'd be comfortable with that," he concluded, shaking his head. "But thanks," he added.

Just as Colm had expected, Mr. Hafferty was more than happy to lend him his ladder. He even offered to come over and hold the base of it while Colm climbed up with the window box. But Colm, not wanting to embroil his elderly neighbor and friend in an unpleasant task, had discouraged him. The base of the ladder was only a few feet beyond where Chester still lay when Colm ascended with the freshly painted window box filled with Miracle-Gro potting soil and young begonia plants.

As he descended, he thought of his mother and wondered how she was doing on the plane. She was not, in her own words, "a good flier." When she flew, which wasn't often, Fiona would stop just as she was boarding the plane and try to get a good look at the pilot. Maybe exchange a few words with him. "How's the weather up there?" she'd say, busily assessing his personality and capabilities. If the pilot had a nice comportment, if he was friendly and projected strength, she could relax. Once, she had turned around and bolted from a plane when a pilot had mumbled his words with her, appearing tense and distracted by a growing stain above his shirt pocket. Colm hoped that the crew aboard their plane to Las Vegas was nice to Fiona.

It was noon and ninety-eight degrees out.

He retracted the ladder and laid it alongside the front of the house. Then he went inside and poured himself a glass of lemonade.

He sat in the kitchen, resting his forehead on the kitchen table, and wondered what to do about Chester. The bruised sensation in his chest lingered, as if a tire had blown out violently inside him, shredding and ripping apart at high speed as it bounced around his rib cage. He took a few shallow breaths.

He'd actually been looking forward to being alone in the house for the week of Fiona and Don's honeymoon. They'd invited him to come with them, but Colm thought someone had to look after the house, and he'd imagined a free week to himself, practicing his guitar, watching TV, organizing his baseball cards.

Even his best friend, Justin, was away, up in New Hampshire, working as a counselor-in-training at a summer camp on Lake Winnipesaukee.

Colm had planned to take advantage of everyone's absence and get started on the laundry room. He was remodeling it as a surprise for his mother's wedding present. He was going to paint the walls and the ceiling, rip out the old linoleum floor, and put down quarry ceramic tile. Also—and Fiona would love this—put a drain in the floor because the soapstone sink by the dryer often clogged with lint and overflowed, driving her crazy.

Five hours later he was still sitting at the kitchen table.

Again he thought of calling Cameron, but now she was probably out. Maybe she was at the lake with her girlfriends. Or at Todd's annual July Fourth party, drinking too much beer and angling for a fight during the annual slow-pitch softball game.

The certain indifference with which she would receive the news about Chester contributed to his reluctance to call her. He recalled, with some annoyance, her suggesting a few months ago that they put Chester down after he had begun to lose control of his bladder. With this heat spell, Colm had been putting him outside to sleep though he missed having him up on his bed with him. Chester had slept with Colm since he was a puppy. Not at the foot of the bed, but right up alongside him, the heavy weight of Chester's sizable body pressed snugly against him through the night.

The front doorbell rang.

He stared, frozen, straight ahead.

"Oo-ooo!" A voice shot down the hallway through the front screen door.

"Colm! Oo-ooo! It's Angie!"

The screen door opened and slammed shut, and Colm heard the click of high heels briskly charging up the hallway.

"I made a lasagna! Thought you might like some company."

Angie, one of Fiona's oldest and best friends, trucked into the kitchen as if she lived there, flung open the oven door, and stuck the lasagna inside. She turned the oven on to 425.

"It'll take just a sec to heat up. How are you, hon?"

Without waiting for an answer, she sat down, joining him, the multitude of bracelets on both wrists jingling as she deposited her shoulder bag and a bucket of margarita mix on the table.

"Hot, huh?"

"Hi, Angie," Colm said.

"So what'd you do today?"

"Not much."

"Heard from Fiona yet? They must be in Vegas by now. Their plane was scheduled to land at one twenty Nevada time." She looked at her watch, frowned, tapped it, and put it to her ear as if it had stopped.

"Not yet," Colm said.

"It's exciting, isn't it? Hard to take it in, it all happened so fast. Whirlwind romance."

Angie sprang up to retrieve a couple of glasses from a cupboard.

"I tell you, I woke up this morning with a smile on my face. That Don is a godsend, a godsend, her life is going to be so much easier now. He's a *little* whiney, a little needy, but that man loves every hair on her body, every hair. He is going to treat her like a princess. Do you want some margarita mix, I haven't put the tequila in yet," she said, parking the glasses down on the table and reaching for a bottle of tequila from out of her bag. "Good God it's hot. We could go down to the VFW later and watch the fireworks if you felt like it."

Colm watched her fill both glasses up with the mix and then add a significant amount of tequila to her glass.

"Here," she said, putting a glass in front of him and sitting down. "I want to ask you something."

Colm looked at her, waiting for her question and realizing at the same time that he'd been sitting in that chair for a very long time. She planted an elbow on the table, holding her drink up in front of her.

"Now be honest," she said, leaning into him with a little gleam in her eye. "What did you think of Walter?"

"Walter?" Colm asked, puzzled.

Angie kept smiling at him, waiting for a response, her mouth open and slyly grinning as if she thought Colm was teasing her by not answering.

"Yes, Walter. *Well?*"

"Who is Walter?"

"Who is Walter?" Angie repeated, disbelievingly. "Who is Walter? Don's brother!" she blurted out. "You sat next to him at the dinner last night! What did you think of him?"

Colm reflected. Walter hadn't made much of an impression on him. He tried to picture him.

"He was okay."

"He asked me out," Angie divulged. "In the elevator, on the way down. I didn't tell Fiona. *Don't tell Fiona* you have to promise."

"I won't."

"I mean . . . I'll tell her. Eventually." She took a swig of her drink and sat back in her chair, smiling to herself and resuming an ongoing internal dialogue.

Angie always wore a lot of perfume, but it seemed that the heat was amplifying the scent, Windsong II. Colm felt it lining his sinuses as he breathed in through his nose.

"Are you all right?" Angie asked.

Colm nodded. He was wondering how he was going to tell her about Chester. He kept waiting for her to notice that he wasn't there. Chester always greeted everyone.

The phone rang.

"Maybe it's Fiona—I'll get it." Angie leapt up and bolted for the living room. Her perfume lingered behind.

"It's for you," she said a few moments later.

"Who is it?" Colm asked, still glued to his seat.

"He wouldn't say. I asked. Got a nice deep voice,"

she said as she grabbed an oven mitt, yanked down the oven door, and reeled back from the onslaught of heat. "Good Christ. As if it's not hot enough in here already."

Colm didn't move.

"Better hurry," she said, poking a fork into the lasagna. "They'll hang up."

Colm peeled himself off the chair and walked slowly down the hall and turned into the living room. Cautiously eyeing the receiver, he picked it up.

"Hello?"

"Don't hang up."

Colm recognized the voice from the call that morning.

"Seventy thousand dollars. I want you to have it."

Out of the corner of his eye, Colm caught sight of a framed photograph on the desk of his mother and Cameron and him taken maybe eight or nine years ago. It was a winter scene. The three of them, all bundled up in long scarves and hats, were holding hands and skating out in the middle of Pontoosuc Lake. Cameron was tossing her head back and laughing. Behind them, off to the right, Chester was trotting toward a man hunched over, sitting on an upside-down bucket, ice fishing.

The picture had hung there for years, but for some reason Colm hadn't really looked at it carefully until now.

"Are you there? Seventy thousand dollars. It's yours, son."

The voice seemed to come from somewhere in the picture, somewhere beyond the tall snow-dusted hemlocks on the far side of the lake, beyond the white rolling hills in the distance. Colm stared at the darkening gray winter sky. His hand tightened around the receiver. He felt a fleeting sharp pain in the back of his head.

"Don't call here again," he said. "Ever. *Never*."

"Wait—"

Colm hung up the phone.

He leaned into the picture a little bit more and studied Chester, who looked so young, so spry and limber, trotting happily across the ice, his head and tail held high.

"It's done!" Angie's voice belted out from the kitchen. Pivoting on his left foot, he turned toward her voice, using it to gain his bearings.

By the time the fireworks were exploding in the distance, they'd eaten most of the lasagna, and Angie had drunk a pitcherful of margaritas.

"You want to go see the fireworks?" Angie asked, turning down the volume of the little television set Fiona kept in the kitchen to watch *Good Morning America*.

Colm shook his head no.

"I'm with you. Seen one, seen 'em all," Angie agreed, turning the volume back up. They were watching the annual Boston Pops July Fourth celebration, but Angie was thinking about Walter. "Maybe he's watching the concert now too," she said, a little agitated, tugging on her necklace.

When Angie finally went home around eleven, Colm was still sitting in the same chair in the kitchen. Fiona hadn't called and he was starting to worry. He pondered turning on the news to see if there was any report of a plane crash.

He got up, but instead of turning the TV back on, he turned off the light. Then he sat back down in the same chair in the dark. Soon he was asleep, his head down on his right arm on the table, elbow bent back.

He awoke with a start around three in the morning. His left hand, resting on the table and looming directly in front of his eye, was bathed in moonlight. For his first waking moments he had trouble recognizing it.

As he squinted his eyes, he became aware of a dim thought stirring and starting to take shape in his mind. *Someone . . . something very bad had happened. . . .* Before he could identify his hand or the thought, he willed himself up and aimed for the door to the cellar.

His boots clattered on the old pine steps as he

purposefully descended the stairs, batting away a large cobweb. He found the garden shovel he was looking for back behind the folded Ping-Pong table that Fiona had bought for ten dollars at a tag sale. Grabbing the shovel with one hand, he unlocked and flung open one door of the hatchway with his other hand. Then he climbed up and out into the brightly moonlit yard.

He walked around the house to the backyard and circled it a few times, studying it from different angles. After a few minutes he picked an open spot between the chain-link fence and the forsythia bush and resolutely began to dig.

At first he didn't even notice the mosquitoes that hovered around him. But after a while he started combating them by tossing shovelfuls of loose dirt up at them. Some of the dirt fell back on him and some of it fell down into the hole. Every now and then he went into a wild frenzy, batting the swarming mosquitoes with the shovel, whipping around and flailing at the air. But he continued to dig a hole that was twice as deep as it needed to be.

From a distance, someone watching might have thought he was alternately digging two holes . . . one below him and one above. One for his dog, and one for his sorrow.

Chapter Three

Fiona called at seven in the morning.

Colm was sleeping on the couch in the living room, so he was able to answer before the machine picked up. He usually woke up around six thirty, but he'd actually just gotten to sleep after burying Chester and then running nine miles.

"Mom?" he asked, eyes barely open.

"I sang! I sang in Las Vegas!"

Colm looked at his watch.

"You're okay?"

"In the lounge of our hotel. Oh, we're at the Desert Sands Hotel. I sang, with a three-piece band, and they want me to sing again tomorrow night! Sweetie, I'm so excited I haven't been able to go to sleep, it's four in the morning. I love this town!"

"How was the flight?"

"The flight? Fine. Could you wait a sec?"

Colm could hear Don asking her a question.

"Huh?" she said to him, and he repeated his question.

"In the outside pocket of the pink carry-on. No, the pink one. *Pink.* Yup. Hi, sweetie." She was back. "How are you doing? I miss you so much. Wait, wait a sec. *What?*"

Don, evidently, was struggling with some task.

Colm rubbed his eyes and headed back to the couch with the phone. He lay down on the tangled bedsheet, straddling one leg up on the back of the couch.

In the background he could hear Bunny start to cry. He suddenly missed his sister badly and wished he could hold her, be with her out on the back porch where they sometimes hung out and have her contentedly pound him until he lay back and she went to sleep on his chest. It was her weight that he was especially yearning for, the very specific ballast of a live body pressed against him. Sometimes the three of them would lie in a pile together—Colm, Bunny, and Chester.

What would they tell Bunny about Chester? Maybe that he'd taken a long walk. That was what Fiona had initially told Colm when he'd started asking questions about his father. Actually, Colm realized, he was around

Bunny's age, just past his first birthday, when his father had left. For the longest time, he wondered where his father was walking. He pictured him walking across large flat continents, across deserts, ice floes, cities. It seemed that at some point surely he would walk all the way around the world and eventually come back to them.

He sensed early on that his mother didn't like discussing the subject, so he didn't bring it up for a long time. When he finally did, she painted a different picture, her explanation for his absence featuring colorful details of his chronic gambling and general nonstop deceit.

"All right." Fiona's voice returned. Then she whispered, "Very sweet but not the sharpest tool in the shed." She was speaking of Don. "I should go, Colm. Don woke Bunny up. So, everything's okay?"

"Fine."

"You're not too lonely?"

Colm didn't answer.

"Sweetie, you're not too lonely?"

"Nope."

"I'll call you tomorrow. Oh, Angie's coming by with a lasagna for you. Don't tell her this, but Don's brother, Walter, is planning to ask her out."

"Mm," Colm said, thinking about Chester. The news of his death was pushing to get out in much the same way that Chester himself used to lean his head against the back door when he wanted to be let out.

Bunny's cries increased in volume.

"Okay, sweetie, I'm hanging up now. I sent you some postcards. *I love you.*"

"I love you, too," Colm said. As he listened to her hang up, he realized he hadn't gotten their phone number. He'd lent her his cell phone because she hadn't paid a phone bill, but she'd neglected to take the charger. He wondered what songs she'd performed.

Fiona's dream had always been to be a nightclub singer. On a cruise ship. Sometimes Colm would accompany her on guitar and it always pulled her out of a bad mood. They'd even performed in public together: once at the grand opening of a Polynesian restaurant on Route 7 and another time at a fund-raiser for the children's health center, an event that was broadcast in its entirety on the local cable channel. For weeks thereafter, local selectmen and other elected officials—the only people who watched the channel—had stopped Fiona all over town and complimented her.

Colm thought his mother had an amazing voice. It was lushly soft with an astonishingly pure tone at the heart of it, and sometimes when she was fooling around, she'd lay a little raspiness on it that cracked him up. She'd tilt her head to the side, bring her shoulder up, roll her eyes, and do that raspy thing, and he'd start bending notes on the guitar till she'd crack up too.

As he stared up from the couch, the ornate molding caught his eye. His great-grandfather, Fiona's grandfather, had built the house in the 1920s, and although from the outside it looked like a modest two-story house, there were many unusual features inside—the hand-carved mahogany banister that matched the fireplace mantel, alcove window seats, pocket doors, an octagonal porthole window in the upstairs hallway, and a small secret room off the first landing of the stairs.

Colm was named after this great-grandfather, Colm McCarthy, and Fiona claimed he'd inherited his building instincts and his "fixing gene" from him. The more Colm worked on the house, the more he felt he came to know his great-grandfather and the more he was inspired to uphold his high standards of craftsmanship. Dismantling sections in the course of repairs, he was often amused by his great-grandfather's sense of humor, revealed in imaginative details and inventive solutions to problems.

Colm lay there, still, for a while, wondering whether to try to go back to sleep or not.

His arms were crossed over his chest to keep the dirt on his hands from getting on the sheet and the couch. It was so hot that the dirt hadn't really caked. He'd left his jeans and boots outside on the back porch with the shovel.

If he went to the early service, he could get back and get a jump start on the laundry room. He was planning on ripping up the linoleum that day, which meant disconnecting the washer and dryer and hauling them out on his hand truck. No telling what he'd find underneath that linoleum. Colm McCarthy had hidden all manner of objects under the floorboards and in the walls of the house—ledgers, newspapers, receipts, letters, little toys, cigar boxes. Colm kept some of the objects in a large fishbowl on the bookshelf in his room.

He got up, showered, and found some clean clothes. A lot of people must have gone away for the long weekend because when he got there, the church was only about a third full. He sat in the next-to-last row, where he always sat. Years ago Fiona used to take him and Cameron to the eleven-o'clock service, but then she started picking up houses to clean on Sundays and got out of the habit. Cameron was thrilled at the opportunity to quit going, but Colm, for reasons he'd never really thought about, kept attending.

27

He looked out the window and saw a man way over by the sidewalk leaning with his back against a tree, eating a sandwich. He was tall and thin and wore a knit wool hat, which, Colm thought, seemed a little odd given how hot it was outside.

A dripping sound caught his attention, and he looked over to see that the wall-mounted air-conditioning unit was leaking. The noise was getting louder, and Colm noticed an electrical outlet underneath, which posed a danger, down near the floor. Should he turn off the unit? He thought for a minute and figured the problem was probably a function of the humidity. He discreetly slipped over and tried sliding the temperature gauge up away from the coolest setting. Sure enough, within minutes the water stopped running. Up front Pastor Steve waved a thanks to him without breaking stride in his sermon.

When Colm went back to sit down, he could see out of the corner of his eye that Melanie Phelps was staring over at him. She went to his high school and was a year ahead of him. She was pretty in an unusual way, or maybe it was her bearing that was unusual. There was something musical in the way she carried herself, something completely self-contained and private and yet connected to everything. She was tuned in to things in a way that made people want to be near her.

Many times, from a distance, Colm had watched Melanie Phelps staring at something, and he always wondered what she was seeing that no one else could see. Once, this past winter, he'd watched her studying a crow that was hopping around on a big dirty snowbank, scavenging for something to eat. It was freezing cold but she had watched that crow for over half an hour. From near a Dumpster across the street, he had watched her watch the crow.

Now she was staring at him.

He tucked his chin down and looked back out the window.

Fiona had sounded happy on the phone. That was good—she was having a good time. He felt like he'd made the right decision not to tell them about Chester until they got back. But . . . he did want to tell *someone*, if only out of respect for Chester.

Maybe Pastor Steve? Possibly, but there was something off-putting about telling someone whose job it was to listen. And even though Colm liked him, he'd observed that Pastor Steve always seemed to perk up at tragic news.

Colm noticed the man out by the tree had finished his sandwich and was now playing with a yo-yo. His wool hat had a curious short visor, like the hat that Radar wore on *M*A*S*H*.

Colm squinted, studying him. He couldn't tell how old the man was, but he cut an odd figure, a grown man playing with a yo-yo. He managed a few standard basic tricks—around the world, walking the dog. When a short, stocky woman pulling a shopping cart paused to watch him, the man flubbed a trick and self-consciously began quickly winding up the string. When he started to put the yo-yo away in his pocket, the woman slapped him on his arm to continue. He glanced over at the church, looked back at her, and suddenly tried executing a bold new trick, kicking his leg out first.

"Colm."

Colm looked ahead to see Mrs. Barnett, ninety-two years old and turned around in her seat, extending her hand toward him.

The sermon was over. People were doing the traditional shake and greet, saying hello and asking nearby parishioners how they were.

"Hello, Mrs. Barnett," Colm said, taking her white porcelain hand and shaking it gently.

"Wonderful sermon, wasn't it?" She smiled.

Colm hadn't listened to the sermon that closely. He had no idea what Pastor Steve had talked about that morning. Relentlessly honest, he didn't want to confirm that something was wonderful that he hadn't paid attention to, but he could see that Mrs. Barnett didn't require an answer.

"Hi, Colm." It was Melanie Phelps. She'd made the effort to walk down several pews and cross the aisle over to him.

Colm had talked to her only twice in his life. He recalled both times well. Once was when he was showing the school janitor how to replace the solenoid in the coffeemaker in the teachers' lounge, and Melanie had peeked in and asked if he knew where the paper for the Xerox machine was kept. Colm knew because he was often called in when the machine broke down. The other time was when, as assistant editor of the school paper, she'd approached him in the hall and asked him to write an article, anything about the junior varsity cross-country team. He'd declined on the spot.

He did try writing something later about running on October Mountain, one particular incident during the state championships, when he and Mike Innes had inadvertently flushed an escaped convict out from hiding, but he didn't think it was good enough to show her.

"Hi," he said.

"So how's your summer going?"

Colm shrugged, achieving a partial grin. She must have been spending some time in the sun, because she was tanned and her hair seemed blonder. He could hardly look at her.

"I heard your mom got married."

"Yeah."

"That's cool."

She stood there, waiting for more of a response from him. He could feel his jaw muscles tightening.

"Did they go on a honeymoon?" she asked, smiling.

"They did. Las Vegas."

"Las Vegas. Wow."

"Yeah."

"You staying for the pancake breakfast?"

"Probably not. Nope."

Again she didn't move, giving him the opportunity to say something more. Completely unnerved, he prayed for something resembling a thought to form in his mind, some few words that he could speak and offer her, something that would pass as conversation.

His heart began to race wildly, pounding against his rib cage. Still seated, he could feel himself breaking into a sweat, and he looked down.

He was conscious that she was still standing there, staring at him, studying him. He could feel his heart throbbing in his ears, and he wondered briefly if she had said something that he hadn't heard. With enormous effort, he glanced up at her, but she seemed to be poised above him in another universe, as if he were staring through the wide lens of a telescope way up at her, at her concerned face that was floating on some distant small round planet, far away.

"Are you?" he finally blurted out.

"Am I what?" she asked gently, almost apologetically. Confused.

"Staying. For the pancake . . ." He didn't finish the thought.

"Oh," she said. Her eyes held him. "Uh . . . I don't know." She shrugged.

"Well, I guess I'm going," he said, suddenly able to stand. He lifted a hand in a parting farewell gesture. Sidestepping his way along the pew without looking back at Melanie Phelps, he hastened down the aisle toward the bright morning light that poured through the open double doors in the church lobby.

"Good morning, Colm," Pastor Steve said by the door, cheerily shaking his hand.

"Good morning," Colm said, bolting down the steps.

"Maybe we'll see you at Bible study this week," Pastor Steve called after him. Colm waved back at him over his shoulder. Every now and then, when pressed to, Colm did show up at Bible study, but he didn't really like it. Sometimes people there interpreted the passages they were studying in ways that didn't seem right to him, and there was no reasoning with some of them.

When he reached the sidewalk at the end of the gravel path, Colm stopped, put his hands on his hips, and caught his breath. His heart was starting to slow down. He took a few more deep breaths, glanced down at the ground, breathed some more, raised his head, and started to walk home.

Suddenly he stopped and turned around, looking over toward the tree where the man with the yo-yo had been. He was gone. Colm looked up the sidewalk for him, across the street, and in the front yards up and down the street in both directions. No sign of him.

As Colm turned and headed once again for home, he felt a sharp pain in the back of his neck. It was the same fleeting pain he'd felt the day before when he was on the phone with Lloyd Henry, studying the wintry landscape in the photograph of his family skating on Pontoosuc Lake.

Colm lowered his head and picked up his pace.

Chapter Four

Newspapers, magazines, and calendars. That's what was stashed under the linoleum, a two-inch layer neatly laid out between the linoleum and the rough wood beneath. They were mostly dated from the spring of 1952, and Colm was pretty sure that his great-grandfather had put them there and not his grandfather, because there were some signature trademarks— several issues of a fishing magazine that his great-grandfather liked. Also pages from calendars of popular golf courses in Ireland and Scotland. Colm had found several old golf balls up under the roof and a small hand towel from St. Andrews golf course in the wall of the downstairs bathroom.

It took Colm all day Sunday to rip up the linoleum, replace a section of rotten boards, put down the plywood, and start nailing down the hardware cloth for the cement.

He'd thought it might get tricky angling the floor for the drain, but he'd realized a quarter-inch slope would suffice, and that wouldn't be problematic when he set the tiles.

Cameron had showed up in the early afternoon. She'd wandered in and taken him completely by surprise when he was down in the basement hooking the PVC pipes to the main waste. He'd already made his cut into the main and was getting the sleeve around it when her voice suddenly spoke from above.

"Why's—?"

"Onh!" His hands jumped around the pipe.

She gave him a moment. Not long.

"Why's the water off?"

He looked up through the hole in the laundry-room floor and saw her face, hair pulled back, peering down at him.

"There's no water," she said, rephrasing her point.

"I turned it off."

"Why?"

"Cameron . . . can't you tell I'm doing something here that might require that I turn off the water?"

"Oh."

She watched him work for a minute.

"I need to borrow some money."

He looked up, and she gave him an imploring look that veered into a smile, Cameron's lopsided grin that slowly inched up the right side of her face.

"P-l-e-ease."

Even upside down it was a smile he couldn't refuse, and she knew it.

"Just a sec. I'll come up."

When he found her in the kitchen, she had emptied a tray of ice into the sink and was rubbing the back of her neck with an ice cube. Cameron usually spent an inordinate amount of time on her makeup and clothes, but today she hadn't given her wardrobe any thought. Wearing no makeup, she looked quite nice, he thought. She was barefoot, in cutoff jean shorts and a plain olive-green T-shirt, and her straight dirty-blond hair was pulled back up in a ponytail the way she used to wear it when she was younger.

He was glad to see her.

"You want some lemonade?" Colm asked.

"I have to go. Jennifer's waiting outside. Colm, I need, just, like fifty dollars. I'll pay you back."

Now she was rubbing the ice cube along one of her arms.

"Where's Todd?" Colm asked.

Cameron shook her head.

"I don't know." She suddenly looked as if she might cry.

He waited for her to say more.

"We had a fight. I don't know." She rolled her eyes. "Whatever."

She and Todd often had fights. Cameron liked to fight—there was no denying it. She liked to go on the attack and get into raging screaming matches the way some people like to shop, or garden. She found it both relaxing and invigorating. Occasionally she would throw things, and twice she was suspended from school for actually punching people. Cameron didn't fight dirty; she threw and landed hard punches. Like Colm, she was athletic, and the two years she'd played girls' varsity basketball in high school, even the referees were wary of her. She was fearless, but she didn't like to lose, and recently Todd had gotten better at fighting back.

Sometimes she'd come home to Palmer Street and stay, and then just as suddenly she'd be gone without a word, back with him.

"Did you hear from Mom?" she asked.

"Yeah. I guess they're having a good time."

She didn't appear to have heard what he said. She was holding the ice cube against her temple, staring at the latch on one of the kitchen cabinets, lost in thought.

"I'll get the money," he said.

She borrowed money from him often, but she always paid him back within a week or so. Right now she had several summer jobs, including one as a cocktail waitress—she'd lied about her age—where she made good money, but she spent it as fast as she took it in. Colm was a saver. He had over two thousand dollars in a savings account, money he'd made from mowing lawns and odd jobs.

He took out a twenty and three tens and turned to see she'd followed him into the living room.

"Here," he said.

She popped the ice cube into her mouth and took the money.

"Thanks. You're okay?" she asked.

"Yeah." He nodded. He was wondering when she would notice Chester was gone. He could see she wanted to leave.

"Next time I come, we'll go get a pizza."

She gave Colm a weak smile, sucking on the ice cube. Then, looking somewhat doleful, she gave him a quick hug and turned to go.

"'Bye," and she was gone.

Later that afternoon, as he was nailing down the hardware cloth, Angie stopped in.

"What do you think?"

He was down on his hands and knees, hammering the metal mesh, nails in his mouth. He looked up.

"Voilà." Angie was wearing a tight lavender dress with small white polka dots and a hot-pink ruffle around the neckline and hem. She taught aqua cardiac and strength classes around the county, and at forty, her petite body was very fit.

"Or . . ." she said suspensefully, teasingly, holding up a finger and walking out.

Ten nails and two minutes later she was back, this time in a mustard-yellow low-cut dress with a long taffeta skirt. She modeled the dress, turning to and fro.

"Or . . ." she said again with a tantalizing there's-more-to-come delivery, and exiting.

Colm folded the mesh back into place and looked over at the roll, wondering if he had enough. This was left over from a spring project when he'd lined all the gutters to keep leaves and debris from clogging them up. Maybe he could improvise with some other material if he ran out. He reached over for some more nails from a Dixie cup.

"Ta-da! We also have *this*," Angie said, making a dramatic entrance in a fringed turquoise short-waisted leather jacket and a short white linen skirt. She modeled once more on a small section of newly installed plywood.

"I know it needs a different camisole. Well? Colm?"

"I like the first dress," Colm mumbled through the nails in his mouth, still down on his knees.

"Really?"

"Uh-huh."

"Hmm."

It didn't look like he'd given her the right answer. She fingered the fringe of the jacket, as if it had let her down.

"By the way, there's no water," she said.

He rolled his eyes and shook his head.

"I turned it off."

"Oh. So . . . I'm going out with Walter tonight," she said, beaming and turning slightly red.

Colm wiped some sweat from his brow.

"I don't know where he's taking me. It's a *surprise*. You really like the first dress best?"

"I do."

"Okay," she said, reluctant but resigned, as if his opinion had settled the matter. "Do you have anything to drink?"

"There's some lemonade in the fridge."

She didn't move, watching him work instead. He wasn't wearing a shirt, and he felt a little uncomfortable with her staring at his back.

"Do you want some?" she said, headed for the kitchen.

"Okay." He pounded a nail in.

After a while, barefoot in overall shorts and a spandex tank top, Angie returned with a glass of lemonade, an opened bottle of red wine, and a mug.

"I'll just have a quick one," she said after giving him the lemonade and pouring herself a mug of wine. She sat down on the plywood, leaning back against the wall.

"I've talked to him three times today on the phone."

Colm gulped down the lemonade, his eyes resting on her tiny bowling-pin earrings.

"He's into trees," she said flatly. "He plants them. Grows them. Sells them."

Angie liked Chester, Colm thought. She'd even ordered Omaha steaks for him three Christmases ago when he could still chew. How could she not notice he wasn't there? Would she notice if the front door were gone? The refrigerator?

Later that night up in his room, Colm realized he didn't want to sleep there now that Chester was gone. Standing in the dark in the upstairs hallway, he looked into Cameron's room, now the guest room, but he didn't want to sleep in there either. Fiona was talking about making that room Bunny's room once she got a little older and outgrew her crib. She'd talked to Colm about stripping the wallpaper and maybe putting up some shelves.

A truck rumbled past the house. Then a motorcycle revved by. It was probably Eddie Siegel, who lived up at the end of the street and would be coming home from his late shift at Plastics Extrusion. The light from a street-lamp flooded through the little octagonal window and flared out down the wall of the staircase.

Colm stood there awhile longer, his bare feet sunk down in the carpet. Sunday had its own particular sound, he thought, listening to nothing. Like no other day of the week. It was the sound of stores being closed, of everything being suspended, on hold. Time felt different on Sundays; minutes were elongated. Interminable. And on holiday weekends Monday was just another Sunday. He realized, annoyed, that Larmon's Hardware would be closed the next day and he wouldn't be able to pick up the cement he needed.

Suddenly a knock broke the silence.

Colm initially couldn't place the geographical location of the sound. It was so loud, flooding the darkness, it seemed as if someone had just knocked on his eardrum.

Another series of knocks made it clear that someone was knocking downstairs on the front door. Who would be stopping by at eleven thirty on a Sunday night?

He gripped the banister and went downstairs. Standing in front of the door, he started to unlock it but then hesitated.

"Cameron?" he asked, loudly enough for her to hear, if it was her.

"I did it again," a voice called from the other side.

Colm opened the door to see Mr. Hafferty, the neighbor, throwing up his arms and shrugging.

"Locked the keys in the car," he said with feigned self-reproach, shaking his head. "What a bonehead, huh?"

Mr. Hafferty was eighty-two and lived alone. He'd given Colm a copy of his house key because every now and then he would lock himself out.

"I'll get my shoes." Colm turned on the hall light to look for them.

"I was at a concert," Mr. Hafferty said, waiting outside on the front porch, his hands clasped behind his back. "Oh, it was *magnificent!*" He tilted his head back and closed his eyes, as if still in Ozawa Hall. Mr. Hafferty was a composer ("An *obscure* composer," he would say with a smile and a wink, as if that were funny) and often went to concerts at Tanglewood, summer home of the Boston Symphony Orchestra. He ushered there so he could go for free, which was good because he had to live frugally off his Social Security and a small pension.

As they walked the short distance, just four houses down, Mr. Hafferty described the concert, swerving slightly with enthusiasm. His longish white hair appeared wilder than usual, standing on end as if electrified by the performance.

It was blessedly cooler out now, and there was even something resembling a breeze. Colm raised his face to receive it, at one point offering his arm to Mr. Hafferty when he tripped over a crack in the sidewalk. They ambled along, arm in arm.

"I'll call Triple A in the morning," Mr. Hafferty said as they arrived at his car, parked in front of his house. He shuffled up to it and stared at the burgundy Ford Escort with detached curiosity. He leaned over and peered in through the passenger window, cupping his hands over his eyes to block the reflection.

"Yup," he said, unperturbed. "They're in the ignition." He grabbed Colm by the elbow and joked, "At least this time I know where they are!"

Colm let him into his house and stayed to replace a few hard-to-reach lightbulbs and also to share a midnight snack. Mr. Hafferty knew Colm liked éclairs and kept a box of them in his refrigerator just for him. They sat at the Formica kitchen table that Colm had repaired and ate two each with a glass of skim milk.

"So, you like this guy?" Mr. Hafferty asked of Don when Colm told him where his mother was and why.

"He's a nurse. A male nurse," Colm answered, chewing.

"Pretty good." Mr. Hafferty nodded thoughtfully, inwardly lamenting the fact that the lovely Fiona Drucker had gotten married. He picked up the carton of milk and silently filled Colm's glass.

Colm took a long way home, making a big sweeping circle past the high school and the General Electric plant to get back to his house. Once home, he opened two of the screened windows in the living room, hoping for a little cross ventilation, and lay down on the couch in the dark. He watched some TV for a while and then turned on a lamp and read through a manual on automobile repair. Even though he wasn't old enough for his learner's permit, he could already take apart and put back together a standard Chevy engine.

When he was done reading, he slid the manual under the couch and turned off the light.

Lying on his back, he brought his arm up over his

face. He thought briefly about his encounter with Melanie Phelps at church that morning. His fist tightened up as he squirmed with discomfort.

He tried to think about something else.

What color was he going to paint the laundry room? He could paint the walls white, the ceiling gray, and the new shelf maybe brown, or black.

An hour later he was still wide-awake.

Exhausted, he kicked his legs out and shook them, banging the backs of his feet up and down on the couch. Then he rolled over onto his stomach and pitched all the cushions onto the floor, flinging them over his shoulder. Heaving back over onto his right side, he got tangled in the sheet.

Suddenly he sat up and, just as swiftly, stood up.

He swayed for a moment or two, free of the couch.

After searching around the house a while, he found a small blue tarp in a cupboard in the back hall closet, and he dragged it and a sleeping bag out into the backyard. He placed the tarp down on the grass so it just overlapped Chester's plot. Then he zipped open the sleeping bag, shook it out, and lay down on his stomach, stretching out his arm. With the palm of his outstretched hand resting on the freshly dug dirt, he closed his eyes and fell sound asleep.

Chapter five

"**W**e're staying another week!"
Fiona exclaimed, excited, on the phone.

It was Friday night.

"Really?" Colm responded, barely concealing his disappointment. He had gone all out to finish the laundry room before they got back on Saturday.

"We called the airline, and there's only a fifty-dollar penalty per ticket. Don said I deserve another week in paradise." Her smile was audible.

"Paradise?" Colm said skeptically.

"I know . . . who would have thought Las Vegas would be so wonderful? Colm, it's not just casinos and bright lights. It's blue skies, the desert, *the west.*"

He could tell she'd been rhapsodizing like that all week. He could just hear her repeating those same phrases over and over to Don and their breakfast waitress

48

and all the many other people she'd encounter, who would be won over by her charms.

"You just feel this sense of opportunity, *possibility*, people are so friendly, not like in New England. It's the complete opposite of Pittsfield, Colm, it's the fastest-growing town in the country. Pittsfield is the fastest-*shrinking* town."

Colm didn't say anything.

"Has Cameron been by again?"

"Not since last weekend."

"She would *love* this place. So—what have you been up to, sweetie? Tell me."

He couldn't speak.

"Colm? What have you been doing?"

His brain had seized up in a logjam. What was he going to tell her?

"Colm?"

"It's a surprise," he said finally. A surge of emotion caught in his throat, and he immediately felt stupid about it.

"A surprise?"

"Yup."

"Aww . . . really? Colm," she said affectionately, as if she surmised it had to do with her wedding present.

He took a deep breath. He was tired. He'd worked

hard every day—laying the tiles, getting the drain right, prepping the walls, sanding the woodwork, caulking the cracks, painting the walls and the ceiling, ripping out the sagging cupboard, putting up shelves, rewiring the new light fixture. And now the room looked so great. He'd played his guitar in there that afternoon before hooking up the washer and dryer.

"Did you sing again?" he asked halfheartedly.

"Every night this week! Colm, I feel like I've died and gone to heaven. Weeknights, it's just Phil on piano, but on weekends Gary, this very debonair amazing drummer, comes by and plays with us. We're doing all the old standards from the thirties and forties. 'Love Me or Leave Me,' 'I Found a Million Dollar Baby,' 'You'd Be So Nice to Come Home To.' The crowd *loves* us."

"Are they paying you?"

"No," she said a tad defensively. "I don't mind."

"They should pay you."

"I won two hundred dollars in a slot machine," she said brightly. "Bunny pulled the lever."

"Mom."

"What?"

He didn't say anything. He wasn't sure what part of that scenario bothered him. Was it the image of Bunny gambling—giggling and squealing as she grabbed hold of the lever in a brightly lit casino—or was it the fact that she was doing all these new things without him?

"What?" Fiona repeated. "Colm, I wish you were here, I miss you so much. Why don't you get on a plane tomorrow and fly out? I could pay for the ticket from here. Do that, sweetie. Get Cameron to drive you to the airport and fly out here."

"I don't think so."

"Give it some thought. I'd love for you to come."

"It's your honeymoon."

"I know. But you're my sweetie."

He took another deep breath, relaxing somewhat. Maybe it wasn't so bad. At least she was having a good time.

"There's all kinds of stuff to do. We could go up in a hot air balloon. We could rent you a dirt bike and drive out to the desert, and you and Don could go dirt biking together. Bunny's made friends with all the chambermaids; she'd love to show you where she hides in the linen closet."

Again, Colm became aware of how much he missed her.

"You got some wedding presents," he said, changing the subject and taking the phone over to the couch. He sat down. "Seven." He had stacked the presents on the coffee table in front of the couch, ready for her to see the next day.

"Really?"

Three had arrived in the mail, and four had been dropped off at the house, including a large hibiscus plant that Colm was watering.

"Gammy sent a box of grapefruit. Pretty weird wedding present."

"It's not a wedding present. It's just grapefruit." After a moment of silence, she admitted, "I haven't told her about Don yet. I'm going to, but . . ." Her voice trailed off.

Gammy was short for *grandmother*. Fiona's parents had retired to Florida years ago, after Lloyd Henry had left, and Gammy had given her the house. Fiona's communication with them was minimal. They'd found religion in Fort Lauderdale, and that had only made them more critical of her. With an almost crazed zeal, their pastor pressured them to witness to as many converts to their faith as possible, as if he thought the numbers would eventually tally up in his own personal convert column.

"We want to witness to you, Fiona," Gammy would say imploringly. ("I need a witness protection program," Fiona would joke to Colm.)

"There're some cards here, too," Colm said, picking up a few envelopes and noticing that he'd neglected to see one was addressed to him. It had no return address, and it was postmarked Pittsfield. He absentmindedly ripped open the envelope.

"We could go rafting. White river rafting."

There was a knock on the door.

"Someone's at the door."

"Who is it?"

"How come no one ever uses the doorbell?" Colm had installed a doorbell a year ago. Maybe he needed to change the placement of it. "Wait a sec. . . ."

He put the receiver down and, taking the letter with him, went to the door.

Angie entered like water through an opened floodgate.

"Walter's outside, talking to some man with a skateboard. He's got Fiona's wedding present, we're just stopping by to deliver it and say hi." Dressed in a black jacket and skirt, she had an oddly corporate air to her. Excited, she winked at Colm and leaned in to whisper, "We're going to a *play* up in Williamstown. How are you, hon?"

"My mom's on the phone."

"Oh, oh, oh, oh, oh," she said, as if popping imaginary balloons with her voice as she aimed for the living room, her black heels clicking across the floor. She looked like she was rushing in to a board meeting.

As Colm heard her say hello to Fiona and start speaking in rapid hushed tones, he stared down at the letter he'd taken out of the envelope. It was written in neat block letters with a black Sharpie.

Dear Son,

I have come to the end of my rope. I have no reason to live. Therefore, I am giving you the opportunity to turn me in for the handsome reward of seventy thousand dollars. Cash. You probably hate me and I don't blame you for that. Maybe if you got to know me, you would hate me even more. But that shouldn't stop you from cashing in.

Please allow me to give my life meaning with this one final gesture. Seventy grand. Tax free. Please call the enclosed telephone number and I will give you the simple easy plan for getting this money.

Sincerely,
Lloyd Henry Drucker

". . . and then we're staying at a B&B up in Bennington." Angie's voice drifted in and out as Colm studied the letter. He read it a few times. Then he turned it over and studied the other side, which was blank.

"Nice guy," a voice said.

Someone cleared his throat.

Colm looked up.

Walter was standing out on the doorstep, holding a large, brightly wrapped present elaborately tied up with a wide gold-flecked ribbon. He was holding it gingerly, as if it were some exotic bird.

"Guy out there. Nice." Walter said, looking a little self-conscious, waiting to be asked inside.

Colm squinted at him, still processing the letter.

"Don't know why he's wearing a wool hat this time of year," Walter said after a pause, just making conversation.

Colm stared at Walter, his brain starting to race into overdrive. Suddenly he bolted past Walter and rushed outside.

"Where is he?" Colm said out beyond the hedge, frantically looking around.

"Huh?"

"The man with the wool hat. Where is he?"

"Oh." Walter couldn't see the road. "He was just there a second ago. Mind if I put this down, Colin?"

"What did he say to you?"

"He said it was a nice day."

"That's all? That it was a nice day?"

Walter, a little flustered, tried to recall exactly.

"Well. He had a skateboard. I asked him if he skateboarded."

"And did he?"

"He said he had just taken it up. Colin, I gotta put this gift down. It's pretty heavy."

From the sidewalk, Colm watched Walter invite himself into the house and disappear. He stood there a moment more and then stepped out onto the street, looking up and down. Seeing no one, his focus gradually went back to the letter.

"Colm!" It was Angie, calling out through the living-room window. "Come and join us! We're having cocktails!"

A car honked. Colm looked up to see that a car had braked directly in front of him. The driver was throwing up his arms in exasperation.

"Sorry," Colm said in a daze. And he wandered back inside.

"Ohmygod ohmygod this is soooo beautiful!" Angie was in the laundry room, looking around with her mouth wide open. "I am stunned! I am speechless!"

"Nice work," Walter said, with the same inflection he had used for "Nice guy."

"You don't understand, Walter." Angie was looking up at the ceiling and spinning around. "This room was a *disaster*. It was dark, crumbling, it *smelled bad*, you felt like your clothes were going to come out dirtier than when you brought them in. You don't understand what this boy has done."

"Nice job," Walter reiterated, with more enthusiasm.

Colm smiled briefly, barely hearing them.

"Fiona is going to die. She is going to *die*," said Angie. "She is just going to die—I want to call her up and tell her."

"Don't," Colm said firmly.

"Don't worry, I won't."

Angie sighed audibly several more times and spun around.

"I feel like I'm in a fancy hotel. I feel like I'm at the Ritz."

"Quite the handyman, eh Colin?"

"His name isn't Colin," said Angie. "It's Colm."

"Mm?"

"Colm. Like 'column,' a Greek column in front of a library. A bank."

"Oh."

"This tile is beautiful. It's *beautiful*. If I paid you a million dollars, would you redo my laundry room?"

Colm was studying the letter again.

"Like Doric," Walter chirped up.

"Yes," Colm said automatically, not looking at him.

"Huh?" Angie was admiring the shelf.

"Doric. Ironic. Corinthian," Walter expounded, pleased with his erudition. "Those are the Greek columns."

Angie suddenly lit up with an idea.

"What do you say we bag the play, order out for pizza, stay here, and watch a video?"

Walter wasn't sure. He looked at her, startled.

"It's such a long drive anyway," said Angie.

After the initial shock, Walter seemed to be adapting slowly. Flexibility didn't seem to be his strong suit.

"Would you like the company, Colm? You look like you could use some company."

"Okay," Colm said. And then, unable to hold back, he corrected Walter, "It's Ionic."

Walter looked at him, baffled.

"The column is Ionic, not ironic."

Walter suddenly laughed out loud, as if Colm had made a joke.

"All right, how about two large—one vegetarian, one meat?" said Angie, heading out. "If I stay in this room any longer, I'm going to have do a load of wash, I just am."

She went off, aiming for the phone in the living room, with Walter following.

Colm stood still for a moment, and then jumped up to sit on the dryer. He leaned over, resting his head in his hands, in a stunned stupor of disbelief.

Colm had no real memory of his father. He had what felt like memories, but they were all just descriptions of events that he'd heard from Fiona. When he thought of his father, which was next to never, the words *liar* and *gambler* came to mind.

He started slowly and methodically tearing the letter up into tiny little pieces, which drifted like flakes of snow down onto the red clay tile.

Every facet of the communication boggled his mind.

He questioned whether it was even authentic, whether someone was playing a joke on him. What grown man could write something so utterly, so colossally stupid? It was like a bad sales promo, the most blatantly obvious scam. And the handwriting. The block print reminded him of pictures he'd seen in *Time* magazine a few years back of letters containing anthrax that were addressed to congressmen. It was the product of a disturbed mind, a simpleton, a psychopath.

How dare he begin "Dear Son"? How dare he

presume to know how Colm felt about him? How dare he intrude on his life?

Now the whole letter was torn up, scattered on the floor. Still sitting up on the dryer, he reached over, dropped the plug into the soapstone sink, and turned both faucets on to full.

If Lloyd Henry Drucker was following him around, if he was stalking him, Colm would get a restraining order. He was tempted to call the police.

It took a while for the sink to overflow, but eventually it did. Once a sufficient amount of water was on the floor, Colm turned off the faucets. From up on the dryer, he looked down to see the tiny pieces of white paper buoyed up by the water and escorted down the new drain.

Colm hopped down and crouched over the hole, his elbows locked around his knees. He looked down, studying the new system. It was draining perfectly.

His great-grandfather would be proud.

"Colm!" Angie's voice belted out from the living room. "Movie's starting! Showtime!"

The last shred of letter circled around and disappeared.

"'I've come to the end of my rope.'" Colm shook his head. Good, he thought. Keep going.

Chapter Six

It was so crowded at church on Sunday that Colm couldn't see whether Melanie Phelps had come or not. Even when he got up to turn on the overhead fan at Pastor Steve's request, lingering by the switch and scanning the crowd, Colm couldn't be sure.

Staring out at the tree where the man with the wool hat had eaten the sandwich and fooled around with a yo-yo the week before, Colm wondered what Melanie was doing for the summer. Last summer, he knew, she'd worked at the boat club on the Stockbridge Bowl, managing the snack bar and helping out with boat rentals.

She'd written an article for the school paper about the evenings Ed Powell had let her ride with him on the town weed boat. The utilitarian boat, a cross between a tank and a paddleboat, was about the size of a dump truck. Melanie waxed eloquent in her descriptions of how it yanked the milfoil weeds up from the depths of the lake, breaking them off and hauling them out of the water in a tangled mess. The boat was bright orange, and venturing out on it was one of the highlights of Melanie's summer.

Colm had saved the story.

It had knocked him out that someone so smart and beautiful would get that excited about a weed boat. He liked that she admired its mechanics and appreciated its rudimentary design; its unhurried passage through the water. It was like a float in a parade, she wrote. The best perch from which to watch the great blue herons, and the fireflies that flickered along the wooded shore as daylight disappeared.

For the darkening ride back to the boat landing, she always brought a hooded sweatshirt. It was an image that had stuck in Colm's mind—Melanie with her hood up, crossing the lake at dusk. Something about that picture transported him.

There was applause. Colm looked up front to see Pastor Steve giving a wet Avery Johnson a congratulatory hug. He had just accepted Jesus Christ as his savior and was laughing self-consciously because he'd gotten some water up his nose. Next in line was Avery's eight-year-old nephew, Pete, who held his arms stiffly by his sides and was already closing his eyes in tense anticipation. Pastor Steve held him firmly and plunged him backward into the tank.

Colm resumed looking out the window.

He didn't see Melanie after the service. For a moment he wondered if his bizarre behavior the Sunday before had put her off coming, but then he realized that his existence was not going to influence Melanie Phelps one way or another.

Walking home, Colm ran into Mr. Hafferty, who was dressed in his favorite bright raspberry pants and his green seersucker blazer. He was headed home with the Sunday *New York Times* tucked under one arm, his house key firmly clenched in his other hand.

"Not done yet," Mr. Hafferty said, hooking his arm through Colm's as he shuffled along, "but it's coming along nicely."

He was composing a fugue for oboe, clarinet, and harpsichord as a wedding present for Fiona. He acknowledged, after humming a few measures of it, that no one would ever hear it, but Fiona had once admired a composition he'd shown her, saying how pretty the notation was, and at the very least she could enjoy the neatly penned notes.

Colm sometimes stared at Mr. Hafferty's eighty-two-year-old head and thought of all the music inside that had never made the leap from Mr. Hafferty's inner concert hall out into the world.

"Key of D major," Mr. Hafferty said, and hummed some more.

As they got closer to his house, Mr. Hafferty slowed down.

"And what does the day hold in store for you?" he asked, looking searchingly into Colm's eyes, as if he were asking a far deeper question.

"Baseball cards," Colm replied, automatically listening for Chester's greeting bark up the street.

"Ahhh." Mr. Hafferty nodded slowly.

He studied Colm a moment more, smiled, raised his key in a triumphant gesture, and shuffled up the walk toward his door. Colm waited and watched to make sure he got in all right, and when half the sections of the bulky Sunday *New York Times* slipped away from under Mr. Hafferty's arm as he fumbled with the lock, Colm was there collecting them as they reached the ground.

At home Colm had three bowls of Cheerios and then, still hungry, made himself a stack of French toast heavily sprinkled with confectioner's sugar.

There was a note on the kitchen table from Cameron.

She could drive him to his mowing jobs on Tuesday, Wednesday, and Friday mornings before ten, but he would have to figure out a way to get back home himself. One of the problems with Fiona's postponed return was that Colm had to find another way to transport his lawn mower to those customers who weren't within walking distance of his house. He'd alerted them all to the fact that he wouldn't be by the week of his mother's honeymoon, but some of them might not be too thrilled if their lawns were permitted to grow an additional week.

Cameron had drawn a smiley face on the note and left fifty dollars under the shot glass with the cinnamon toothpicks.

There was a P.S. "Out of paper towels."

Unbelievable, he thought, mounting the stairs to change out of his church clothes. She notices the paper towels are gone but not the family dog. He wondered if *he* were to suddenly disappear how long it would take before anyone would notice.

Barefoot in cargo pants and a T-shirt, he rifled through his closet, digging through a mess to retrieve his baseball cards. With no one home, he planned to bring all his boxes and binders downstairs and take over the living room. He had about 220 new cards to file into the system, and he also wanted to comb through the majority of his old ones, a semiannual housekeeping of his collection.

First he would divide new cards up into what was and wasn't valuable, something he could usually ascertain by eye, but he also used a *Beckett's Price Guide* for reference. He alphabetized all the nonstars and stored them in case some sort of flaw or colorful detail emerged that might suddenly render one valuable. (For example, the Billy Ripken card where someone had written FUCK FACE on the bottom of the bat, a flourish no one had noticed at first.)

Then he'd go through his star collection with the price guides and record the adjusted value in his color-coded notebooks. He'd also cull out rookie cards, generally more valuable, and put them along with his star cards in a binder. Gradually many star cards, especially rookies, turned into nonstar cards as promise went unfulfilled. These then needed to come out of the binder and go into the alphabetized boxes.

Colm enjoyed poring over his cards and directing them along their paths. It was a soothing pastime that had figured as a steady and ongoing focus in his life since he was five.

A conservative estimate, he calculated, put his collection at close to four thousand dollars.

He cleared the wedding presents off the coffee table in the living room, stacking them by the television. Then he pushed the table forward, clearing enough space to sit on the floor and lean back comfortably against the couch with the boxes of cards in a semicircle in front of him.

Three hours had passed when the doorbell rang.

At last, he thought to himself. *Someone is finally using the doorbell.* As he went to answer the door, he wondered not so much who was there, but who, after all this time, was the person who had chosen to use the bell.

"Hello, Colm." It was Audrey Robertson, wilting in the heat, her mustard-yellow Century 21 blazer draped over her arm.

"Hello," said Colm.

"How are you?" Even her smile was wilted.

"Did you hear my mom's gone for another week?"

"Yes, your mother called me. So"—she took a breath, panting slightly—"I just showed a house up in Dalton and I'm on my way down to Lenox. Thought I'd stop by and just take a peek around."

Colm assumed she had come to drop off a wedding present. Fiona had cleaned Audrey's house once every two weeks for almost twelve years.

"You're on town water, aren't you?" she asked.

"Yes, we are."

"And is that your property line, at the end of the hedge there?"

Her face was red and mottled. She was a big woman and appeared to be losing her battle with the heat on every front.

"Yes, it is. And that's the other line there," he said helpfully, pointing it out for her.

"Do you mind if I come in and take a quick look-see?"

Colm didn't quite catch her last few words, but he assumed she wanted to come in and use the bathroom.

"Sure. Would you like a glass of cold water?"

"No, thanks," she said, entering, visibly relieved to get out of the sun. Sweating and aiming for the staircase, she continued, "I'll show myself around, don't worry."

"There's a bathroom right off the kitchen," Colm said, pointing the way so she wouldn't have to hike up the stairs.

"Half bath?" she asked.

"I guess so." He thought. "Yeah."

She nodded and continued her labored ascent up the stairs, lugging her purse up with her as if it were a suitcase, and gripping the banister for dear life with each step. Colm went back into the living room.

He was down on the floor, studying rookie cards of Barry Bonds and Randy Johnson, when she stuck her head in the doorway about ten minutes later.

"Just a couple quick questions?"

He looked up. He'd forgotten she was in the house.

"First off, your house is in great shape."

"Thanks."

"Have you had your land perked recently?"

He thought for a moment.

"No."

She nodded, making a mental note, and then leaned in to share a secret with him, holding on to the doorframe as if she were bracing for an earthquake.

"Let me just warn you. Don't do it till you're sure you want to sell, because if you fail the test, they make you install a new septic tank within two years." She gave him a wink along with the tip. "And then you're talking twenty grand."

Colm blinked at her a few times.

"Baseboard heating, right?"

"Pardon?"

"I forgot to look upstairs. You've got baseboard heat upstairs too?" she said, looking around the living room.

"Yes," Colm said, perplexed.

"Righty-o. I'm off," she said, disengaging from the doorway. "I left a card on the table. Thanks, Colm," and she turned to go.

Colm stared down at Randy Johnson and, after a moment, jumped up and went to the door. Audrey, in an ongoing effort to conserve her own energy, had left it open.

"Why?" he called out to her.

"Mm?" Audrey said, as she stepped down off the last step onto the walk.

"Why do you want to know all those things?"

Looking back at him, she had to shade her eyes from the sun.

"Your mom was just curious."

"Curious about what?"

"She just wondered what your house might go for on the market these days."

Colm looked at her intently.

"Just wondered aloud," Audrey smiled, squinting.

"She called you?"

"Yup. She called to say she wouldn't be coming this week, and the conversation just went from there. It's a seller's market," she added confidently.

"When?"

"When what?"

"When did you talk to her?"

"Oh . . . last night."

Colm just nodded, thought for a few moments, turned, and went back into the house.

"Toodles," he heard her sing out as he closed the door.

Inside, he saw her card on the little table by the phone. He picked it up and stared at it, holding the Randy Johnson card in his other hand. It was about half the size of the baseball card, with an entirely different set of statistics.

He went into the living room and called Fiona.

"Desert Sands Hotel," a voice answered, brightly. "How may I help you?"

"Room 423, please," Colm said.

"I'll connect you."

As the phone rang, Colm remembered he needed to water the begonias up in the window box.

The phone continued ringing.

Colm stared down at his bare feet and wound the cord around his arm a few times.

After a long time, the hotel operator finally picked up.

"No one is answering!" she said in a bright, almost

congratulatory tone. It was a voice from a land where everyone was a winner.

"Could I leave a message?"

"Certainly!"

"The message is to call Colm. Right away."

"How do you spell that, please?"

"C-o-l-m."

"C-o-l-m?"

"That's correct."

There was silence.

"I think I missed a vowel."

"You didn't."

"Hm," she said. "And how do you pronounce that again?" No response. "Okay!" she suddenly blurted out, as if his name had been approved.

"What time is it there now?" Colm asked.

"It's twelve forty-five. Sir." She wasn't about to try to pronounce his name.

"So they'll get the message?"

"I'll make sure Mr. and Mrs. Schroeder get the message!"

"Good."

It was odd hearing his mother referred to as Mrs. Schroeder.

Colm wondered what Mr. and Mrs. Schroeder and

Bunny DeCavalho were doing in Las Vegas on a Sunday afternoon at twelve forty-five. (DeCavalho was the last name of Fiona's second husband, who had returned to Portugal.)

Maybe they were out by the pool with their new beach towels and sunglasses. Or at one of those all-you-can-eat buffets Don had written him about on a postcard, listing everything he had eaten at a brunch buffet and everything he'd been too full to eat and had brought back to their hotel room wrapped in paper napkins.

"A seller's market." Colm turned and stared at the doorway where Audrey had loomed, trying to remember everything else she'd said. Fiona would probably be amused to hear that some remark she'd made had prompted Audrey to stop by and appraise the house.

He glanced over at his cards, stacked in piles on the carpet, and was seized with a strong urge to go outside. He slipped on his sneakers without tying the laces, grabbed a grape Popsicle out of the freezer, and went out into the yard.

The hose was lying coiled by the spigot near the hatchway, and he dragged it over beneath the window box. Adjusting the nozzle, he aimed a fine spray up so it rained down on the young begonia plants in the box.

This side of the house looked pretty good, he thought, eating the Popsicle and checking it out.

They had painted it just last summer. For the past three years—after Fiona had received an estimate of six thousand dollars to have the whole house painted—Colm had painted one side of the house each summer. Fiona paid him five hundred dollars for each side, and this August, Colm and his best friend, Justin, were going to paint the back, the last side. The plan was to keep going and continue painting one side a year.

Colm went around the yard and watered everything, dead or alive. He rolled up his sleeping bag and started to water the forsythia bush near Chester's grave but then thought better of it as he imagined the water seeping down.

He'd wondered whether to put some sort of marker on the grave—a few of the rounded stones from Cape Cod, or the weathered Tiki figurine back near the barbecue—but then he thought that was something they'd all figure out together when everyone got back from Las Vegas.

They'd have some kind of ceremony for Chester.

Chewing on the Popsicle stick, he coiled the hose back up near the hatchway. The faucet could use a new washer, he observed as he turned off the water.

Oddly restless, he did up his laces, grabbed his bike helmet from off the back porch railing, and jumped on his bike.

Cruising past the high school, he circled in front of Billy Kiger's house to see if Billy wanted to go for a ride with him, but there was no car in the driveway, and no one appeared to be home.

He biked over to Route 7 and zipped up a few miles to the entrance of the Berkshire Mall and the Ashuwillticook Trail, a bike path paved over an old railroad bed that extended eleven miles north along the Hoosic River, all the way up to North Adams. Colm sped along, passing skateboarders, joggers, and other bikers, not having to worry about cars and trying not to worry about anything else.

About five miles into the trail, the sound of Audrey's voice caught up with him, ringing in his ear like a cheap bicycle bell. "It's a seller's market. It's a seller's market."

By the time he'd biked to the end of the paved trail, a growing anxiety had gained an urgency he couldn't ignore. He'd been looking forward to buying a quart of ice cream in North Adams and eating it by the overpass, but now he decided against it.

He needed to get home.

There was no denying that Fiona often acted on

impulse and later regretted it. As he cycled along, he could think of dozens of poor decisions she'd made in the heat of excitement, often with the best of intentions. He needed to talk to her.

A couple of blocks from his house, he passed a few people huddled around a man who had evidently fallen off his bicycle. It was hard for Colm to tell what had happened as he sped by, but the man was on the ground, leaning over, cradling one arm with the other. Maybe it was broken.

Just out of the corner of his eye, Colm caught a fleeting glimpse of a car nearby parked at an odd angle. Maybe the cyclist had been hit. At least he was wearing a bike helmet, Colm thought, zipping by and dodging a squirrel. He considered stopping to offer assistance but the man was clearly receiving help. A police car was approaching and Colm could hear the wail of an ambulance in the distance.

After skidding a tight turn into the driveway, Colm rode his bike right up to the back porch and jumped off.

There were no messages on the answering machine.

He picked up the phone and dialed.

"Desert Sands Hotel." A man answered this time.

"Room 423, please."

"I'll connect you."

After a few rings, Fiona picked up.

"Mom."

"Colm! Bunny has been saying your name all day! It was the first word out of her mouth this morning."

This information caught him completely off guard.

"She must have known you were going to call."

"I did call. Did you get my message?"

"What message?"

"My message to call."

"Oh. Yes! I was going to call. No, honey, don't put that in your mouth." Colm could hear Bunny making grunting sounds in the background.

"Audrey Robertson was here," Colm said, straight out.

"Really?"

"She's putting together an appraisal of the house."

"Of our house?" Fiona sounded surprised, but he could tell she wasn't.

In many ways Colm understood his mother better than she did, understood her the way he grasped the inner workings of computers and other complex machines. All his antennae were now poised to pick up every shading of color in her voice.

And already he was hearing things he didn't like.

"Yes, our house," he said. "Why is she doing that?"

"Oh, just ignore her, sweetie."

"Did you ask her to?"

"No."

"You didn't?"

"Well . . ." She hesitated. There it was. The reveal he was looking for, the dead giveaway he was dreading. It was a tiny piece of evidence—a brief hesitation—but from it he constructed a whole world.

"Well what?"

"Oops! Bunny just grabbed Don's water bottle. You want to say hi to Bunny?"

"Mom."

"It's Colm, Bun-Bun, say hi."

"Mom."

There was silence.

Colm could hear some labored breathing, and he realized with a sharp pang that Fiona had put Bunny on the phone. He closed his eyes, sensing his baby sister's presence in the dark. Even at fourteen months, Bunny had full-blown personality and great charm, and Colm adored her. Listening to the rise and fall of her shallow breaths, Colm found himself breathing along with her. Joined in this deep communion, his head almost reeled from the profound comfort of it.

Bunny had said his name. She'd never said his name before.

"Colm?" Fiona had taken the receiver back.

Reluctantly he opened his eyes.

"Mom, why did you ask Audrey Robertson to appraise our house?"

"It's just . . . Really it's nothing."

"The more you talk, the more I know it's something."

"It's just . . . Well, Don got this offer at the hospital."

"What?"

"As a travel nurse."

"Don applied for a job at the hospital there?"

"Not really. Well, yes. He was just checking it out, sweetie."

"Checking out a job? In Las Vegas?"

"Just for fun. We'd seen this condo for sale, and—"

"You're looking at condos?"

Colm sank down into a squat, leaning back against the wall.

"We got an inside tip. It's not on the market yet. We met this woman in a buffet line—"

"You're looking at a condo? To buy?"

"Colm, calm down. You're overreacting."

He *was* calm, he realized. He was very calm.

"You're not selling this house," he said matter-of-factly.

"I know. Of course not."

"You're not."

"I know."

"You're *not*," he repeated bluntly.

"Colm. Don't talk to me like that." Now her tone was transparently defensive. She made a pathetic attempt to disguise it in a parental scolding voice she rarely used with him. "It is my house, after all."

She was reaching for straws now. He didn't even respond.

"Listen, sweetie"—her voice was genuinely warmer—"I didn't ask Audrey to come by, I really didn't. I just asked her what she thought the house would be worth. Colm? I was just . . . curious. I'm sorry. Don't worry, Colm, sweetie. Really. We're not selling the house. Relax."

Colm didn't say anything. He knew her so well. He had the big picture now.

"Colm? Colm?" Silence. "I'm buying you a ticket to come out here, I want you to come out and have a vacation with us. I'm sending it express mail. *Colm*. Say something."

"I'm buying the house."

"Mm?"

"I said I'm buying the house."

"You're buying the house? Our house?"

"Yes."

There was a pause.

"Fine. But we're not selling. We're not selling our house."

Colm didn't say anything.

"We're not selling our house." The more she said it, the more he believed otherwise.

"Don wants to say hello. You want to say hello to Don? Colm?"

Colm didn't say anything.

"Sweetie, don't be upset."

"I'm hanging up now."

"Don't hang up."

"I'm buying the house."

There was a silence. Then she spoke.

"Okay."

"'Bye."

And he hung up.

Still in a crouch and leaning back against the wall, he dropped his head down into his hands. His eyes were tightly closed, with his thumbs pressed up against the bridge of his nose.

He knew what he had to do.

Chapter Seven

By one o'clock the next afternoon, Colm had spoken on the phone with Audrey Robertson, two other Realtors, one lawyer, three bankers, and four baseball card stores in Springfield, Hartford, and Albany.

He had also spoken with a nurse who had called Colm early in the morning on behalf of Mr. Hafferty, who was laid up in the hospital, recovering from a concussion, a broken collarbone and three cracked ribs. Unfortunately it was Mr. Hafferty who had driven into the cyclist Colm had seen the day before, and subsequently hit a telephone pole.

Colm sat in the hospital waiting room, wearing his one dress jacket and tie for a later appointment at a bank, reviewing some figures in a spiral notebook.

A large cup of Dunkin' Donuts coffee was on the

floor by his feet, and a plastic grocery bag containing a box of Entenmann's éclairs. Mr. Hafferty loved Dunkin' Donuts coffee, and even if he wasn't allowed to drink it in his current condition, Colm hoped he would enjoy having the cup with its familiar cheerful logo on it.

Audrey had stunned him with her off-the-cuff appraisal of their house—$240,000—but the two other Realtors confirmed that the estimate was probably well within the ballpark, based on other recent sales in the neighborhood. Both Realtors were eager to stop by and tour the house, but he adamantly said no, repeating several times that there was already a buyer in the picture.

He studied the numbers on his notepad. Most likely the bank would want at least ten percent down— $24,000. Interest rates were currently quite low, and after looking through ads in two local newspapers, he thought he could get a 30-year mortgage with a fixed rate of 6.25 percent. That would make for monthly payments of $637.20, and if he rented out two of the upstairs bedrooms at three hundred dollars a month each, that would just about cover the mortgage payments.

If he finished the downstairs screened-in porch as a bedroom for himself, he could even rent the third upstairs bedroom. But three tenants on the second floor all sharing the same bathroom might get a little crowded. Better if he was up there, keeping an eye on things.

Of course, this was all until Fiona's misbegotten adventure in Las Vegas fell apart, and she was home again.

The hard part was going to be coming up with the down payment, the twenty-four grand. If he sold his entire baseball card collection, his electric guitar and amp, his stereo, table saw, generator, and a few other items, he calculated that—along with his savings—he could come up with roughly eight thousand dollars.

He doodled with a pencil around the eight-thousand-dollar figure, pondering.

Maybe he could keep *some* of the more valuable cards. His favorites.

"Mr. Drucker?" She had to say it again. "Mr. Drucker?"

He looked up to see a middle-aged nurse with a clipboard looking over at him.

"Mr. Hafferty can receive visitors now."

Behind her was a small sign on the nurse's station in needlepoint announcing that visitors under eighteen had to be accompanied by an adult. Colm had been eyeing the sign with a mixture of annoyance and concern ever since he'd gotten there.

"I'll show you where he is. I'm headed that way myself."

Picking up the coffee and the bag with the éclairs, Colm hurried to follow her through the double doors and down and around the long green hallway. Wrestling with whether to tell her or not, he finally said to her quietly from behind, "Excuse me, I'm only fifteen."

"What?" she asked, turning suddenly around, which caused her glasses to slide from the top of her head down onto her nose.

"I'm fifteen." He stopped, stepping out of the way of a patient being briskly wheeled by on a gurney, and she stopped too.

She studied him. Dressed in his pressed jacket, tie, and polished shoes, clutching the cup of Dunkin' Donuts coffee, Colm looked as if he could be an earnest young premed student.

"And your point?" the nurse asked, sliding her glasses back up.

"The sign said minors have to be accompanied by an adult."

"What sign?"

"The sign in the waiting room."

She tilted her head, squinted, and studied him some more. He realized he was probably being stupid, but he didn't want a scene to be created later in Mr. Hafferty's room because of his not having followed the rule.

"You're not fifteen," she said finally.

"I am. "

She didn't look convinced.

"You're fifteen?"

He nodded.

"Well," she said, giving it some thought, "I'm an adult. And I'm accompanying you."

Colm nodded and proceeded to follow her past an elderly woman in a wheelchair hooked up to various tubes, and a man in a SpongeBob bathrobe and slippers struggling along on a pair of crutches.

"Last stop," said the nurse outside a room at the end of the hall, gesturing for Colm to enter.

"Thank you."

The three beds in the room were separated by bright yellow curtains hanging from rods off the ceiling. Colm was disturbed to see, on the far side of the room by the window, Mr. Hafferty's head wrapped up in a white bandage, sunk back into a pillow and peeking up over a white blanket. After a few moments he walked over.

"Mr. Hafferty, " Colm said quietly, standing by the bed. There was no response. "Mr. Hafferty . . ."

Slowly Mr. Hafferty rolled his head until his watery eyes were looking up at him.

"Oh boy," he said, smiling wanly. "Am I glad to see you."

The whole right side of his face was bruised a deep mottled purple around his eye and cheekbone all the way down to his jaw. The bandage on his head was wound snugly around his forehead, so he appeared to be wearing a close-fitting white Himalayan Sherpa hat. The contrast between the bright white and deep purple was stark.

"Wow," Colm couldn't help but mutter.

"They told me I had a visitor," Mr. Hafferty said, drooling slightly. "Have a seat."

Colm didn't move. He wondered if Mr. Hafferty had had a chance to look at himself in a mirror.

"I brought you some coffee," he said finally, placing the cup on the bedside table.

Mr. Hafferty was visibly pleased.

"That ought to wake me up," he said, closing his eyes and then opening them up partway. "They got me all drugged up."

With some effort he pulled his hand out from under the covers, slowly raised it to his face, and wiped his chin with the back of it.

"I wish I had an éclair to offer you," he lamented, gazing around.

Colm took the box of éclairs out of the bag and held it within his view. Deeply touched, Mr. Hafferty shook his head slowly back and forth as his eyes filled with tears.

"My sister came," he said. "What did she bring me? Toothpaste and nail clippers. You, you bring me exactly what I need."

"Would you like one?" asked Colm.

Mr. Hafferty waved a no with his hand. "Please. Help yourself. Enjoy."

Colm lifted an éclair out of the box, dragged a chair toward the bed, sat down, and took a small bite.

"I feel so bad," said Mr. Hafferty.

"Where?" Colm asked.

The whole right side of Mr. Hafferty's face looked as if it were in dark shadow, like the north face of a mountain on a late winter afternoon. Colm wondered which hurt worse, the cracked ribs or the broken collarbone.

"I hit that poor man on the bicycle."

"Oh," said Colm, realizing he was referring to his mental, not his physical state.

"They say he came and visited me, but I don't remember. I was all drugged up."

He sighed. Colm could see Mr. Hafferty's foot move a little under the blanket.

"That poor man. He looked *so confused*. . . ."

Colm had never seen Mr. Hafferty so upset. It was going to be impossible to pretend to enjoy eating the éclair. He wiped off a little bit of cream filling that had fallen onto his tie.

"If only I could tell him how sorry I am. Apologize."

He looked at Colm dolefully.

"We can probably find out who he is," said Colm.

"How? I've been trying to think. Take out a classified?"

Colm pondered.

"I could go check the police record."

"Really?" Mr. Hafferty's left eye opened up all the way. "Ohhh," he sighed. "If we could do that . . . that would be *terrific*."

"We can do that. I'll do that."

"I'll pay you."

"You don't have to pay me."

"I know."

Mr. Hafferty sighed again and closed his eyes.

He breathed audibly through his open mouth, a raw scraping sound.

"He came right at me. Out of nowhere. This great

white helmet on his head. Like a big bird. I don't think that man could ride a bicycle very well."

"I'm sure it wasn't your fault."

"It *was* my fault. I was listening to Prokofiev's Fifth Symphony. The Erich Leinsdorf Boston Symphony recording. So sublime."

"You want some coffee?"

"Please."

Colm got up to pick up the coffee cup, but when he looked back over at Mr. Hafferty, he was sound asleep. Snoring lightly.

Colm put the coffee back on the table and sat back down again, waiting for him to wake up.

An hour and a half later Colm was at the Pittsfield Cooperative Bank, sitting on a straight-backed armchair, waiting for a Mrs. Howe, ten minutes early for his appointment. He'd ridden his bike over from the hospital and had locked it up two blocks away so that no one at the bank could look out the window and see his means of transportation. Likewise he had left his backpack at home.

The sitting area was off to one side of the central lobby, a large vaulted room.

From there Colm watched the bank tellers at their windows. It was not a busy time of day, and Colm could

hear the ticking of the grandfather clock near the receptionist's desk. The receptionist, ostensibly freezing from
the air-conditioning, was hunched over with a thick
mohair shawl wrapped around her bare shoulders. A
young woman in her early twenties, she glanced over at
Colm several times while he waited.

He realized that all he had eaten that day was half
a bowl of Cheerios, all that remained in the cereal box,
and a small portion of an éclair.

"Mr. Drucker?"

It was the second time that day Colm had been
addressed in that manner.

Mrs. Howe, neatly coiffed and wearing a sky-blue
pantsuit, beckoned him to follow her. She walked with
her head perfectly level, placing one foot in front of the
other as if she were walking on a tightrope across the
thickly carpeted floor. Even though she took small minc-
ing steps, she covered a lot of territory quickly.

"Come on in," she said, standing by the door to her
office and gesturing for Colm to enter.

He ventured in, carrying his notebook and pen. A
large oak desk consumed much of the small room, and two
chairs for customers faced the desk. The upholstery of the
chairs matched the busy floral pattern of the wallpaper,
so they almost disappeared from view except for the oak

legs and the large brass tacks attaching the fabric.

"Have a seat."

Colm took stock and aimed for the chair that was closer to the desk. His pant legs were a little short—he had definitely outgrown these pants—and the closer he sat to the desk, the less likely she was to see his socks when he sat down. He waited for her to come in and sit before he did.

"You have an account with us?"

"No."

Mrs. Howe closed the door, went around behind the desk, and deposited herself in the black leather executive chair, leaning forward and folding her hands on the smooth polished surface. A smile suddenly hopped on her face like a little bird jumping up onto a ledge.

"So," she said. "You're interested in acquiring a mortgage?"

"I'm buying my mother's house."

Mrs. Howe tilted her head slightly, as if she were a little hard of hearing.

"Actually it's the family home. My great-grandfather built it."

"Oh?"

Colm straightened his tie.

"I saw your ad in the *Berkshire Eagle*," he said.

"Regarding interest rates."

"Your mother is selling her house?"

"She's in Las Vegas."

Mrs. Howe's smile lingered on her face, although her thoughts seemed to have migrated on.

"You're offering a thirty-year mortgage at a fixed rate of six point two five percent?"

"That's correct. We are. Have you ever applied for a mortgage before, Mr. Drucker?"

"No."

"Well," she said, with a hint of condescension, "you know, it's *quite* complicated."

"Mrs. Howe," Colm responded, "your bank is the first of several I'm interviewing this week. At this point I'm basically just doing some comparison shopping."

The tone of his voice knocked the smile off her face with the precision of a perfectly aimed snowball.

"Yes. Well. Of course."

She leaned back, reached for the brass handle of the top drawer, and yanked it toward her.

"Have you established any kind of credit?" she asked, taking out some materials.

Colm didn't respond.

"You have a credit card? Have you ever taken out a loan before?" She opened the bottom drawer and took out three pamphlets. These she placed next to a new yellow legal pad and a long tapered pen with the bank's logo emblazoned on it.

"No."

"You are, of course, eighteen?"

As she assembled the various pamphlets and sheets of paper in front of her, Colm rammed the tip of his tongue into a little pocket between two back molars. He kept it anchored there as he wrestled with his answer. Every fiber in his body had lurched forward, poised to answer truthfully.

She looked up at him and repeated the question.

"You're eighteen?"

Through the wide rectangular window behind her, he could see the bank's parking lot and the neatly landscaped border that separated it from the street beyond. What if he said no? If he told her the truth, would she escort him briskly out of the room and send him on his way?

Over her shoulder, he could see a blue Honda Civic pull into the parking lot. From his perspective, it appeared to drive straight through her head, entering into her left ear and coming out her right.

"Two hundred and forty thousand dollars," he said, in as deep and mature a voice as he could muster, locking eyes with her.

"Mm?"

"That's the asking price. Two hundred and forty thousand dollars."

He waited for her response.

"Oh." She blinked a few times.

"If I made a down payment of, say, seventy thousand dollars, what are some possible payment plans?"

She stopped blinking.

Whatever concerns she might have had about his age suddenly vanished. The eighteen in question vaporized once the seventy thousand was floated, the larger number consuming the smaller like a whale snacking on a small herring. All of Mrs. Howe's banker instincts were fully aroused, and she picked up the pen and leaned over to her calculator, her fingers already tap-dancing on the keypad.

Colm hadn't planned to talk about a seventy-thousand-dollar down payment. He'd planned to talk about a twenty-four-thousand-dollar down payment.

He cleared his throat and sat there, gently bobbing up and down in the wake of his remark.

Seventy thousand dollars. The number had risen up out of him like a methane bubble surfacing from a deep bog. He had just tossed it out into the room in a purely offensive move, but now that the figure was there, he found himself examining it. Recalling its source.

Since he had torn up and flushed Lloyd Henry's letter down the new drain in the laundry room, Colm hadn't given his offer a second thought. It had seemed so preposterous, so odiously entangled. Now . . . it seemed like a lot of money. If it was real.

He tugged his pant legs down and sat there, watching Mrs. Howe busily jotting down numbers in four neat columns. Over the top of her head, the blue Honda Civic drove back the other way. Something in him was doing a reverse, too. Or beginning to. The turning radius made it difficult, as if he were about to turn a long barge around in a narrow canal.

Seventy thousand dollars. Given the stakes, maybe he should check it out.

Chapter Eight

Colm had several stops to make on his way home from the bank, including the Stop & Shop for groceries, Brooks Pharmacy for a NO TRESPASS-ING sign to keep Realtors away, and the police station where he wanted to check out the accident report for Mr. Hafferty.

But first he rode his bike over to Radio Shack to buy a caller ID. If only they'd already had one hooked up, he'd have a number for Lloyd Henry. As it was, Colm couldn't even be sure the man would ever call again. The letter he'd sent was postmarked from Pittsfield, but maybe he was just passing through town and had long since vanished.

Next Colm stopped in at Blount, Dowling & Frangione to speak with a lawyer whose lawn he mowed and who had offered to give him some legal advice regarding purchasing the house. In ten minutes Colm learned pretty much what he needed to know and also received the sixty dollars Mr. Frangione owed him for two mowings.

"I feel bad taking this money," Colm said, looking down at the handful of bills.

"Why?"

"You just gave me all this information for free. I should pay you."

"Tell you what, Colm, " said Mr. Frangione. "If you could take a look at that damned fan over there and tell me why it stopped working, we'll call it even."

Colm aimed straight for the outlet behind his desk and unplugged the fan.

"Red Sox are looking pretty good this year," Mr. Frangione said, leaning over and untying his shoes.

Colm had taken out his Swiss Army knife and was already unscrewing the screws in the plug.

"Pitching's strong."

In less than a minute, Colm had reattached a loose wire in the plug. He plugged it back into the wall, and the fan immediately started working.

"Hallelujah," said Mr. Frangione, throwing up his arms and reveling in the breeze. "You're a *genius*, Colm."

"You should use the on/off switch, Mr. Frangione,"

Colm said, folding up his pocketknife and putting it away.

"But that means I have to get up out of this chair and walk all the way over there."

"Yanking the plug to turn it off could cause a short. Start a fire."

Mr. Frangione was leaning back, happy as a clam, his feet in mismatched argyle socks up on the file cabinet near the desk.

"Shadow buyer," Colm mused in the doorway before taking off.

"Yup. That's what you want," Mr. Frangione said, settling in for an afternoon snooze. "Good luck. Call me for the closing."

"I will. Thank you."

Later, speeding over to the supermarket on his bike, Colm took off his tie and wrapped it around the grips of his handlebars, holding on to both ends of the tie as he pedaled along. He felt he'd made some progress that day, and with the wind on his face, he relaxed and enjoyed his ride.

According to Mr. Frangione, Colm's name could be on the deed, the instrument of ownership, but because he was under eighteen, he wasn't old enough to sign a mortgage. He'd have to find a shadow buyer, someone whose name would appear on the mortgage and also on the deed. That person had to show a steady income, have good credit, and "be someone you can trust, *really* trust."

Colm cruised into the Stop & Shop parking lot and locked his bike in the shade by the main entrance. He grabbed a cart and pushed it inside, jumping up onto the back of it and rolling into the store.

Angie might be a good candidate to be a shadow buyer, he thought, wandering down the cereal aisle, although he wasn't sure how good her credit was. Mr. Hafferty would sign a mortgage for him in a heartbeat, but he didn't have a substantial income beyond his small pension and Social Security. Thinking of Mr. Hafferty, Colm remembered he had to go to the police station.

In the checkout line, he realized he was starving and noticed that his cart was filled with far more food than he'd planned to buy. He picked up two candy bars while he waited and ate them both, showing the cashier the empty wrappers.

As he headed out the door carrying two full bags of groceries, he ran straight into Melanie Phelps out on the sidewalk.

"Hi," she said, smiling, as he stepped back.

"Sorry. I didn't see you."

"That's okay. I saw you."

There was a slightly awkward silence.

"Getting some groceries?" she asked.

"Uh-huh."

"My mom's inside."

"Oh?" He cleared his throat.

"I got my learner's permit. I drove her over here."

"Really."

Another silence. Colm couldn't believe how wonderful she looked.

"So what are you doing this summer?" she asked.

Ten possible answers collided between his brain and his tongue.

"Oh. You know. Things."

She nodded and studied him, that amazing brain of hers clicking away. Her brain could eat his for lunch, he thought.

"I'm buying my mother's house," he volunteered suddenly.

"Really?"

"Yup." Colm was stunned he'd said it.

"Why?"

He could feel a few items shifting in the left bag. The carton of chocolate milk. The package of sliced American cheese. He adjusted his grip and held the bag closer.

"Why?" Melanie repeated after a while.

"So she won't sell it."

"Oh."

She seemed satisfied with this answer. Again she smiled.

Her sun-streaked brown hair was piled loosely on her head, but several long strands fell down onto her collarbone and bare arms. The turquoise blue of her sleeveless cotton top appeared to be reflected in her already remarkably blue eyes.

Neither of them said anything or moved. After a few moments, she flicked a fly away from her face without taking her eyes off him. They stood there awhile longer, staring at each other, neither speaking.

Something in her gaze, in the way she was looking at him, was so riveting, so unusual, that he couldn't stop staring into her eyes. Summoning all his intuition, he was trying simply to fathom what it was that he was staring at.

"There's my mom," she said suddenly, glancing over at the far exit of the supermarket.

Before he could turn to look over at her mother, Melanie had stood up on her toes and kissed him. On the lips.

She pulled back a little, her face still close to his.

Still up on her toes, she studied his response, her eyes darting back and forth. Her face broke into just a hint of a smile, seemingly illuminated by some small discovery, and then suddenly she took off.

"Call me," she said, backing up and hurrying over to her mother, who was pushing a cart out into the parking lot.

Colm didn't say anything. He didn't move.

He stayed put and watched as, in the distance, Melanie helped her mother load groceries into the back of their station wagon. He stayed and watched as Melanie pushed the empty cart over to the striped awning by the store where the carts were kept, and he watched as she opened the door to the driver's side, got in, and drove away.

As the car made a left turn out of the parking lot, an arm appeared out the driver's window. Raised high and waving.

If Colm's feet had been made out of concrete and had been poured at the same time as the sidewalk, he wouldn't have been more rooted to the spot.

The same fly that had buzzed around Melanie now came and landed on his cheek, but he didn't notice.

It was only after a few people had passed by and given him questioning looks that he finally stirred.

"So what'd you forget?" one woman joked. "Soda? Chips?"

As soon as he got home, he hooked up the caller ID and called Cameron, asking her to call back so he could see if it worked. She wasn't home, so he just left a message.

There were three messages on their answering machine, all from Fiona, telling him how much she missed him and that she'd express-mailed a Southwest airplane ticket for the next day.

"*Please*, Colm. Come out. It'll be fun."

Colm wandered into the kitchen and cooked himself a few cheeseburgers, now wearing only his Oxford shirt and boxer shorts. He'd bought four packs of baseball cards, but he left them unopened on the counter near the NO TRESPASSING sign while he ate.

That evening he watched a little TV, but soon found himself nodding off on the couch, even though it was barely dark out. His head felt unusually heavy.

When he finally got up to go to bed, he didn't aim for the back door and the yard. For the first time since Chester had died, he felt like climbing up the stairs and crawling into his own bed.

Entering his room with a mounting exhaustion, he fumbled with his shirt buttons and dropped the shirt on a large pile of dirty laundry on the floor.

In bed he stared at the moonlight that flooded

through his window onto the wall. The shadow from the oak tree just outside was in dark relief in the white-washed light.

He opened his mouth as if to yawn, but then closed it again, as if he couldn't quite remember how.

For some reason he was having difficulty reviewing the events of the day.

He was buying a house. And Melanie Phelps had kissed him. *Melanie Phelps had kissed him.*

Colm closed his eyes, and the instant he closed them, he saw Melanie's eyes, staring at him. It was as if he hadn't closed his eyes but opened them . . . wider.

Chapter Nine

"**C**olm!"

"Hrm?"

"Colm! Colm, get up!"

Colm opened his eyes. Cameron was glaring down at him.

"You've got three minutes."

She put three fingers over his face.

He glanced over at the clock and remembered in a flash they'd arranged for her to give him a lift down to Lenox. He'd forgotten to set the alarm.

"Three minutes and I'm leaving."

It took Colm three and a half minutes to get ready, and two of those minutes were spent loading his bulky power lawn mower into the back of Cameron's 1982 Jeep, which was packed with beach towels, folded lawn chairs, mounds of loose laundry, and trash bags filled with refundable bottles and cans.

"I'm going," Cameron warned, revving the engine and yelling back at him from the driver's seat as he struggled with the handle of the lawn mower.

"Ten seconds," she said. "Nine . . ."

As proof of her intentions, she suddenly lurched the Jeep forward a foot.

"Cameron!" Colm wailed, falling forward. He yanked out a trash bag of refundables and flung it to the ground by the driveway to clear space. Likewise a lawn chair. He was finally able to pound the handle free, tilt the lawn mower back enough to shove it in sideways, and then close the door, race around to the passenger door, and climb in as Cameron shifted from first to second and sped out the driveway.

Sitting in the passenger seat, Colm finished lacing up his boots, lamenting that he hadn't had time to grab a pair of socks. He also hadn't had a chance to eat anything, and he knew that he probably wouldn't for hours. Bleary-eyed and slightly disoriented, he sat back and ran his tongue over his unbrushed teeth.

Not fully awake, much of his mind was still embroiled in his dream. He'd dreamed that he and Chester were riding out on the weed boat that Melanie Phelps had written about. They were sitting, side by side, on the bench seat atop the slowly moving harvester, hauling up weeds. At first it was a still summer day, but then it had begun snowing.

Way off in the distance, on the far shore of the lake, Fiona and Cameron were standing by the water's edge, waiting to be rescued. The snow squall picked up, and through the whirling curlicues of snow Colm could see them both jumping up and down, waving to show him their whereabouts. He was trying to make the boat go faster, but the whole scene started to freeze over. The weeds were turning into long icicles that were freezing up the belts.

"Shit." Cameron, whose mission in life was to avoid all traffic lights, braked abruptly for a red light.

Colm gazed sleepily over at her and then back out his window.

His dream reminded him of the photograph of the three of them out on Pontoosuc Lake, the photograph he'd studied in the living room when he was on the phone with Lloyd Henry. Fiona was wearing the same puffy purple ski jacket in his dream, and Cameron was dressed in the same red wool coat and the crazy multicolored scarf she'd crocheted in fourth grade.

"You don't know where Lloyd Henry lives, do you?" Colm scratched his elbow.

"Who?" Cameron asked, after a few moments.

"Lloyd Henry."

She slowly turned and stared at him.

"Well. Do you?" Colm asked.

"No."

"Do you know if Mom does?"

He must have still been half asleep, because he was not heeding classic Cameron warning signals. If she were a porcupine, she was now provoked, barbed quills raised and threatening.

"Why?" she asked suddenly. Aggressively.

He didn't say anything.

"Why?" she repeated.

"I just wondered."

"You just wondered," she echoed nastily.

Colm, his radar systems awake now and functioning, felt his stomach start to knot up. He knew he was in for it, and he turned his body away from her to stare out the passenger window, hunkering down. Unfortunately they were at least ten minutes away from the Flannerys, his best customers, who owned two and a half acres of flat landscaped lawn and who tipped generously.

"You know . . ." she said, ramping up, "I think there is something *seriously* wrong with you, Colm."

"Oh really?" He knew if he didn't say something back, her rate of nuclear detonation would accelerate.

"Yes. What in God's name would lead you to believe I would a) have any information about where that asshole scumbag lives, and b) that I would even enter into a conversation about him. Furthermore—"

"Cameron . . ." he said, trying to hold her back. She must have been in a bad mood to start with. He should never have brought up Lloyd Henry without carefully checking her out first.

"Furthermore . . . I think you should go see a psychiatrist. I think you're losing your *grip*, Colm. Mom says you're thinking of buying the house."

He turned back toward her.

"Is that true? *Is that true?*" she asked. "Because if it is . . . if it is . . . then you are seriously deranged."

"Mom told you that?"

"Yes, she did, and she's concerned, and frankly so am I. That is just so *demented* and . . . *weird*. That is totally more than alarming delusional behavior for a sophomore in high school. Colm, people who are fifteen don't buy houses."

"Well . . . she's looking at buying a condo."

"So?"

"So. She thinks she wants to move to Las Vegas."

"What's wrong with that? It's better than living in this hellhole."

"She told you she wants to move there?" Colm zeroed in, more focused now on gathering information than ducking a Cameron firestorm.

"You sit around that house like some wacko . . . like an old man. You are *old*, Colm, you're just a kid but you're old . . . you're old like Chester, I'm surprised *your* bladder doesn't leak."

"Pull over."

"You're always fixing something, fixing or building or futzing with the house . . . puttering around like some old retired man. . . . It's perverse. You never drink, you're so goddamned serious. Why don't you get a girl-friend? I think you don't even like girls."

"Pull over."

"It's like you have this sick relationship with that house."

"It's the family home."

"Colm, I hate to break this to you . . . but it's not the family home. The family isn't home. The family moved out. The only one who's home is you."

"PULL OVER!"

Colm unfastened his seat belt and opened the door, fighting a fifty-mile-an-hour wind.

Cameron, stunned that her brother had yelled at her, braked and swerved into the entrance of a Jiffy Lube just south of Pittsfield along a commercial strip.

Colm put his hand on the dashboard to brace for the jerking sudden stop. Then he leapt out, stormed around to the back, and flung open the back door. He hauled out the lawn mower and set it on the ground, dragging out a beach towel and a bikini top along with it. These he kicked furiously under the Jeep before coming around and slamming the passenger door shut.

Cameron, not one to be outslammed, opened her door, scrambled up, and started screaming at him over the roof of the Jeep.

"That's the last time I'm giving you a ride anywhere! Ever again! You're *sick*, Colm! *Sick!*"

Colm grabbed the handle of his lawn mower with both hands, leaned forward, and began pushing it along the sidewalk as if he were hell-bent on mowing inches off the concrete. The men at the Jiffy Lube, fully entertained, stared from their open bays at Cameron, whose cherry-red lipstick could be seen from a mile away.

"Go back to the family home!!" she screamed. "You're an old man, Colm, an OLD MAN!"

One of the Jiffy Lube guys made a remark that made the others laugh. At the sound of their laughter, Cameron whipped her head around like a fifty-caliber on a swivel mount and fired a menacing glare at them. One lanky bald guy threw both his hands up, dropping his wrench, and cowered as if he were terrified of her, making his buddies laugh even more. Pissed off, she gave them the finger, plunged down into the driver's seat, and screeched away.

Colm kept walking in the other direction, his own steam fueling the lawn mower's drive like high-octane gas. If the brake had been on, it wouldn't have slowed him down.

After some distance he calmed down enough to realize he was heading north, back up toward Pittsfield. He halted abruptly in front of Guido's market, flung his hands free of the handle, paced around, stopped, and stared out at the traffic without really seeing it. At least fifty cars had sped by before he furiously kicked off a plastic bag attached to his boot and then crouched down, leaned back against a telephone pole, and pondered his options.

It would take him at least an hour to walk down to the Flannerys. And then at least another two hours to walk home after he'd mowed their lawn. Mrs. Flannery might be around to pay him and maybe give him a lift back in her SUV, but what if she wasn't home? Feeling hungry, he reached for his back pocket and realized that in his haste to get ready that morning, he'd neglected to grab his wallet. He had no money. Despondent, he slid all the way down the telephone pole onto the grass.

What a jerk his sister was. He was glad she'd

moved out. And to think he'd been feeling badly that Lloyd Henry had written to him and not her, had offered him that gargantuan sum of money. Now he certainly wasn't going to give any of it to her. None. He wouldn't even tell her about it.

A boy of about ten shuffled past him on the sidewalk eating a donut. Cameron's beach towel that had fallen out of her Jeep was draped around his shoulders, and he had threaded her crimson red bikini top through the belt loops of his cargo pants. But it was the donut that had Colm's attention.

He could go into Guido's to see if his friend Andrew was working that morning. Andrew was his biology lab partner and had achieved some notoriety that spring getting suspended for making a documentary entitled *Sweat—How the Body Perspires and the Psychological Causes and Ramifications.* Though it was initially conceived as a science project, Andrew came to consider it a postmodern art film on angst. He had posted his evocative results, including charts and myriad graphic photographs, on the Internet. The close-up of the high school band leader's wet armpits alone had been enough to land him in the assistant principal's office.

He had a summer job bagging groceries and helping out in the produce department, chopping up mountains of cantaloupes, watermelon, and other fruit for the quart-size plastic fruit salad containers. Colm thought about asking him if he could borrow some money, or maybe Andrew could get him a muffin. Guido's had delicious blueberry muffins.

He looked back at the store longingly. Then he looked at his lawn mower. He picked up a rock, made a fist around it, and banged it down hard on the ground a few times.

Resigned, he got up, hauled his lawn mower across Route 7, and began pushing it along the right-hand side of the road, traveling in the familiar bike lane.

Without socks, his feet chafed in his boots and he soon felt a couple of hot spots, sure signs of the beginnings of blisters. Like all roads in the Berkshires, Route 7 was hilly, and he trudged along, pushing the lawn mower up and down the winding road, his arms outstretched, staring down at the pavement, ignoring the drivers who occasionally honked at him or yelled wisecracks out their windows as they drove by.

Fifteen minutes later someone in an old yellow pickup truck stopped and gave him a ride partway home. He sat in the truck bed in the back with his lawn mower even though the driver had invited him to come sit up front. Leaning back against the cab with his legs stretched out, rocking back and forth, Colm watched the road and the paycheck he was counting on retreat in front of him. Mrs. Flannery was pretty fussy about her lawn. He hoped she wouldn't be too mad.

He closed his eyes and remembered his dream from that morning, riding the weed boat out on the lake with Chester by his side. It struck him that the weed boat was essentially a giant lawn mower that mowed the bottom of the lake. He wondered what Melanie Phelps would think about that.

He pictured her the way he had countless times, riding back to the dock at dusk, her hooded sweatshirt pulled up over her head. Even though he'd never actually seen her like that, the image was stored away in his mind, more real in some ways than the memory of her kissing him. Remembering the kiss, he opened his eyes, startled.

At that moment the driver stopped near Park Square, and Colm scrambled out. There could be no more unwieldy an object than a lawn mower, Colm thought, arduously hoisting the base out of the truck bed and settling it down out on the sidewalk. Hauling out a drunken man would have been easier.

He pushed the mower for many blocks through downtown Pittsfield, maneuvering it up and down the curbs, past the CVS drugstore, the boarded-up

Woolworth's, the thrift shop, and used-book stores.

Colm had gone a few blocks past the police station before remembering about Mr. Hafferty and the accident report. He wheeled around and went back, wondering if it would be safe to leave his lawn mower outside while he went in. Who would steal a lawn mower from in front of a police station?

He debated what to do. What would the police think if they saw someone coming through the front door pulling a lawn mower?

Hungry and frustrated, he was aware his brain wasn't working too well. He finally backed up the lawn mower, wheeled it around, and proceeded to steer it home. After another mile, he took off his right boot, the heel of which had created a nasty blister on his ankle, and put it up on the lawn mower, where it rode like a hood ornament. With one bare foot, he strode for another mile or so through town, trying to avoid broken glass and small stones.

The first thing he did when he got home was check his messages and the caller ID. There was a number with an unfamiliar area code, but it turned out to be his grandmother calling from Florida to see if the grapefruit had arrived. There was a message from Angie, asking him if he needed any groceries—she was cooking dinner for Walter that evening and was going shopping, and one from

Fiona, wondering if the plane ticket had arrived. The caller ID had worked, but there was no number for Lloyd Henry.

He went into the kitchen and made himself a large stack of French toast, also eating a couple of donuts, a quarter of a watermelon, and several tablespoons of peanut butter. What would he do if Lloyd Henry never called? How could he possibly get in touch with him? Should he ask Fiona if she knew anything about him? Or would she go nuts on him like Cameron had?

He pondered. There was no denying it . . . he *was* about to consort with the enemy.

Sitting at the kitchen table, he wiped his mouth with the dish towel and leaned back in the chair.

No denying it.

He threw the dish towel across the room into the kitchen sink.

After washing up his dishes and the skillet, he went out into the hall and settled on the bottom step of the staircase to put some first-aid cream and several Band-Aids on his blisters.

Resting back on his elbows, he stared at the narrow frosted windowpanes on the top half of the front door and realized how quiet it was. The house suddenly felt enormous, like an ill-fitting coat—all those rooms and no one else in them.

He got up and climbed the stairs to the first landing. Sitting on the top step, he reached over to the bottom right corner of a panel on the wall and pressed. The corner of the panel depressed slightly and then sprang back. It was a secret door to a small cedar-paneled four-foot-square room that Colm had discovered when he was three, following Chester up the staircase. He and Chester had slept together in there many times on an old army surplus sleeping bag.

Fiona had wanted to use the little room to store the old tennis rackets, the badminton net, and all the outdoor toys, and Cameron had tried to claim it a few times, but Colm had adamantly defended his turf.

It had been a long time since he'd been in there. He bent over and ducked inside, squatting on the braided carpet he'd scavenged out of a Dumpster. There was a pull chain for a light in the ceiling, and he gave it a tug but the lightbulb had long since burnt out. He could dimly see a pile of pillows at the end, Tinkertoy models, action figures, and other familiar toys.

Colm sat on the carpet, leaned up against the wall, and pushed the door until it was almost shut, leaving open a crack to let a little light in. When he'd been a kid, this room had been big enough to jump around in, but now he could neither stand up nor lie down. Sitting there, he felt too big for the room in a way similar to how he'd just felt too small for the house.

Wherever he was, he was out of proportion.

He reached under his right thigh and picked up a small object. He knew immediately, feeling it in the dark, what it was—a little top that his great-grandfather had carved out of the same mahogany he'd used to carve the banister and the mantelpiece. It was in the shape of an apple, the rounded bottom curving to a slightly raised point. Colm could feel the fine cross-hatching on the two leaves that sprouted near the apple's stem.

Holding the top in the palm of his hand, he thought of his great-grandfather and immediately sensed him in the room with him, a powerful presence.

"Chester died."

It was the first time Colm had spoken the words.

He'd thought them so many times, he'd actually wondered over the last ten days if he had in fact said them out loud. But the way it felt to finally voice them made him sure he hadn't.

As soon as he spoke, his eyes teared up.

He banged his head back against the wall and gritted his teeth.

Leaning forward, he pushed the door shut so he was in complete darkness. He sat back and after a split second broke down, letting loose tears that had been on hold for ten days since his dog had died. He cried for several minutes and then pulled off his T-shirt and wiped his face with it. Then he blew his nose into the shirt and threw it down.

Every muscle in his body went limp as he dropped his head forward, his elbows resting on his knees. He felt as if he were somersaulting forward, suspended in total darkness. He thought of a pilot he'd read about who had inadvertently flown into the ground in the pitch-black of night because his instrument panel didn't work and he'd assumed he was the other way up.

Colm took a couple of deep breaths.

It amazed him that the scent of the cedar had lingered for all these years, as if the wood were still alive. In some ways, he thought, this little chamber was the heart of the house.

Maybe it was true. Maybe everyone in the family had moved out except him. But if he didn't hold on to the house, *how could any of them ever come home?*

He picked up the mahogany apple top his great-grandfather had carved, gripped it, and started rubbing his thumb in circles around the smooth polished surface. It fitted snugly in the palm of his hand.

Five minutes later, he pulled the door open and scrambled out onto the landing, blinking at the dust-filled shaft of sunlight that shone down through the octagonal window onto his face. Straightening up, he continued up the staircase to take a shower and put on some clean clothes.

Then he went into Fiona's bedroom and turned on Don's computer, which was temporarily set up on a hope chest by her bureau. Sitting on a footstool next to a large box of diapers, Colm went online and Googled Lloyd Henry Drucker. Forty-three sites came up, including a Lloyd Drucker who lived in Australia and ran a scuba diving school, but nothing seemed remotely connected to the person who was his father.

Not that it would be easy for him to tell. He himself, he thought, wasn't remotely connected to the person who was his father.

He went off-line and turned off the computer after staring briefly at Don's screen saver, a picture of an antique Coca-Cola cooler. Don liked to buy Coca-Cola antiques on eBay.

Down in the kitchen, Colm polished off a quart container of lemonade and ate three more honey-dipped donuts. Then he put on his sneakers, giving his blisters a break from his boots, and went outside, hopped on his bike, and headed back over to the police station. He was planning to stop by the hospital that evening and bring Mr. Hafferty his mail, his Walkman, and the information from the accident report.

He locked his bike up to a snow-emergency signpost in front of the station and climbed two steps at a time up to the front door.

Just inside the doorway, Colm noticed a brown wallet on the tiled floor. He picked it up and handed it to the young cop sitting behind the front counter, who was engrossed in his computer screen.

"What's this?" the cop asked.

"It was on the floor."

"On the floor?"

"Yeah. By the door,"

"What was it doing on the floor?" the cop asked, suspicious.

"I don't know. Someone dropped it."

The young cop opened up the wallet and examined a significant amount of cash and several credit cards inside. He eyed Colm warily.

"Can I have your name?" he said, flattening his hair down with several vigorous strokes of the palm of his hand before picking up a pen.

"My name?"

"Yes. Your name."

"Colm Drucker."

The cop frowned and looked up at him, unable to spell what he'd just heard but unwilling to admit it. He scribbled something down and stared back at his computer screen as if he were finished with Colm.

"I need some information from an accident report," Colm said, not at all hopeful at this point of getting it.

His instincts proved right. After a series of tiresome questions, the cop informed Colm that he needed a letter signed by Mr. Hafferty authorizing him to receive the information from the report before he could give it to him.

"Unless you're a relative," the cop said. "Are you a relative?"

Colm just stared at him, blankly, and turned to leave.

"Hey, Colm!" an older police officer called out to him from the doorway of an adjoining office. It was Walt Hayes, Justin's uncle, who rented the other half of a duplex from Justin's parents. He was on the phone and was energetically beckoning Colm to come over. Colm hovered, reluctant to engage anymore with the nincompoop who was guarding the gate.

"Houlihan," Walt called out to the young cop, covering the phone receiver with his hand, "let him in. Let him in!"

Sourly the young cop lifted up a section of the counter, and Colm entered and walked back to Walt, who put his arm around Colm's shoulder and smoothly guided him into his office.

"No, no, no," he said into the phone. "It was a four iron. *A four iron.* Matt, I was there."

Walt continued to be engrossed in his golf conversation as he picked up a large Larmon's Hardware paper bag and poured the contents out onto his desk . . . a wide variety of brand-new plumbing parts for a toilet, easily forty dollars' worth. Looking at Colm, Walt pointed back and forth between a bathroom off the office and the new parts on the desk. Then he mimed jiggling the handle of a toilet that won't stop running.

"Five-o'clock tee time is good. Yeah."

Colm collected all the new parts and disappeared into the bathroom.

It took him two minutes and no new parts to repair the toilet.

Ten minutes later he and Walt were standing side by side out at the front counter, and Walt was rifling through a heavy black notebook, bulging with papers jammed into it.

"Heard from Justin?" he asked, licking his fingers and turning the pages.

"No," said Colm.

"I haven't either. Guess he's having a good time."

Walt gave Colm a wry smile as he flipped through the reports and eventually found Mr. Hafferty's accident report.

"Here it is."

He turned the notebook around so Colm could take a look at it. The victim's name was listed below Mr. Hafferty's with his home address and telephone number.

Colm picked up a pen from the counter.

"Do you have a piece of scrap paper?" Colm asked, glancing up at the clock on the wall.

Walt looked around for something for him to write on, first rummaging through a nearby wastepaper basket and then tearing off a corner from the sports page before finally just giving him a yellow Post-it.

"Houlihan!" Walt suddenly exclaimed, delighted. "You found my wallet! Son of a gun. That's *fantastic*. I take back everything I said about you this morning."

Colm didn't even look over to see the young cop's smug smile. He'd written the victim's first name on the Post-it and was staring down at it. Stunned.

The inexperienced rider on the bicycle whom Mr. Hafferty had nailed in his burgundy Ford Escort while listening to Prokofiev's Fifth Symphony, the white-helmeted birdlike specter who was haunting him now as he lay stiffly between the starched white sheets of his hospital bed, the victim Colm's elderly friend was so desperate to apologize to . . . was none other than Lloyd Henry Drucker.

Chapter Ten

"Coffee?"

"No, thanks."

"Sure?"

"I don't drink coffee."

"Wow, really? I couldn't live without coffee."

The young waitress lingered to watch Colm pour more maple syrup on the last of his banana buckwheat pancakes. He'd arrived at the International House of Pancakes an hour early in order to get a good table, eat, get focused, and prepare for his meeting with Lloyd Henry. He'd already had two cheeseburgers with bacon, a large order of fries, and two thick strawberry milk shakes with extra ice cream.

"Can I get you anything else?" The waitress with the short-cropped blue hair was currently devoting all her serving skills to the handsome young man at table twelve. The place was nearly deserted anyway.

"Maybe some more water."

Cradling the brown IHOP coffeepot against her chest, the waitress rocked back on her heels, smiled, and took off, propelled by the prospect of returning shortly.

Colm peeled the little paper off a portion of butter and pushed it onto the remaining pancake with his thumb, spreading it around with the back of his spoon. By the time he was done, the waitress was back with the water pitcher and a fresh application of lipstick.

"So your friend's not going to be eating?" she asked, fishing for information, filling his glass up as slowly as she could.

"I don't know," Colm said, taking a bite of syrup-drenched pancake. "He's not my friend," he added.

"Oh?" the waitress asked, keenly interested. "By the way, you have great hair. I bet girls tell you that all the time."

Before she had a chance to watch Colm ignore her remark, she turned to see who had tapped her on the back of her shoulder. She seemed almost offended at the man's request for service.

"All right," she said huffily, putting Colm's filled water glass down on the table and following the frustrated man back to his booth, where his wife was hauling their wailing two-year-old child up from under the table while their four-year-old stabbed the wall repeatedly with a fork.

It was around three thirty in the afternoon. He'd gotten there at three. After carefully studying the layout of the dining room, Colm had chosen the booth that commanded the best view of the parking lot. Sitting by the window, he also had a clear shot of the entryway and the front door. He wanted to be as prepared as possible, to minimize any opportunity for surprise that might put him at a disadvantage.

Everything he'd ever heard about Lloyd Henry—from his penchant for lying to his compulsive gambling to his smooth charm—made Colm exceedingly wary.

Fiona had many horrific but entertaining stories of how he'd frittered away their savings and belongings, betting on boxing matches, football games, and other sporting events. He bet compulsively—on the horses, on greyhounds, the weather, movie listings, and the color of the Jell-O in the school menu in the Friday paper. He bet on elections, ambulance routes, fall foliage, tick bites, and traffic. If there was someone around willing to take him up on a bet, Lloyd Henry could come up with one.

He and Frank Coyne had once stayed up all night in the middle of February, drinking bourbon and shining a flashlight through the kitchen window at the outside thermometer every ten minutes on a bet that the temperature wouldn't drop below twenty-six degrees. He made two-dollar bets, and he made twenty-thousand-dollar bets. Sometimes he won, but just as often he lost. Fiona had come home from the hospital when Colm was born to find their brand-new maple bedroom set gone, payment for a bad bet.

Lloyd Henry was now driving down from Keene, New Hampshire, where Colm had reached him by telephone the evening before. He'd answered the phone at the start of the first ring, which had caught Colm off guard.

Their conversation had been short, under two minutes, and was confined primarily to the time and location of their rendezvous, though the father had done his best to launch a more convivial conversation in any of several directions. But Colm would have none of it. This was about money, nothing else.

"I know you must hate me," his father had said, after Colm had cut him off abruptly a few times.

"I don't hate you," Colm said. "So . . . four o'clock."

"I would hate me if I were you."

"I don't anything you. Zero," Colm had countered. "How can you hate someone who doesn't exist?"

His father hadn't quite known how to respond to that. Even Colm was surprised by his own remark and wondered for a second if it made any sense.

"Four o'clock," Colm reiterated. "No bullshit."

"Okay," Lloyd Henry had said. "Okay."

"'Bye."

"Okay. See you."

Staring out now across the parking lot, over at the Allendale shopping center beyond four busy lanes of traffic, Colm squinted and wondered if he was making a mistake. Most likely there was no seventy thousand dollars and this would prove to be a colossal waste of his time. He realized he needed to keep strategizing about other ways to buy the house.

An old red Chevy pickup truck pulled in and parked in a space not far from the entrance. Colm sat up and watched intently as a stocky young man with tattoos on his arms and up around his neck jumped out and headed for the USA Today vending machine. Colm slid back down in his seat, absently watching the man enter the restaurant.

Colm glanced down at his watch. It was ten to four. The waitress had cleared everything except his water glass. All he had to do now was wait.

He had called his grandmother in Florida that morning. He'd been thinking she might qualify to be the shadow buyer he needed to purchase the house, though of course he didn't even begin to broach that subject with her. Fiona still hadn't called her parents, either to thank them for the grapefruit or to inform them of her recent marriage.

"So they were Ruby Red? The grapefruit?"

"Uh-huh," Colm had said. "I had one. It was very good."

"That's good. That's good," she sounded relieved, as if she had had bad experiences sending fruit. "Fiona's not there?"

"Not now."

"Well." She sighed plaintively. "Have her call me." She didn't sound too hopeful.

"I will."

"And how's your walk with Jesus going, hon? Still going to church every Sunday?"

"Pretty much."

"You're a good boy. We love you, you know that."

"I love you, too," Colm had said, slightly uncomfortable. Every time his grandmother brought up his walk with Jesus, he pictured her on an entirely different walk than his. Gammy walked with Jesus in a beautiful park with soft ambient lighting and sweet furry animals. Her relationship with Jesus had no component of mystery about it, unlike his, as if she might suddenly decide to send Jesus a box of grapefruit and call him up later to chat or complain. Colm's instincts were to try to emulate Jesus but also not to bother him.

He was remembering, too, the last time she'd been up to Massachusetts for the fall foliage and had railed on and on about Lloyd Henry after Fiona had made some rare oblique reference to him. Gammy thought that Lloyd Henry was a helpmate of Satan's, evil and rotten to the core. (Though Colm had found a foot-high trophy in a box in the garage with both Gammy's and Lloyd Henry's names engraved on it. Apparently they'd teamed up and won first prize in some bridge championship tournament.)

What would Gammy think if she knew he was sitting here at the International House of Pancakes, waiting for "the worst mistake Fiona ever made" to show up?

He took the little mahogany apple that his great-grandfather had carved out of his pocket, twirled the stem forcefully with his thumb and forefinger, and dropped it, setting the top spinning on the table. It spun beautifully.

Colm thought again of Cameron's remarks about the house and how everyone had moved out. Lloyd Henry had never moved out, because he'd never lived there.

Staring at the top, admiring its stability and simple

design, his mind spun too and suddenly turned up Melanie Phelps. He pictured her out on the sidewalk in front of the supermarket after he'd bumped into her, standing in the shade of the overhang, petunias and other trailing plants for sale hanging nearby. She had the same surprised, pleased look now in his mind.

It had occurred to him when he'd woken up that morning that Melanie had said something to him right as she was taking off to go join her mother in the parking lot. He could distinctly remember the soft sensation of her lips on his; he could remember in great detail her expression, her eyebrows raised in expectation, what she was wearing, how she'd skipped backward a couple of steps, but he could not for the life of him remember what she'd said.

The top fell onto its side and rolled around the table. Colm grabbed it.

His waitress stopped by with the water pitcher, and just then he smelled something burning.

"There's a fire in the kitchen," she volunteered, mildly amused.

"A fire?" Colm asked.

"Whatever. Smoke."

Colm took a moment.

"Is it smoke, or is it a fire?"

"Well. A ton of smoke. I'm thinking of calling the fire department."

Colm studied her, actually seeing her for the first time.

"Where's the manager?" he asked.

"He's not here." She shrugged. "He was supposed to be back twenty minutes ago." She smiled, aware that at last he was beginning to see her.

"Is anybody back there?" Colm asked.

"Yeah, but he doesn't speak English too well."

Colm drummed his fingers on the table, somewhat annoyed with this development.

"There's only one person back there?"

"Well . . . one *and a half.*" She rolled her eyes.

He looked out at the parking lot.

Reluctantly Colm got up and headed for the kitchen, slipping the mahogany top back into his pocket. Pushing through the swinging kitchen doors, he saw a high school kid throwing water on the smoking grill while a slight, bearded man, extremely upset, was talking rapidly in a foreign language to someone on the phone.

It was, as Colm suspected, a simple grease fire and the water was only making it worse, causing billows of black smoke to fill up the kitchen. Whatever was cooking on the grill was at this point burnt and smoking as well.

"Stop, stop," he said to the kid, grabbing a couple of oven mitts and moving through the smoke toward the grill. The acrid, stinging smoke made his eyes water, and he ducked his head down as he reached for the grease pan under the grill and cautiously pulled it out.

"Whoa!" The kid was impressed with the flames that erupted on exposure to air.

"Grab the baking soda," Colm called over to him, noticing a can of it up on a shelf. "Throw it on the fire, throw it all."

In less than two minutes the baking soda had smothered the fire, and the slight bearded man was simultaneously wiping away tears and applauding, in thankful relief. Colm poured the grease into a pail on the floor for that purpose and then slid the tray back as the boy, mindlessly rotating the stud in his left ear, watched.

"You might lower the heat a little on the grill," Colm said as diplomatically as he could to the bearded man. "And make sure someone empties the grease tray."

Exiting the kitchen, Colm noticed some grease splattered on his T-shirt and pants. Great, he thought.

He headed across the dining room back to his booth and stopped halfway when he saw a man and a woman sitting there, opposite where he'd been sitting. The man was wearing an olive-green wool hat and had a cast on his right arm, which he rested on the table. He'd been engaged in a chatty conversation with Colm's waitress, but as soon as Colm halted, his eyes shot across the room and fixed intently on Colm. After a charged moment, he suddenly broke into a smile and waved, as if he were hailing an old friend.

Colm didn't move.

The man waved again, beckoning him to come over, as if there were something interesting he wanted to show him. There was a built-in familiarity in his wave, as if they were all on vacation together somewhere.

With each step that Colm took toward the couple, he took two steps back in his mind. This was insane. What on earth had he been thinking? For a moment he considered veering past them and heading straight out the front door, but his feet stayed on course, moving toward the booth.

"Felicity's been taking care of us," the man said, now standing and cradling his right arm in the cast with his left arm. "She told us all about you."

It gradually dawned on Colm that Felicity was the name of his waitress.

"Sit. Sit." The man gestured cheerfully to Colm's seat.

Colm blinked a couple of times and sat down.

"So."

The man sat back down, wincing slightly as he

carefully deposited his cast on the table, and grinned at Colm, who was in a mild state of shock. It was uncanny. This man had Cameron's lopsided grin; the same pronounced cheekbones and blue-gray eyes.

"I'll bring you your coffee," Felicity said, winking at the man and then looking at Colm saucily before taking off.

Colm gripped his seat with both hands.

"This is Donna," the man said, wrapping his left arm around the demure woman at his side and pulling her close. She looked to be about twenty years younger than him and seemed extremely shy.

"She's a physical therapist," the man said, giving her a squeeze and smiling Cameron's lopsided grin at her. "Good thing," he said, glancing down at his cast. "Gonna need it!" He laughed and looked over at Colm, who still hadn't spoken one word.

He had just spent an hour at this table, staking it out, but now, after only minutes, it belonged to the enemy.

"Donna, do me a favor and light me a cigarette?"

Donna compliantly opened her purse and took out a pack of cigarettes.

"Broke my arm this week," the man explained, as if Colm had shown great interest in it. "Couple days ago. Interesting story, actually . . ."

Colm caught a strong whiff of something rancid and realized after a moment that it was him. After his recent escapade in the kitchen, he smelled of burnt food.

He closed his eyes for a few moments, as if doing so might remove him to another place far from here, and reluctantly opened them.

The man in front of him was still talking. Colm was trying to connect the name "Lloyd Henry" with this person. It wasn't easy. The concept of "Lloyd Henry" was so much larger, so much more amorphous and far-reaching than the middle-aged man in front of him in the black-and-white striped short-sleeve shirt now taking a puff on the cigarette that Donna the physical therapist had handed him.

When Colm was a little boy, "Lloyd Henry" had walked across continents in his mind, had walked around and around the planet, and the more he'd traveled in Colm's mind, the more space he took up, like a snowball growing on its way down a snowy mountainside. He was bigger than life, a legend, like Paul Bunyan, only notorious. "Lloyd Henry" was made out of stories.

Like the story of how he'd been arrested at the airport in Florida with Fiona and her two babies after he'd snuck them out of the Orlando Holiday Inn without paying for their weeklong stay.

Or the story of the time Fiona had received a notice in the mail, along with a giant fur-trimmed valentine from Lloyd Henry, informing her that the deed to their house had been transferred to a man in upstate New York.

Lloyd Henry was the story of when he and Fiona were on the front page of the society section of the *Berkshire Eagle* after winning the dance contest at a New Year's Eve ball in Newport, Rhode Island. "Area Couple Steps Out."

And he was the story of the time that Fiona went to pick him up at the Pittsfield bus station after a gambling binge in Atlantic City, not long after they'd lost their house, and he never got off the bus, and they never saw him again.

"So what's the deal?" Colm said suddenly, interrupting the story of how Lloyd Henry had been hit while on a bicycle by an elderly man who seemed to be aiming right for him.

They were the first words Colm ever uttered face-to-face to his father. And the way things were going, they could prove to be the last. Lloyd Henry, halted abruptly in his anecdote, looked blankly at Colm.

Colm stood up. Ready to leave.

"Deal?" Lloyd Henry asked.

"The seventy thousand."

"Oh."

Colm noticed that the hand holding the cigarette was shaking, but his mind was racing too fast to begin to assimilate what that meant.

"What about it?"

"You tell me."

"Simple."

"What is it?"

"Turn me in. You get seventy grand." He punctuated his remark with a sound remarkably like a bowling ball traveling down a hardwood lane, followed by the strike and rattle of pins. He smiled.

Donna melted into shy giggles of admiration and pleasure.

Inspired by her response, he launched into the sound effects of a Ping-Pong ball being hit back and forth, and then, without skipping a beat, he adjusted the opening of his mouth to produce the meatier sound of a tennis ball being played in a heated match.

"Out!" he called, watching the imaginary ball fly across the room. He looked back, grinning at Colm, who appeared both cautiously perplexed and alarmed.

"Turn you in to . . . ?" Colm asked, staying on track.

Lloyd Henry inhaled deeply on his cigarette and held the smoke in his lungs for a long time before exhaling.

"Frank."

"Frank who?"

"Frank who's offering seventy grand for my head."

"Who is he?"

"He wants me."

"Why?"

"I can't tell you."

"Why?"

"Let's put it this way . . . I pissed him off."

"What did you do?"

"What did I do?" Lloyd Henry looked at Donna. "Kid's persistent. I like that." He smiled. "Good-looking kid, huh?"

She nodded shyly but enthusiastically.

"What did you do?"

"I can't tell you what I did."

"Why not?"

Lloyd Henry shook his head again, tilted it, and shrugged.

"Why not?" Colm pressed.

"I'm ashamed." And there was Cameron's grin again, easing up the right side of his face, which was turning slightly red.

"Here you go," the waitress said, putting two cups on the table and filling them with coffee.

"Thank you, Felicity," Lloyd Henry said with great warmth, as if Felicity had served him his afternoon coffee every day for the last five years.

"Excuse me, do you have any soy milk?" Donna asked Felicity, speaking for the first time and revealing a curiously high-pitched voice. "I'm lactose intolerant."

"No. Sorry," Felicity said, giving her blue bob a shake. "Leaving?" she asked Colm, who was still standing up.

"Felicity, could you bring us some pancakes?" Lloyd Henry suddenly asked, looking up at Colm as if that terrific idea would surely make him want to sit down and stay.

"What kind?" Felicity asked.

"Any kind. Your favorite." He smiled with assurance, as if he had entrusted her with such decisions many times before. She returned his smile and, to Colm's disgust, winked again at Lloyd Henry.

"So," he said to Colm. "Up for an adventure?"

Lloyd Henry reached for an imaginary handle in the air and pulled it down, achieving a perfect imitation of an all-aboard train whistle.

"Are you wanted by the law?" Colm asked sternly.

"The law? No."

"You're not wanted by the law?"

"He isn't," piped up Donna in her falsetto voice, a look of deep and earnest sincerity on her face as she held on to Lloyd Henry's left arm with both her hands.

"Just Frank," said Colm, grilling him.

"Just Frank."

"Is Frank in the Mafia?"

"Frank?" Lloyd Henry laughed a little at the thought. "No."

"He's not in the mob?"

"No. Frank is his own mob."

Colm wished he were doing anything but this.

"I can give you Frank's number. You can call him. He'll be thrilled to hear that we're coming."

"How long has he wanted you?"

"Years."

"What did you do to piss him off?"

"I can't tell you."

"You owe him money?"

Lloyd Henry grabbed the visor on his wool cap and yanked it up and down a few times. "It's complicated."

"I thought you said it was simple."

"From your point of view . . . it is."

"Where does Frank live?"

"Bakersfield."

"Bakersfield?" Donna asked, surprised.

"Yeah." Lloyd Henry smiled. "Road trip."

"I turn you in to Frank, he gives me seventy thousand dollars."

"On the spot."

Colm studied him. He had absolutely no idea whether this man was lying or not. And that irked him.

"You don't look like you're at the end of your rope," he said.

"Trust me. I am."

"I don't trust you."

Lloyd Henry tilted his head, pondering this.

Colm held his ground.

"Let me ask you this," Lloyd Henry offered after a while. "What have you got to lose?"

He had a point.

Lloyd Henry and Colm stared at each other while Donna suddenly reached for a napkin and caught the falling ash from Lloyd Henry's cigarette.

"That number I called you at . . . that's your cell phone number?" Colm eventually asked.

"It is."

Colm picked up his backpack, slung it over his shoulder, and stared at Lloyd Henry with a cold, detached gaze.

"I'll think about it. I'll call you tonight."

"Okay. It'll be fun."

"And stop following me around."

"Okay."

"I mean it. Don't follow me."

Lloyd Henry nodded.

"I know you have been following me."

Lloyd Henry shrugged with an affable, almost boyish look of culpability.

And then Colm said something he hadn't planned to say.

"I know the man who hit you with his car."

It was the low-key assured way Colm spoke, inadvertently but nonetheless undeniably implying a greater involvement in the event than was true, that sent the admission ricocheting around the table.

Donna gasped.

Lloyd Henry's left eye squinted slightly, studying Colm with new intensity. Colm was picturing Mr. Hafferty, filled with guilt and remorse, lying on his back in his white hospital bed. It struck Colm again just how bizarre it was that Mr. Hafferty was now permanently and fatefully entwined with the legendary Lloyd Henry.

"I don't blame you, son."

"Don't call me son."

"I don't blame you," said Lloyd Henry with almost

maudlin empathy. His grinning, easygoing nonchalance had been annoying enough, but this unchecked display of emotion was intolerable.

"I'm going."

"Okay."

Colm edged his way along the table and stepped away from it, relieved to be able finally to straighten his legs.

"I'll call you tonight."

"I won't follow you," Lloyd Henry promised, glancing down at his cast.

Looking remorseful, Lloyd Henry thought for a few moments and then gently elbowed Donna with his good arm. "How 'bout that?" he asked quietly, beaming slightly, as if proud of his son's enterprising bold nature.

She shook her head as if they were both crazy.

Colm was reluctant to leave. He still felt unsure about the offer and no better informed to make the right decision.

"If you're lying to me . . ." Colm said, staring at Lloyd Henry with all the gravity he could muster.

Whether or not Colm intended to complete his sentence they would never know, for at that very moment a fork came flying through the air, lobbed from some distance, and finished it for him. The airborne fork arced gracefully high over Colm's left shoulder and dropped prongs first into Lloyd Henry's cast, where it stayed, as fixed as a dart in a dartboard.

"Sorry." The tremulous voice of a small child drifted from across the room.

None of them turned to look toward the child, who was already being reprimanded by his parents. Given the circumstances, the child's role in this stabbing event seemed negligible.

Lloyd Henry, Donna the physical therapist, and Colm all stared at the fork sticking up out of the cast. No one made a move to remove the utensil. No one spoke. It was a transcendent moment, both extremely silly and awesome, and all three witnesses were frozen in a kind of stunned stupor.

At the very least, it assuaged in Colm any need to ask more questions. The fork in the cast served as some kind of closing statement, an unambiguous finale to an otherwise unsatisfactory encounter. If he left now, he thought, he would at least be leaving in a position of strength.

Lloyd Henry stared up in wonderment at Colm, who was fighting an irrational urge to apologize. He didn't apologize, nor (as with Lloyd Henry's accident) did he deny any complicity in the event, though the perfect timing of the four-pronged weapon implicated him resoundingly.

Out of the corner of his eye Colm caught sight of the blue-haired Felicity hurrying toward them, buoyantly carrying a tray with a plate of Swedish pancakes, lingonberry syrup on the side.

Without even looking at Lloyd Henry, Colm took a step backward and turned toward the front door. Repositioning his backpack over his shoulder, he walked away, leaving his mother's first husband to twist around for possibly the last glimpse he would ever have of his teenage son.

It took Colm an hour to walk home, enough time to process the new information and reappraise the situation. By the time he reached 43 Palmer Street, he had decided against having anything to do with Lloyd Henry. There had to be other avenues he could pursue besides dealing with him.

As he walked up the sidewalk to the front gate, Colm found himself missing his mother. He wished she were home and he could go inside and head up to his room and not have to think about buying the house. He could just fool around with his baseball cards while she and Angie made a chef's salad together and laughed downstairs in the kitchen.

He turned and walked up the path to the front door,

imagining her waiting inside for him with a pitcher of lemonade, or a box of Kentucky Fried Chicken. If she was done cleaning houses for the day, she might be reading a magazine out in the backyard, her feet in the kiddie pool they set up for Chester to cool off in, listening to a Bonnie Raitt CD. She'd be happy to see him.

As he reached for the front screen door, he caught sight of three cards stuck between the door and the doorjamb.

He took them out and examined them. Two were from the Realtors he had called to get a sense of Audrey Robertson's estimate of the selling price of the house, and the third was from Audrey Robertson herself. All three Realtors had scribbled notes on the cards requesting to see and show the house.

Colm's heart sank. He leaned his head against the screen door, despondent, and stood there for a couple of minutes.

Wearily he went inside and called all three numbers, leaving messages since it was after five, admonishing all three Realtors *never* to come by the house again or he would have them arrested for trespassing.

Next he went into the back hall to check the two locks on the back door. After tightening the screws on one, he went down to the basement, where he mounted a second slide-bolt lock onto one of the hatchway doors. After going around and checking all the downstairs window locks, he parked himself on the couch and watched the last part of an Adam Sandler movie and the first six innings of a Red Sox game before getting up and calling Lloyd Henry.

"Hello?" Again Lloyd Henry answered before the first ring was done.

"We're leaving tonight," Colm said matter-of-factly.

"Tonight?"

"Pick me up at my house in two hours."

"Really?"

"Two hours."

There was a pause.

"Uh . . . can we make it three?"

"No." Colm hung up without waiting to hear a response and went back to the couch to settle in and watch the rest of the game.

Chapter Eleven

Lloyd Henry didn't show up in two hours. He didn't show up in three. It was five hours before a brand-new black Ford Explorer crept slowly up the other side of the street and came to a halt beneath the streetlamp, idling awhile before the engine was turned off.

It was after midnight.

Colm was sitting at the top of the front steps with a Rand McNally road atlas on his knees. He had thrown an extra T-shirt, shorts and underwear into his pack, expecting that they would be back the next evening. Or rather that *he* would be back, having deposited Lloyd Henry somewhere up in New Hampshire.

Colm had turned the overhead porch light off to redirect the multitude of moths and other flying insects to the light at the end of the walk. He watched them hovering madly around the lamp post, a little cloud of busy aerial activity. Though it was July, some June bugs were still around, and every now and then one would buzz past Colm like a small helicopter, banging into the screen door and temporarily stalling out.

He was thinking about the summer three years ago when he and Fiona and Angie were all hanging out on the front steps late one night waiting for Cameron to come home from the movies, and Angie had fallen backward off the steps onto the grass after a June bug had tried to fly into her neck. The three of them were all laughing so hard that when Cameron showed up, she thought something terrible had happened because Fiona had tears streaming down her face.

Colm heard a car door shut. Lloyd Henry slowly appeared out on the sidewalk and stopped beyond the front gate, recessed and framed on either side by the hedge. He waited a moment to speak.

"Sorry it took so long," he said very quietly, though his voice carried clearly up the long walk. "Had a few things to do."

He hung back, as if there were yellow police DO NOT CROSS tape hung across the path. Even in the dark, Colm sensed his manner was more restrained than his outgoing behavior that afternoon at the IHOP.

"It's almost midnight," Colm said.

"I know. I'm sorry. I had to put Donna on a bus."

"Why?"

"She has to work in the morning."

That didn't really make sense to Colm, who was disappointed there wasn't going to be a third person coming along to act as a buffer.

Lloyd Henry cleared his throat.

Colm could barely make out his outline.

"Is anybody else home?" This question, tentatively posed, contained an undeniable trace of anxiety, possibly even fear.

And why wouldn't he be fearful? His first wife and daughter might be inside the dark house, might even now be staring down out of an upstairs window at the figure hiding in the shadows.

"No one's home. There's no Bakersfield in New Hampshire," Colm said.

"No?" Lloyd Henry's voice was calmer now.

"It's not in the Rand McNally road atlas."

"You got an atlas. Hey, that's great! You want to drive?"

Colm could hear the jingling of a set of keys coming toward him, and he reached out in the dark to grab them.

"Nice catch."

"I don't have my license," Colm said, standing up.

He picked up his pack, hoisted it over his shoulder, and started walking down the path toward the street. He was actually kind of glad it was midnight. Something about the late-night hour lent an air of unreality to the whole venture. Also, in a way it felt like they were getting an early start on the next day, and he would be home that much sooner.

"No license, no kidding?"

"I'm only fifteen," Colm said, reaching Lloyd Henry, standing uncomfortably close to him as he handed him back the car keys.

Lloyd Henry was taller than Colm, but only by a couple of inches. Colm was disconcerted to realize that some part of him was assessing his ability to beat up his father if he had to. He could feel his muscles imagining taking him down.

Colm bolted across the street to the black SUV.

"Right," Lloyd Henry said, following behind. "Well . . . might take us a little longer."

"Why isn't Bakersfield on the map?" Colm asked, standing by the back door, relieved the car was new and not some decrepit vehicle.

"Were you thinking of sitting in the front?"

"No."

Lloyd Henry looked down at his feet.

"If you could sit in the front," he said quietly, "it would be a big help."

Colm eyed him warily.

"The cast makes it a little difficult to shift. I could use some help. Shifting."

Colm stared at the white cast, which Lloyd Henry was holding as he always did with his left arm, now glowing an iridescent snowy blue under the harsh streetlight.

"It's a standard."

"Standard?"

Colm was looking at the green wool cap with the visor, wondering why Lloyd Henry always wore it. Maybe he was bald, or maybe he had a scar or disfigurement of some sort on his forehead that he was concealing. Maybe he'd spent some time in prison.

"Yup. So I have to reach across my body . . ." Wincing slightly, Lloyd Henry demonstrated reaching with his left hand across his body toward an imaginary gearshift on the floor. "Once we hit the freeway . . . won't be a problem. Put it in fifth, we'll be all set."

Colm's brow was furrowed.

"Road trip," Lloyd Henry said, upbeat. "Gonna be fun!"

"Why isn't Bakersfield on the map?"

"It is."

"No, it's not."

Lloyd Henry took the atlas from Colm, rested his cast on the hood of the car, and then rested the atlas partly on the cast as he started flipping through the pages. He fumbled briefly to take his reading glasses out of his shirt pocket, smiling a little sheepishly as he placed them crookedly on his nose.

Resisting the urge to straighten the glasses, Colm was struck once again by his uncanny resemblance to Cameron.

"Right here," said Lloyd Henry.

Colm looked.

"That's California."

"Yup."

Colm's eye went over to Los Angeles, and then up to San Francisco, and then up to Lloyd Henry's face.

"Bakersfield is in California," Lloyd Henry said assuredly.

Colm squinted at him, processing the information.

"What?"

"Yeah, Bakersfield—" Lloyd Henry began.

They both suddenly stepped toward the car as a Boar's Head delivery truck rumbled past them.

"Bakersfield is in California?"

"Uh-huh."

Colm was dumbfounded, unable to speak. He stared at Lloyd Henry, flummoxed.

"I thought you knew."

"You thought I knew Bakersfield is in California?" Colm shook his head in disbelief.

"Yeah."

"You think I'm driving all the way to California with you? Are you out of your mind!?"

"I told you." Lloyd Henry cleared his throat. "Bakersfield."

Colm watched him shuffle in place, shifting his weight back and forth from one foot to the other.

Without saying a word, Colm took the atlas, turned, and walked back across the street. He headed up the walk to the house, unclipped the carabiner that had his keys on it from his pant loop, unlocked the front door, and went in, closing the door behind him.

Inside, he took off his backpack and threw it with great force through the living-room doorway, unfazed by the sound of the stack of wedding presents crashing into the television set on the other side of the wall.

He kicked off his shoes, went into the kitchen, and filled a glass with tap water, leaning against the sink. After swigging it down, he got an unopened half-gallon container of Breyer's cherry vanilla ice cream out of the freezer and took it into the new laundry room. There he sat down on the Mexican tile floor and began eating the ice cream slowly, with a soup spoon.

A mouse darted out from behind the washing machine, raced toward the drain, circled it tightly three times, and raced back, disappearing behind the dryer. Colm stared straight ahead, his gaze unwavering, methodically consuming the ice cream.

He could hear the sound of the refrigerator kicking on in the kitchen, making the high-pitched whining noise that signaled the need for another repair.

When Colm had eaten half the container, leveling off the ice cream perfectly as if he were skim coating a wall, he got up and put it back into the freezer. He flicked off the kitchen light and went upstairs to the bathroom, where he brushed his teeth in the dark and splashed cold water onto his face.

In his own room he climbed into bed, fully clothed, and pulled the sheet up over his head.

Closing his eyes, he heard a motorcycle zooming by, probably Eddie Siegel on his way home from his night shift at Plastics Extrusion.

He lay there not moving, his eyes closed, his mind blank.

* * *

Several hours later Lloyd Henry woke from a deep sleep in the driver's seat of the Ford Explorer when Colm knocked hard several times on his window. He had to turn the key in the ignition in order to roll down the window, tilting his head back from his sunken position only as much as was needed to gaze up at his son.

"I"ll meet you in Las Vegas this weekend," Colm said, the Rand McNally atlas rolled up under his arm. He had called Southwest Airlines and learned that for twenty-five dollars he could use the ticket Fiona had sent him and fly out that day. After studying the atlas, he'd discovered that Las Vegas was actually en route to Bakersfield. Colm's plan was to spend a couple of nights with his family and then meet up with Lloyd Henry and drive the remaining three hundred miles to Bakersfield together.

"Uh . . ." Lloyd Henry, now sitting up, struggled to get his thoughts together. "I don't think I can get to Las Vegas by myself this weekend."

"Why not?"

Lloyd Henry blinked a few times and looked down at his cast. He stared at it ruefully.

Colm glared at the cast with animosity, unwilling to cede to it any power that would allow it to impinge on *his* plans.

"Don't you have anyone you could drive with?"

Lloyd Henry sniffed a couple of times.

"On such short notice? I don't think so."

Colm bit his lower lip. "How long would it take you drive to Las Vegas?"

"Mm. Maybe . . . Five days?"

Fiona would be back in five days. It was early Thursday morning, and they were flying back on Sunday night. The idea of meeting up with them all in Las Vegas was becoming more and more appealing to Colm—hanging out by the pool with Bunny, watching Fiona sing in the hotel lounge, seeing a saguaro cactus for the first time in his life. He was becoming increasingly more determined to make it happen.

"You could buy a plane ticket."

"Sorry." Lloyd Henry shook his head.

"Sorry what?"

"I don't fly."

"Why not?"

"I don't do . . . planes."

"You don't *do* them?"

"Bad experience."

Colm looked skeptical.

"I almost died."

"How can you almost die in a plane?"

"Emergency landing. Foam on the runway. Fire trucks. Sorry . . . no can do."

Colm took a deep breath, frustrated.

"Sorry. I'm really sorry." Lloyd Henry seemed embarrassed by his unmanly admission.

"You know . . ." Colm said, growing more irritated.

Lloyd Henry, tilting his head away as if he were about to be admonished, waited for Colm to finish his sentence. When he didn't, he busied himself by staring over at the empty passenger seat as if something of great importance were going on there that required his attention.

"We could stop at the Grand Canyon," Lloyd Henry said, perking up, turning back. "Ever seen the Grand Cany—?"

"Does Frank know we're coming?" Colm cut him off.

"Mm?"

"Have you called Frank yet?"

"Frank? Not yet. No."

"How do you know he'll be there when we get there?"

"Oh, he'll be there."

"When are you going to call him?"

"I'll call him."

"When?"

"I'll call him . . . when we're in Nevada."

"Nevada . . ."

Colm felt like he had six jigsaw puzzle pieces from six different puzzles in his mind. None of the pieces fitted together, and as he fumbled with them, he had a strong sense that if he wasn't very careful, he could do something really, really stupid.

He tried to concentrate. He could fly to Las Vegas later that day, be with his family, and meet up with Lloyd Henry after the weekend, on Monday or Tuesday. If he showed up. And he'd have to tell Fiona about the whole enterprise. Of course, he realized, he'd have to tell her that regardless.

"If you drove," Lloyd Henry said, "we'd be there in two and a half days. Saturday. Drive straight through."

"You didn't hear me," Colm said angrily. "I don't have my license."

"So what?"

"So maybe you don't mind breaking laws and lying and stealing, but I do."

Lloyd Henry looked stung. He turned away, working his mouth around with his lips pressed tightly together, as if he were trying to dislodge a bit of food stuck to his front teeth. He was clearly wounded, but eventually he came around. "I don't blame you, kid. I don't blame you."

Colm stared up at the night sky, uncertain what to do. Should he forget the whole thing and tell Lloyd Henry to disappear? Or should he just jump in the car with him and head for California, maybe picking up another driver along the way?

Seventy thousand dollars.

How was it that he'd come to find himself in this predicament?

He was unaccustomed to not knowing what to do, and he didn't like the feeling. There was no manual in which he could look up the right answer. No part he could pick up at Larmon's Hardware that would unclog this impasse and restore flow.

"Hey," Lloyd Henry said suddenly. "How's Chester doing?"

Colm looked at him blankly.

"Chester. Little brown puppy?"

Colm said nothing, his mind suddenly wired to his heart.

"Course," Lloyd Henry muttered, ". . . not a puppy anymore."

Colm still didn't speak.

Lloyd Henry nodded, as if somehow responding to his own question.

"Yup. " He appeared lost in thought. "Cute little mutt."

It was the combination of Cameron's face asking about Chester that had momentarily thrown Colm, vaulting him across the vast continent that separated him from his father and uniting them for half a second in a place of deep familiarity.

"Why do you wear that stupid hat all the time?" Colm finally blurted out.

"Mm?"

"It's the middle of summer. Why do you wear it?"

He was squeezing the mahogany top in his pocket so hard that the point almost penetrated the palm of his right hand.

"I've got my reasons," Lloyd Henry said, looking away.

Colm grabbed the side-view mirror with his left hand and worked it back and forth a couple of times as he stared over the roof of the car. Suddenly he turned and crossed the street, once again leaving his father without saying a word and retreating into the house.

This time he left the front door open.

Twenty minutes later Colm reappeared in the doorway carrying a packed duffel bag, his jacket, his backpack, and the box of Florida grapefruit. When he closed the front door, he double-checked it a couple of times to make sure it was locked. Passing by the lamppost down by the walk, he hung the NO TRESPASSING sign on an unused plant hook.

Then he crossed the street and knocked on the roof of the car, because the window was open and in that short period of time Lloyd Henry had managed to fall back into the sleep of the dead.

Colm rapped on the roof again. Hard.

"Who . . . ?" Lloyd Henry responded, without opening his eyes.

His body had slid down under the steering wheel, and his head was sunk down in his shoulders like a turtle's that has retreated partially into its shell.

"Okay, these are the rules. Listen up."

With enormous effort Lloyd Henry managed to force his eyes half open.

"No talking on this trip," Colm said.

Lloyd Henry looked deeply disoriented.

"I don't want to know anything about you. Nothing. And I'm not going to tell you anything about me."

Realizing he needed to focus here, Lloyd Henry made a big effort to sit up and pay attention.

"No talking," Colm repeated.

"Okay."

"I'm not kidding."

"I can see."

"No conversations."

"Fine."

"And another thing . . ."

"Yes?"

"If I don't come home with seventy thousand dollars . . ."

"You will."

"If I don't . . ."

"I know, I know." With his left hand, Lloyd Henry described the arc of the fork flying through the air and landing on his cast. He smiled sleepily. Colm didn't. He opened the back door and stared briefly at the baseball bat, ball, two gloves, and unopened kite that were on the backseat. He threw the duffel bag, his jacket and backpack, and the box of grapefruit on top of them. Then he closed the door, came around to the passenger door, and got in.

"Cool," Lloyd Henry said, watching Colm do up his seat belt.

Colm glared at him.

"Fine, okay." Lloyd Henry mimed zipping up his mouth and tossing away the key.

They both looked forward and sat in silence for a few moments. Still, but with an inexplicable halted momentum behind them. It was almost as if they had just arrived from a long journey, had just driven three thousand miles across the country, and were now sitting there, staring at the Pacific Ocean.

Eventually Lloyd Henry spoke quietly, almost in a whisper.

"Are we going?"

"We're going," Colm said flatly.

Lloyd Henry reached around in front of the steering wheel with great difficulty and turned the key to the ignition.

"Ow," he said, grimacing slightly. "Okay . . . when I nod, put it in first."

"Where's first?"

Lloyd Henry demonstrated with his left hand. "First . . . second . . . third . . . fourth. Like an H. Then fifth. When we're cruising."

Colm nodded. Cameron's Jeep was a standard.

"All right. First. *Ow,*" Lloyd Henry winced again, in pain now that he wasn't holding the cast with his left arm.

"Why aren't you wearing a sling?" Colm asked critically.

"Mm?"

"A sling. For your cast."

"Oh."

"So you don't have to hold it all the time. Didn't they give you a sling?"

Lloyd Henry appeared momentarily stumped. Before he could retrieve an answer, Colm had already unbuckled his seat belt, reached around back to his duffel bag, and taken out a towel.

"Turn this way," Colm said. "More. *Turn.*"

Complying like a small child, Lloyd Henry twisted around in the driver's seat toward Colm who fashioned him a perfect sling, tying a knot in the folded towel up behind Lloyd Henry's head.

"Wow. Thanks," he said, staring down at the new arrangement, enormously pleased. "Wow. That feels *great*. Thanks." He couldn't stop admiring it.

"Step on the clutch," Colm said, doing up his seat belt again and studying the gearshift on the floor.

Lloyd Henry, trying to conceal the smile that had begun to form while his son was making him a sling, stepped on the clutch, and Colm slipped it into first.

"Good. Very good," said Lloyd Henry, waking up more and more as the reality of what was happening caught up with him. "Now, second."

Colm brought the gearshift down into second gear as Lloyd Henry pulled the car away from the curb.

"Perfect. Excellent," he said, letting go of the steering

wheel for a second to reach up and adjust the rearview mirror. "We're a team!"

"We're *not* a team!"

"We're not a team, okay."

"No team."

"Got it. Okay, third."

Colm shifted into third.

"Good. Good."

The Ford Explorer picked up speed, the only moving vehicle out at that hour on Palmer Street, heading toward one of the main streets of Pittsfield. It was five thirty in the morning and the sky was getting light.

"I just realized something," Lloyd Henry said.

"I don't want to know."

"Okay."

Lloyd Henry nodded, but Colm could sense he wasn't through.

"Sure?" Lloyd Henry asked.

"This is *exactly* what I'm talking about," Colm said firmly. "I don't want to know anything . . . what you're realizing . . . what you're not realizing. Nothing. I don't want to hear *anything* from you."

"Roger. Dodger."

Colm reached over and turned on the radio. Out of the corner of his eye he could see a little smile forming again on Lloyd Henry's mouth. In an effort to turn down the smile, Colm turned up the volume on the radio.

He leaned back, folded his arms, and looked out the window. He was going to California.

He hadn't told anyone what he was doing . . . not his mother, his sister. Justin. Angie. Mr. Hafferty. No one.

"Could I ask you a favor?" Lloyd Henry shouted over the music.

"No."

"What?" He leaned in toward Colm to hear better.

"NO!"

Lloyd Henry nodded agreeably and sat back, resting his left hand up on the wheel, his right arm snugly held by the towel sling.

Colm rolled down the window and let the warm July air hit his face.

He hadn't slept all night, but he was wide-awake. He turned and reached around into the back and grabbed a grapefruit out of the box, unwrapping it from the crinkly tissue paper that enclosed each one. Sticking his thumbnail in and carving a small circle to peel it, he thought of his grandmother. What would Gammy think now to see him sitting next to Satan's helpmate, en route to Las Vegas?

He felt a tap on his left shoulder. He looked over

to see Lloyd Henry pointing to the gearshift and then holding up one finger. They had come to a stop at their first intersection and needed to begin the shifting sequence again. Lloyd Henry had ridden the clutch to a halt.

Holding the grapefruit like a softball in his right hand, Colm grabbed the gearshift with his left hand and slipped it into first. Pretty soon Lloyd Henry held two fingers up, but he needn't have. Colm was already getting the rhythm and had shifted smoothly into second. Lloyd Henry was right, he thought. Whether he cared to admit it or not, they were a team.

olm, his back to Lloyd Henry, stared in the side mirror at the reflection of a wasp clinging upside down on his window.

He was trying to remember his last long trip.

He'd been on a few long road trips with his mother and his sister, but they'd always headed either south, down to Florida to visit Gammy, or up to the Maine coast, where Fiona always said she would move if she won the lottery. He'd never been west of Massachusetts except for when they went to pick apples in the orchards over the border in Claverack, New York.

Two summers ago Fiona and Angie had looked briefly into starting a frozen apple pie business after they'd bought a used commercial freezer together at Meissner's auction. For three weeks that September the refrigerator was jammed with bowls of sliced-up apples drenched in lemon juice with cinnamon, nutmeg, allspice, and Fiona's "secret" ingredient. Although she claimed there was such an ingredient, based on the response of her male customers Colm always thought the secret ingredient was Fiona and the enthusiastic way she talked about the pies.

At one point there were 112 frozen deep-dish apple pies in the large freezer and their two smaller refrigerator freezers, and orders were coming in for additional pies, but the whole enterprise turned out to be too labor-intensive.

Colm designed an apple peeler for them that worked better than the ones on the market, but picking, coring, and peeling the bushels of apples required to turn a reasonable profit was something neither Angie nor Fiona felt was her true calling. You just couldn't core more than one apple at a time. Colm had come close to figuring out a way, placing six apples in a section of adjusted gutter and penetrating them with a rotating piece of motorized copper tubing, but the apples just weren't uniform enough to core efficiently.

The wasp suddenly flew up and zigzagged out the window.

Colm yawned. He stretched his legs out in the roomy SUV, his left hand finally off the gearshift. There was no need to shift anymore, because they were cruising along in fifth gear at seventy miles an hour on the New York State Thruway, bound for New Jersey, then Pennsylvania and points west.

That afternoon he would call Audrey Robertson and tell her that he'd be putting a down payment of seventy thousand dollars on the house the next week. It wasn't that he had that much confidence in her Realtor skills, but he figured if she perceived herself to be working for him, she'd be less inclined to drive potential buyers by the house and show it off while Fiona was gone. Summer months were especially active ones in the real estate business in the Berkshires.

And he'd call Mr. Frangione, his mowing client and lawyer, to tell him that the closing would be some time before the end of July. Maybe Justin's father would agree to be the shadow buyer. Justin had been Colm's best friend for years, and Colm couldn't think of any reason why Mr. Hagen, who liked him, wouldn't be trustworthy or why his credit would be bad.

Better to wait a day to call his mother. He wasn't sure what he was going to tell her, although he was sure that it wasn't going to be much. He could simply say that he was aiming to show up in Las Vegas sometime on Saturday. That was certainly true, and furthermore she'd be happy to hear it.

One nagging detail in his loosely formed plan was that while he spent Saturday night and Sunday with his family, Lloyd Henry would be on the loose in Las Vegas till they hooked up again Sunday night. Lloyd Henry and Las Vegas did not sound like a good combination, but right now Colm wasn't going to worry about it.

He stared out the window at the rolling farmland, glowing a golden pink in the morning light, and yawned again. There was really nothing more he could plan at this point.

Now that his mind was empty of house-buying details, it didn't take long for it to start filling up rapidly with something else. He was becoming increasingly aware that as Pittsfield receded steadily behind them, they were also driving seventy miles an hour away from Melanie Phelps. Every five hours, he calculated, they would be 350 miles farther away from her.

His body was moving west, but his mind was gazing east, already looking forward to when he would be back in Pittsfield, back in the place where crossing paths with her was always a possibility.

He realized, as he pictured her locking up her bike at the bike racks in front of school, that thinking about Melanie Phelps was different now ever since he'd run into her at the supermarket. For so long he'd been able to stare at her from a distance and just enjoy watching her. From behind, for instance—at church, her brown hair pulled back, sitting lost in thought while everyone else was standing up singing a hymn; or at football games, her head tilted back watching a flock of geese overhead instead of the game; or in assembly at school, head down, overcome with emotion after a movie about Martin Luther King Day.

But now he had these new memories of her studying *him*, taking him into *her* world. It was as if he had been watching her safely from behind a hedge and she had somehow jumped over the hedge. Now she was watching him, taking in every detail with that formidable brain of hers.

Why had she kissed him? It just felt like a mistake, her kiss. As if she'd dropped something by accident in the parking lot that he had inadvertently picked up.

Colm became aware of a noise that cut through the traffic report on the radio. It sounded like a helicopter was whirring nearby, and he looked out the window for one. Unable to locate it, he glanced over at Lloyd Henry and realized the sound was coming from his mouth, his lips snapping repeatedly together as he seemed to be sucking in air and rapidly working his tongue in and out.

"Not talking," Lloyd Henry paused to mouth the

words quickly, smiling briefly over at Colm, before going back to the helicopter, adjusting the volume so it sounded remarkably like a chopper flying by.

Gazing stone-faced at him, Colm resolved on the spot to change his last name. If Fiona Schroeder and Bunny DeCavalho didn't have it, why should he? Let Cameron be saddled with Drucker. After all, she looked just like him.

Colm contemplated a few possibilities for a different last name and then suddenly realized he could change it to his great-grandfather's . . . McCarthy. What a great idea!

Excited by this plan, Colm felt an overwhelming urge to tell Lloyd Henry. He would just *love* right then and there to tell him he was planning on rejecting his name. But he resisted, and turned away instead to look out the window at the passing billboards of Melanie Phelps that filled his mind.

He wondered what she was doing at that moment. Was she driving her mother somewhere, or was she walking along by herself, lost in thought in contemplation of some interesting curiosity? She might be still asleep. He imagined her head resting on a pillow, a sheet pulled up over her shoulders, her mouth slightly open, her eyes flickering under her eyelids as her brain conjured dreams beyond his ability to imagine.

He lingered with this particular image of her until, two hours later, they stopped for gas.

Stirring from his reverie, Colm jumped out, mumbling that he would pump the gas as Lloyd Henry opened his door, rocked himself out of his seat, and headed toward the convenience store to pay.

"Want anything?" Lloyd Henry called out across the pumps in a chipper, friendly voice. "Coke? Pepsi?" Thinking that Colm hadn't heard him, he whistled a phenomenally loud ear-piercing whistle that made everyone in the store rush to the window and look out. Then he illustrated his question for Colm, putting his thumb to his mouth, tilting his head back, and miming swigging a drink. When he raised his left arm in a giant shrugging questioning gesture, Colm turned away as if he didn't know him.

Colm McCarthy, he thought, pumping the gas. What a terrific idea. Colm McCarthy. Why hadn't he thought of that before? He wondered how old you had to be before you could legally change your name. Maybe Mr. Frangione could help him get it changed in time to appear on his title to the house.

As Colm was pumping the last of the gas, he became aware that Lloyd Henry was standing next to him. Colm sensed him trying hard to get his attention.

Putting the nozzle back, Colm carefully avoided looking at him. He grabbed the gas cap, screwed it on, and was about to walk around to the passenger seat, but in the split second that Lloyd Henry caught his eye, he couldn't help but see him take a candy bar out from his sling and grin at Colm surreptitiously, like a kid who doesn't want to be accused of showing off but who has just made a nice move on his skateboard.

Colm stopped.

He looked at the candy bar Lloyd Henry held upright, like a candle at a vigil.

"What's that?" Colm asked, momentarily perplexed.

"Candy bar. Oh Henry!"

Colm watched Cameron's grin slip up the right side of Lloyd Henry's face and stay there, waiting for some kind of appreciative acknowledgment of his action.

"You stole it?" Colm asked in disbelief.

Lloyd Henry shrugged, playing down his accomplishment, and started to move toward the driver's door before Colm's tone stopped him.

"You stole that candy bar?"

"Shhh," Lloyd Henry said, grinning, turning around to see if anyone was listening, but the man in the fuchsia tank top and the Yankee baseball cap pumping gas was oblivious to them.

"Put it back."

"Huh?"

"Put it back."

"Yeah, right. Funny."

"It's not funny."

Lloyd Henry looked at Colm and realized he was serious.

"You're kidding, right?"

"No."

Cameron's grin slid back down and flattened out like the monitor of a person whose heart has recently stopped.

"Go back in there and put the candy bar back."

Lloyd Henry walked a few steps away, frowning and shaking his head and smiling all at once, embarrassed now. He held the Oh Henry! bar down by his side, glancing around.

"I'm telling you . . . go back in the store and put it back." Colm was pointing to the store.

Lloyd Henry stepped in tightly next to him.

"I'm not gonna put it back," he said emphatically, in a hushed, low tone.

"Yes, you are."

"I'm *not* gonna put it back."

"Yes, you are." Colm said, growing visibly angry.

He was upset not so much at the petty theft but at Lloyd Henry's deceit. Colm was working hard to believe the man he was driving cross-country with could be trusted, and this just made it that much more difficult. If he could steal, he could lie, and if he could lie, he could lie about anything, including the seventy thousand dollars.

Not to mention the fact that Colm had made the sling used in the crime. And it was his towel. He could just imagine Gammy shaking her head.

"It's a candy bar, for God's sake."

"So?"

"It's a candy bar!" Lloyd Henry said in an urgent whisper, bending his knees and pummeling the air with the Oh Henry!

"Put it back."

Lloyd Henry licked his upper lip for a while.

He slid his tongue back and forth quickly, studying Colm before he looked away, thought briefly, slipped the candy bar back into his sling on top of the cast, and reached for the car door handle with his left hand.

In one sharp movement with his hip, Colm bumped him away from the door, knocking Lloyd Henry hard toward the rear of the car, where he steadied himself on the roof with his one hand and, in an instant, spun around and reflexively raised a fist.

"If you don't go back in there," Colm said adamantly, "I'm going to go in and tell them what you did."

"You're going to . . . *what!?*"

Lloyd Henry stood there with his fist raised, as if he didn't realize it was up there.

"What is *wrong* with you?!" he said finally.

"What's wrong with me is you stole a candy bar."

Lloyd Henry awkwardly lowered his fist and paced around between the car and the gas pumps.

"I don't believe . . ." he said, shaking his head and looking around, getting more red-faced and self-conscious. "I don't believe . . ."

Suddenly Colm stepped forward, reached into the sling, grabbed the candy bar, and marched solemnly back toward the store.

Lloyd Henry watched him go, incredulous. He continued watching, motionless, after Colm disappeared into the store. Then, glancing around again, he grabbed the door handle, opened the door, and got in, sinking down in his seat.

Three minutes later Colm came out of the store empty-handed, walked calmly over to the passenger door, and got in. Silent and brooding, Lloyd Henry turned his head to watch him do up his seat belt.

"Let's go," Colm said, not looking at him.

Lloyd Henry didn't move.

"You happy now?" he asked finally.

Colm didn't respond.

"You happy?"

"No," Colm said, looking him squarely in the eyes. "I'm not happy. I'm not happy at all."

"You know," Lloyd Henry countered defensively, "what you said last night, about me breaking laws and lying and stealing . . . it's not true. It's not true."

"What's not true?"

"I don't break laws and I don't steal."

"You don't steal."

"I don't steal."

"You just stole a candy bar."

"I wasn't stealing a candy bar!" he said, practically shouting. He quickly rolled up his window.

"What were you doing?"

"I was just . . ." He shook his head and chewed on his tongue before exploding with the right word. *"Playing!"*

"Playing?"

"With you! Playing! You know . . ."

"I don't know."

"You *play* a game. You *play* . . . catch. *Play!*"

Lloyd Henry's frustration was on a par with Colm's disgust, neither of them backing down.

"I don't think so," Colm said, not buying any of it.

"Look. I gave that establishment forty-five dollars' worth of my business. Forty-five dollars; that candy bar cost nothing. It cost nothing. And it's not like it's a mom-and-pop operation," he added, gesturing toward the convenience store. "It's Mobil oil, for chrissakes, it's a *corporation!*"

Suddenly exhausted by his conviction of his own innocence, Lloyd Henry sank back, took a deep breath, and turned to gaze forward out the windshield.

He appeared to have imploded. His lack of sleep from the past two nights caught up with him, flooding his face with a weariness that made him look older than his fifty years.

Deflated, he glanced over at the convenience store and took another deep breath.

"Okay," he mumbled, staring off. "Okay."

He turned back, reached around in front of the steering wheel for the key, and started the engine.

Silent and disgusted, Colm stared forward and grimly put his hand on the gearshift, ready to put it into first.

"Oka-ay." Lloyd Henry almost sang the word on one

note, quietly, and stepped on the clutch.

Together they shifted smoothly into first, second, third, and fourth until they had left the rest stop behind and were cruising along the highway in fifth gear, not far from the Pennsylvania border.

Within a few minutes a state trooper pulled up alongside them on the left, staying with them as he looked over a few times.

Lloyd Henry glanced several times furtively over at the trooper and then, his eyebrows raised ever so slightly, looked slowly over at Colm, the unspoken question hanging in the air between them: Had Colm reported him back in the convenience store? The reverberations from the flying fork at the IHOP resonated as well, like overtones from a tuning fork.

Colm said and revealed nothing, not even the tiny glimmer of pleasure that flashed through him as he perceived Lloyd Henry's apprehension about the possibility of getting arrested.

Eventually the state trooper accelerated and passed them.

Lloyd Henry exhaled a long shallow breath. The two of them continued on in gloomy silence. For the next six hours neither spoke a word.

Chapter Thirteen

When they stopped to eat at a rest stop on Route 70, Colm had planned to get takeout so they wouldn't lose any time, but once they were inside the bustling lobby, Lloyd Henry and Colm bolted from each other, each aiming for a different fast food restaurant.

Colm was sitting alone now at a table in the Burger King. He had two cheeseburgers in front of him that were getting cold, a large order of fries, and a strawberry milk shake that was almost gone.

Greatly dispirited, he was having serious second thoughts about this whole trip.

He hadn't done much hitchhiking in his life, but he was considering crossing the four-lane freeway to the rest stop on the other side and trying to get a ride east. If he hung out by the gas pumps, maybe he could befriend a truck driver. Maybe offer some money.

Hammering the bottom of the ketchup bottle over his fries, he wished he knew what crime Lloyd Henry had committed to make someone offer seventy thousand dollars for him. How bad a person was he?

Colm picked up one of the cheeseburgers, took a bite, and started methodically chewing as he stared down at the opened road atlas by his elbow.

They were just outside of Claysville, Pennsylvania, and could be across West Virginia and in Ohio within an hour. After their rift over the candy bar, Lloyd Henry, in a sullen mood, had stepped up the speed, and they were averaging closer to eighty miles an hour.

Then there would be six states between them and Nevada. After Ohio, there was Indiana, then Illinois, Missouri, Kansas, Colorado, Utah, and finally Nevada. Their route was simple. They would take Route 70 west all the way to Route 15 in Utah, which hooked straight down to Las Vegas. Some ketchup dropped off his cheeseburger onto Las Vegas, and he smeared it away with his elbow, leaving an ominous stain on Nevada. He dripped some water onto the stain and tried to wipe it off.

After their weekend in Las Vegas, they could continue on Route 15 south down to Route 40, which offered a straight shot west into Bakersfield.

Colm ate a french fry and studied Bakersfield on the map.

It appeared to be a fairly large city, just west of the Mojave Desert. Some of the surrounding towns had exotic names like Tehachapi, Weed Patch, Caliente, Pumpkin Center, and Old River. It seemed strange to deposit Lloyd Henry, who was from New Jersey, in the vicinity of towns with names like that. Colm tried to picture him in his wool hat with the visor, the apricot short-sleeved shirt he was wearing now, chinos, black leather shoes, and his cast standing out by the Mojave Desert.

He couldn't even pass for a tourist, Colm thought.

He wondered if Lloyd Henry had ever been to Bakersfield before, and whether Colm was returning him to the site of a crime he'd committed. What if Lloyd Henry was planning to bolt from him as soon as they got there? Maybe the SUV was packed with heroin and Colm was spending the start of his summer helping a convicted felon transport drugs across state lines.

He finished off both cheeseburgers, slurped up the last of his strawberry milk shake, and pondered ordering another one, but before he did that, he got up and headed over to a pay phone.

There were four messages. Two were from Fiona and

another was from Justin, who was calling him from the weather station on top of Mount Washington. He'd just hiked up from Pinkerton Notch with ten campers and a counselor who'd thrown up three times on the way up. It was the first Colm had heard from Justin since he'd gone off to camp, and listening to his friend describe the details of the counselor's intestinal agony was music to his ears.

In that one phone message Justin gave Colm a minute and a half of his old life back.

Colm replayed the message twice, thinking how he'd give *anything* to be up on Mount Washington with Justin and a bunch of campers right then instead of in a rest stop in western Pennsylvania with Lloyd Henry. He covered his other ear to block out the noise and the voices of people using pay phones on either side of him.

The last message was from Cameron.

"Please call me, Colm. *Please.*" She sounded upset. "It's important."

Colm hadn't spoken to Cameron since the lawn mower incident. In a way that fight was useful now to justify his lack of communication with her. He wasn't mad at her anymore, but he was reluctant to call her because she'd see from her caller ID that he wasn't in Massachusetts. Once she got wind of that, she'd be all over trying to find out what he was up to.

After leaving messages for Audrey Robertson and Mr. Frangione, he talked briefly with Mr. Hafferty, who was still in the hospital.

"Colm?"

"Yes."

"Is this you?"

Mr. Hafferty sounded like he was still being heavily sedated.

"This is me. I'm out of town," Colm tried to explain slowly and clearly. "I'll be back in five or six days."

"You don't sound like Colm."

"I'm tired, Mr. Hafferty," Colm said, suddenly feeling exhausted.

"Did you get the name of the man I hit?"

Colm pondered his response. He not only had the name, he had the man. How was he going to answer?

"I need to apologize to him," Mr. Hafferty said, with some urgency.

"I know you do." Colm closed his eyes. "When I get home."

"Where are you?"

"Pennsylvania."

"Pennsylvania?" Mr. Hafferty sounded skeptical. There was a long pause.

"Mr. Hafferty? Mr. Hafferty?"

Suddenly there was a click. Mr. Hafferty had hung up.

Colm kept the receiver to his ear, not moving.

It seemed infinitely easier to stay there than to hang up and have to continue with his journey. He rested both elbows on the phone book on the little shelf beneath and leaned his head forward against the phone, still holding the receiver to his ear. Eyes closed, he felt capable of falling into the deepest sleep of his life.

He might actually have slept a minute or two before a child's shriek roused him. He raised his head, hung up the phone, headed over to the Burger King counter, and bought two chocolate milk shakes and the first cup of coffee he had ever ordered.

Back at his table someone had cleared away his tray with the uneaten fries, but he didn't care.

He gulped down half of one milk shake, poured the cup of coffee into it, and was almost finished with it when he felt a tap on his shoulder.

"Excuse me?"

Colm looked up to see an older woman in a red-checked cowgirl outfit and a red cowboy hat with a daisy bouncing on a coiled stem scrutinizing him.

"Are you Cohen Drucker?"

Colm kept sipping, looking at her. Her eyebrows appeared to be entirely artificial, severe black lines drawn way too high above her small hazel eyes. He wondered, briefly, what the function of eyebrows was and why a person would feel a compulsion to try to represent them where they could not possibly be, in the middle of one's forehead.

"Well, are you?"

"Maybe," he said, reluctantly.

"Your father just passed out over at the Roy Rogers?"

At first Colm thought she was asking him a question but then, after she repeated it, he realized she had that way of inflecting the end of a sentence so it sounded like a question.

He was not quick to respond.

"Fell off his chair?" she said after a while in a much louder voice, as if Colm were hard of hearing. "Hit the floor?" She seemed dismayed that Colm wasn't responding with more concern.

Colm slurped up what remained of the milk shake and swished it around his teeth as if he were rinsing his mouth out with mouthwash. Staring blankly ahead at a group of teenagers clustered around a video game, he appeared to be lost in thought, but in fact he wasn't thinking at all. He had stopped thinking.

Moments before, he'd still been contemplating the possibility of cutting himself loose of this whole enterprise, bolting across the highway and trying to hitchhike home. Now, with the arrival of this piece of news, he knew he had no such option.

He had no options at all.

In his extreme exhaustion, he sensed it was not his own fate that was playing out here. Lloyd Henry's fate had engulfed his own, swept him up in much the same way it had Mr. Hafferty. Lloyd Henry hooked people through his vulnerabilities, his weaknesses. His knack for riding a bicycle ineptly had landed Mr. Hafferty in the hospital. Now he had passed out in a rest stop at the precise moment when Colm was gearing up to leave him.

The missing pieces, the cracks and holes in Lloyd Henry's character, created a vacuum that sucked people in; this was something that Colm had known instinctively about his father even as a small child. He had sensed this space that he now felt himself drawn into; this vortex felt deeply familiar somehow. After all, he had lived his whole life in the space that Lloyd Henry had left behind when he'd abandoned the family.

"You could hurry? Cohen?"

The waitress cleared her throat, staring at Colm as if he

were the worst son in the world. Her penciled eyebrows, now frowning, pointed at each other at a ninety-degree angle, and the daisy in her hat bobbed from tension below.

He reached over and grabbed a napkin from a stack on the next table and slowly wiped his mouth with it before picking up his knapsack and his atlas. He stood, turned, and faced the precise direction where Lloyd Henry was now enacting whatever drama was required to further his own misbegotten story line.

The waitress was deluded if she thought she led the way for the tall young man following behind. At that moment Colm could have found Lloyd Henry blindfolded. He walked through the busy lobby with his eyes half closed. He was numbly calm, prepared for anything—the sight of Lloyd Henry lying on the floor, his head in a pool of blood. The sight of medics, firemen, an oxygen tank, all the elements of a rescue drama.

What he saw when he turned into the Roy Rogers restaurant—past the restrooms, the souvenir shop, and the TCBY counter—was Lloyd Henry comfortably seated at a table, leaning back against the wall, being attended to by three middle-aged women. One, in a short skirt and knee-high black boots, was at that very moment placing a cup of hot tea in front of him. Another,

in a long blue leather coat, was sitting next to him, holding his good hand up on the table and listening to him,
absorbed. And the third, another waitress also in cowgirl getup, was awkwardly leaning over holding an ice
pack up against his cheek.

All three women looked concerned. Lloyd Henry
appeared relaxed and cheerful, if pale. He was regaling them with some story.

Colm walked up to the table.

"How ya feeling, hon?" This was asked by Colm's
escort, who now intruded herself into the scene with a
proprietary manner, having been the one to first dis-
cover Lloyd Henry on the floor.

"Hey!" Lloyd Henry said, brightly, looking up at
Colm.

"Found him for you?" the waitress announced in her
interrogatory inflection, basking in Lloyd Henry's enthusiasm.

"Sip just a little." The woman in the short skirt raised
the teacup up for Lloyd Henry while sharply eyeing the
woman holding his hand, signaling her to release it. She
didn't, so the woman in the short skirt very carefully held
the cup up in front of Lloyd Henry's mouth. He leaned
forward slightly and obliged her by gingerly sipping a
little bit of the hot brew.

"Your dad is gonna have one helluva shiner," said the waitress who held the ice pack against his cheek. She pulled it off to show Colm the bruise that was already forming on his cheekbone.

Colm said nothing.

"Okay!" announced Lloyd Henry, moving a little as an overture to scatter the women. They all jumped back slightly, like birds at a feeder responding to some nearby sudden movement.

"Time to hit the road. Ladies, my deepest most heartfelt thanks. Merci beaucoup," he said, retracting his hand from the grip of the woman with the blue leather coat, and taking the ice pack from the waitress. He slid along the vinyl bench without the use of his hands, scuttling sideways with his feet.

The knot that Colm had tied in the towel sling was still holding up.

"Now you're *not* driving," cautioned the woman with the teacup.

"You should take him to the hospital. The emergency room?" said the waitress who had corralled Colm. She spoke to him now with that same schoolteacher tone, as if Colm were six. "He passed out, you know. He was unconscious?"

"Ladies," said Lloyd Henry, moving toward the

door, "a pleasure. If Pennsylvania had a state flower, it would be each and every one of you."

They all simultaneously took a half step toward him.

"His son is adorable," Colm heard one of them say to another. "I'm dying to touch his hair."

Colm stood in place, one of this small throng who watched, riveted, from the restaurant's outermost boundary as Lloyd Henry navigated his way through the crowded rest stop toward the exit. They might have all been onshore, watching a tacking sailboat venturing out to sea, soon to be swallowed up by the horizon.

"Aren't you going with him? Cohen?"

Without saying a word, Colm put one foot in front of the other and started moving toward the door. The crowd parted for him, offering him a direct route. Though his father had worked his way back and forth through the busy throng, Colm was somehow able to navigate a straight line, moving steadfastly toward his destiny.

Out in the parking lot, Lloyd Henry was leaning over, sliding everything on the backseat of the SUV down onto the floor—clothing, some trash, empty beverage cups, Colm's duffel bag, the unopened kite, the baseball gloves and ball. Colm stood watching from a few feet behind.

They had parked next to a Minnie Winnie Winnebago, and a bald man in a fishnet undershirt was shaking out a large, unwieldy piece of AstroTurf from the top step of the doorway, kicking it vigorously from behind.

"What are you doing?" Colm addressed Lloyd Henry's back.

"I need some sleep."

"What happened back there?"

"Just three, four hours. That's all I need."

"What happened in the restaurant?"

"When?"

"What do you mean when? Just now."

"What happened?"

"Did you really pass out?"

Lloyd Henry was wrestling with the box of grapefruit. It was stuck somehow in a crease in the seat, but he finally managed with his left arm to dislodge and pitch it over onto the floor. Several grapefruit rolled out.

"Can you hand me my ice?"

"Huh?"

"My ice. It's on the roof."

Colm looked up and saw the blue ice pack. He handed it to Lloyd Henry, who reached back for it and fell forward in a heap onto the backseat.

"Ow," he said, shifting over more onto his left side away from his broken arm. He temporarily placed the ice pack on the seat in front of his stomach, hoisted himself up sideways, torqued, and with great effort pulled the door shut after giving Colm a fleeting partial wave. It was as if he had bid him good night and closed the door of his bedroom.

Colm immediately opened it.

Lloyd Henry was curled up, hurtling toward sleep.

"Why did you pass out?"

Lloyd Henry, his forehead burrowed into the backseat, had placed the ice pack under his face. Colm could see his eyes were closed.

"Just a couple hours' sleep. I'll be fine."

"I'm not letting you sleep till you tell me why you passed out."

"I thought you didn't want me to talk to you."

"Are you sick?" Colm asked.

"No. It's just a thing I have."

"What thing?"

"A swallowing thing. When I drink."

"You were drinking?" Colm asked, immediately assuming Lloyd Henry meant alcohol.

"Sometimes I can't drink. When I'm standing up. Some weird thing, I black out."

"You weren't standing up. You were sitting down."

Lloyd Henry moaned slightly and shifted to get more comfortable.

"You were sitting down," Colm repeated more forcefully.

"Okay. You're right. I didn't pass out. Could you please close the door, I just need . . . three hours' . . . three hours' sleep."

"Are you terminally ill?"

"Terminally ill?"

"Are you?"

Lloyd Henry raised his head a little and squinted back up at Colm.

"Would you care?" Lloyd Henry asked.

"No," Colm responded instantly.

Lloyd Henry looked at him for a moment and then put his head back down.

After several minutes Colm placed both hands on the back door and pushed it shut.

"Hey, pal. Could you help me fold up my yard here? Woo-oo!"

Colm realized someone was talking to him. He turned and saw the bald man from the Winnebago, wrestling awkwardly with his AstroTurf.

"Could you lend a hand?"

Colm stepped over, grabbed two corners of the bright-green material, and brought them together like the corners of a sheet. Together they folded up the portable grass.

"Thanks," the man said, embracing it and lugging it up the small collapsible steps into his Winnebago. "Can't have cocktail hour and watch the sunset without my front lawn."

Colm turned back and looked at the SUV.

He felt a strong urge to sit down on the pavement, but instead he opened the front door, and got in, sinking into the seat. He closed the door and leaned his head back against the headrest.

"Colm?"

Colm didn't respond.

"Colm?"

Without moving his head, Colm glanced up into the rearview mirror, but Lloyd Henry was out of view, lying prone beneath the sight line.

"Would you mind opening some windows? It's hot as hell in here."

Colm heard the keys, tossed from behind, thwack against the ceiling before they dropped in his lap. He stared down at them, overcome with exhaustion, and remembered a time in fourth grade when Justin's father had taken them to a ball game at Fenway Park and Colm had slumped asleep against the shoulder of the stranger to his left.

He picked up the keys and for the first time noticed the key chain, a miniature orange flip-flop with a fuzzzy yellow pom-pom attached. That was odd, he thought. He tried to imagine Lloyd Henry choosing and purchasing that keychain in a convenience store along with his breath-freshening gum.

It *was* hot in the car. Stifling.

Inserting the larger of the keys into the ignition, he turned it more than necessary and the engine started right up.

He located the controls for the windows, and one by one he rolled them all down. Then he rolled them all up again, then down.

Lloyd Henry was snoring.

"What a stupid thing to say. 'If Pennsylvania had a state flower . . .'" He imitated Lloyd Henry's voice speaking to those women, pouring on the charm.

"Pennsylvania *has* a state flower."

Colm shook his head, disgusted.

"God, that was stupid."

He turned on the air-conditioning and then fooled around with the wipers, spraying the windshield a few times. It took a while for the remnants of a bug to disappear, but eventually the last trace was wiped clean. Colm studied the temperature gauge, the oil pressure, and the odometer. Bleary-eyed, he looked over at the glove compartment. After a while he leaned over and popped it open. A white rectangular piece of paper fell out onto the passenger seat, and he picked it up. It was the registration for the SUV in the name of Donna Kimball, 283 Lewis Ave., Nashua, New Hampshire.

Donna. He stared at the word, trying to comprehend it.

If he was processing this information accurately, Lloyd Henry didn't own this vehicle. Donna the physical therapist owned it. Had Lloyd Henry stolen it from her? Had he really put her on the bus back to New Hampshire, or had he mugged her?

Colm turned around and looked at Lloyd Henry crumpled on the backseat. In a heap, he looked like a worn stage prop dummy that has been poorly folded and squeezed into a drawer. He had grabbed one of the baseball gloves and was using it for a pillow, with the ice pack tucked into the webbing.

Studying him, Colm wondered how he'd ever thought they could possibly get to Las Vegas on Saturday, just two days from now. Lloyd Henry would probably sleep till Saturday. They'd arrive sometime Monday or Tuesday, long after Fiona and Bunny had left.

If only he had his learner's permit.

Turning back around, he jerked his legs over and accidentally kicked the clutch. Staring straight ahead, he mindlessly picked up his left foot, stepped on the clutch pedal, and depressed it. Then he released it and pressed down again. Then he stepped over onto the brake. Then he put his right foot on the gas and revved the engine slightly a few times. It reminded him of pulling the choke out on his lawn mower.

Although he had never driven before, never even sat behind a steering wheel, Colm now released the hand brake, depressed the clutch, and smoothly slipped it into first as if he'd been driving all his life. The SUV rolled forward toward the woods that bordered the parking lot. Colm turned the wheel gently and, going about ten miles an hour, straightened out and shifted into second, traveling slowly along the edge of the woods.

He had no intention of *driving*, of trying to make up any distance they would lose while Lloyd Henry slept. A natural mechanic, he was simply caught up with the operation of the vehicle. At this point, the car was driving *him*.

Nearing the entrance to the freeway, he turned around and drove back the entire length of the rest stop, past the restaurant, past the gas station, way out to the end of the parking lot on the other side where cars and trucks were entering. Then he circled around behind the gas station, behind the restaurant, past the row of parked eighteen-wheelers, many of them with diesel engines idling. He approached the freeway again, his head still resting back against the headrest, and navigated an even wider circle around the same route. For about five minutes, he drove slowly all around the parking lot, at the far ends carving elongated half-moons back and forth the way he did on his hockey skates.

Once he stopped and put it into reverse and stalled out, but he just started the engine up again and backed up nimbly between two parked cars. He went forward and backward several times, using the rearview mirror and the side mirrors and looking back through the rear window over Lloyd Henry's sleeping body. He circled around the entire rest stop a few more times and then, without thinking, he accelerated, shifted into third, and within a minute had driven onto the freeway, merging with the speeding traffic.

He stayed in the right lane, curious to see how it felt to go faster and slip into fourth, which he did, and eventually fifth. He'd been shifting all day for Lloyd Henry, so he knew exactly where all the positions were. He glanced down at the speedometer and saw they were going sixty-five, the speed limit.

The wind was whipping through all the open windows, and he rested his left elbow out the window, still keeping both hands on the wheel.

It was so easy.

He experienced an extraordinary sensation of relief, of liberation. It was surprisingly different from riding in the passenger seat. Utterly relaxed and in control now, he felt like he was cruising along on his bicycle, except the landscape was flying by.

It felt like a dream. He accelerated and pulled over into the passing lane.

Before this he hadn't particularly been looking forward to getting his license, but now he calculated the months until he'd be able to go for his learner's permit. And then it struck him: What would it be like to be cruising along like this with Melanie Phelps sitting beside him? What would it be like if they were driving up to Vermont? Or to Cape Cod? They could park by the National Seashore and bring sleeping bags and a tent and camp out in the dunes; they could take a ferry to Nantucket for the day and bicycle around the island and eat ice cream and fried clams on the pier. They could go anywhere they wanted. New York. They could drive down to New York City and go to some museums; she'd like that. He could show her the diorama of Berkshire County in the Museum of Natural History. He imagined her in the passenger seat now, her hair flying back in the breeze as she stared out the window, daydreaming. Happy.

He smiled and glanced down at the speedometer. They were going *eighty-five*.

Alarmed, he abruptly lifted his foot off the accelerator, sat up and gripped the wheel, causing the Explorer to swerve back and forth slightly. It was strange; it hadn't felt that much faster. A truck, bearing down on them from behind, honked several times as Colm watched the speedometer retreat back down to seventy-five, seventy, sixty-five, sixty. As the car slowed down, his own heart rate sped up, adrenalin pumping through him. His arms and hands were trembling slightly as he waited for an opportunity to get back into the right lane.

The truck driver kept honking and flashing his lights, and Colm kept looking in the rearview mirror, and the side mirror, and twisting around to look out the rear and side windows to make sure it was clear in the right lane. After one aborted attempt at shifting lanes, he jerked over and regained control as the truck barreled by. His heart was pounding. How had this happened?

This was the first time in his life he could recall breaking a law, doing something he wasn't supposed to.

Lloyd Henry produced a rapid series of snorts from the back and was quiet.

Colm thought of Gammy. This is exactly what she would have predicted. That Lloyd Henry's evil nature would have infiltrated Colm's, setting up shop like a virus, a rust spot that would rapidly spread and corrode.

He couldn't continue. This was illegal.

Even though all the windows were rolled down, he turned the air conditioner on high, aiming the chilly blast at his face through several vents to help keep him awake and alert. His tired bleary eyes were wide open, as if propped open by the cold air. He turned the radio on, local news, and cranked the volume up.

When the exit sign loomed up ahead, Colm flicked the windshield wipers on by mistake and subsequently scrambled to figure out how to turn on the directionals. The next exit was three miles away, but Colm kept the directional clicking steadily for several minutes until he could slow down and pull off.

With some difficulty, he followed the signs over a bridge and through a series of turns to get to the entrance ramp for 70 heading east. His instinct was to go back, to return to the rest stop where he'd started, as quickly as possible; to erase this incident, this crime.

One sign in particular was confusing and poorly placed, Colm thought, turning at the last second onto the entrance ramp. This time, merging with the traffic was more daunting and he sat up rigidly as he tried to gauge the right moment to proceed. After resolutely accelerating, he maintained a cautious speed just under sixty and stayed in the right lane, white knuckled and gripping the steering wheel.

The local traffic report was now on the radio, and after briefly listening to a description of a four-car accident involving an overturned eighteen wheeler, apparently not far away, Colm pressed the seek button for the next station and kept it there even though the reception was terrible. He didn't mind the loud static; it was more important to keep both hands on the wheel than to keep searching.

His eyes were darting up and down, up and down, from the road to the speedometer, to the road to the speedometer, careful to make sure he wasn't inadvertently speeding up.

Lloyd Henry remained sound asleep, dead to the world.

Finally an exit arrived and Colm pulled off. Finding

his way back around to 70 heading west was even more complicated this time. At twenty miles an hour, he crept through the back streets of the outskirts of a town, blanching at the sight of a police officer writing out what was probably a parking ticket. At one point Colm had to drive across some railroad tracks, and he looked back and forth half a dozen times to make sure a train wasn't coming before he haltingly lurched forward.

Once he got back on 70 heading west, it felt like an eternity before they reached their rest stop, though it was only sixteen miles away. He was going forty-five, cars and trucks whizzing past him, because he wanted to make sure he didn't miss the turnoff. If he missed the turnoff and had to drive all the way around again, he would be sunk. The sustained rush of adrenalin had ripped out what little store of energy he'd had in him, and sitting stiffly, his whole body felt pulverized. Shot.

He leaned forward slightly, back straight and rigid.

Just to pass the time, he pictured the geometric shapes of all the lawns of his customers. He even mowed one particular lawn in his mind; back and forth, back and forth; front yard, side yard, backyard.

Finally a sign designating a rest area appeared. He slowed down even more, but once he veered off onto the turnoff, he suddenly gunned the accelerator, just for a few moments, as if giving himself and the car a quick transfusion.

The parking space where Lloyd Henry had parked was still vacant, although the Minnie Winnie Winnebago was gone. Colm pulled in to the exact same spot, facing in the exact same direction they'd been in before, and turned the engine off.

With colossal effort he reached over and turned off the radio.

The bright afternoon sun was on his face, even though the visor was down. The thought occurred to him to grab a T-shirt out of his duffel bag and put it over his face, but before he could follow through, he had crashed, asleep, Donna's little orange flip-flop dangling off the key chain on the tip of his upturned index finger.

Chapter Fourteen

"**I** never much cared for fruit."

"No?"

"Nope."

"I've always loved fruit."

"Huh."

"My favorite food group."

"Really?"

"Peaches. I love peaches."

"I'm not big on peaches."

"Kiwis. Grapes."

"If I'm sick, I can eat a canned peach. If I'm sick."

"Pineapple. Cherries. Love cherry pie."

"Well now, fruit *in a pie*. That's a different story."

"Blueberries."

"My first wife . . . she could make an amazing apple pie."

"Is that right? I love a good apple pie."

"Well then, you would *love* my first wife's apple pie. I'm telling you . . ."

It was curious.

As Colm lay there, eyes closed, drifting out of a deep sleep, it seemed that Lloyd Henry was having a conversation with the radio. There was a weather report in the background with a lot of static, but the voices were coming through loud and clear.

"Yup. She had a secret ingredient. Secret ingredient."

"Highs today in the low nineties . . ."

"I love vegetables, too."

"That's good," Lloyd Henry was saying to the man in the radio. "Vegetables are good for you."

"There's not one vegetable I don't love."

"Wish I could say the same."

"Chance of scattered showers this evening . . ."

And that wasn't the only curious thing. Though he didn't have any difficulty remembering where he was—driving cross-country with Lloyd Henry—it did seem strange that he was as comfortable as he was, especially since he had fallen asleep in the front seat. He was unbelievably comfortable. So comfortable that he was reluctant to wake up, reluctant to twitch a muscle and disturb his profoundly relaxed state. It was as if he were floating.

He lingered, eyes still closed, hovering somewhere between sleep and consciousness as long as he could, like a plane that circles the sky in a holding pattern, the landing strip somewhere far below.

"Broccoli. Brussels sprouts."

"I like meat."

There was a pillow under his head. How on earth did a pillow get under his head?

"Steak. Ribs. Chops."

He opened his eyes.

"Do you like to barbecue?"

"Never happier."

Colm sat up.

"Hey! Look who showed up," Lloyd Henry called out cheerily. "Good morning!"

Colm was staring straight ahead at himself in the rearview mirror, blinking and confused, completely disoriented. He was in the backseat. Lloyd Henry was up front in the passenger seat, and a large, balding, bearded man with terry-cloth wristbands on both his wrists was driving.

"This is my son, Eugene. Colm, this is Eugene."

"Morning." Eugene waved in the rearview mirror. "I owe you a few bucks. Ate a couple of your grapefruits— hope you don't mind."

"He doesn't mind."

"They were fantastic. Juicy and sweet."

"Where are we?" Colm asked, his voice perforating their conversation like a bullet.

"We are in tornado country," said Lloyd Henry. "Watch out for falling houses!"

"Auntie Em! Auntie Em!" Eugene piped up in a falsetto voice. He chuckled, wiped his brow with one of his wristbands, and picked up a Dr Pepper bottle from the cup holder.

"We're in *Kansas?*"

"Check it out," said Eugene, taking a swig of Dr Pepper and looking out his side window.

Colm stared out the window. He had never seen a landscape so flat, so immense. It went on and on and on, forever, and there were no buildings or houses in any direction except for one distant farmhouse, surrounded by the only trees in sight. They were clustered like tall sailboat masts docked at some distant marina.

"We're in Kansas?" Colm repeated. He couldn't believe it.

"Halfway across," said Lloyd Henry. "Right on schedule."

Colm blinked a few times.

"What day is it?" he asked with the same severity, as if he were interrogating two suspects.

"The day after Ohio," Lloyd Henry said, and both he and Eugene laughed.

"Tell you what, you are a *good* sleeper," said Eugene. "A good sleeper. I used to be able to sleep like that," he added wistfully, shaking his head.

"It's Friday?"

"Friday. You slept through Ohio, Colm," said Lloyd Henry, yawning but ostensibly in good spirits. "And Indiana, Illinois, and Missouri."

"Let me ask you something, Colm," said Eugene, pronouncing his name surprisingly well, as though he had heard it many times. "Are those grapefruit from Florida?"

Colm looked at Eugene, in profile from behind. It was hard to respond to a person who had essentially materialized out of thin air. Still getting his bearings, Colm studied him with the same incredulity he'd given the passing landscape.

It was as if this Eugene person had dropped into their world out of the sky, like Dorothy's house, and yet he seemed so comfortably settled in the driver's seat, drinking his Dr Pepper, now flicking on the blinker to pass the car ahead with the relaxed assuredness of a professional bus driver.

"Ye-es," Colm said cautiously, in response to his question.

"I knew it! I knew it! Had to be," said Eugene, thumping the steering wheel a couple of times with the ball of one hand. "A grapefruit that good."

According to the car clock, it was ten A.M. When Colm had fallen asleep the evening before, it was still light out. He must have slept close to sixteen hours, and they appeared to have driven straight through the night.

"Eugene wants to see the Grand Canyon," said Lloyd Henry, yawning again and slipping down in the passenger seat a little. "He's been there before, but he'd like to go again."

"I don't need to," said Eugene.

"Well, maybe you don't need to," said Lloyd Henry, with a familiarity that bespoke a long friendship, "but you said you'd like to. You did say that." Lloyd Henry gave Eugene a friendly smile.

"I wouldn't mind," Eugene said affably, shrugging.

"And we've got time, Colm," said Lloyd Henry, twisting around. "We've got time to zip over, catch the Grand Canyon, and be in Las Vegas tomorrow afternoon. Just like you wanted. Right on schedule."

"I need to make a phone call," said Colm. Halfway across Kansas in the backseat of a possibly stolen SUV with two strange men, Colm felt a need to touch base with his mother.

"You can use my cell phone," said Lloyd Henry.

"I don't think so."

Colm was trying to remember when he'd spoken to his mother last. Not for a couple of days. It had been a short conversation because she and Don were just heading out of their hotel room with half-price tickets to a magician's matinée show.

"Sure you can," Lloyd Henry said, leaning over and reaching for his phone out of his windbreaker.

"I need a pay phone."

"Here," Lloyd Henry said, holding the cell phone back for him over his left shoulder.

"No."

"Go ahead."

"No."

With his mouth, Lloyd Henry made the touch-tone sounds of a phone number being dialed, including the one plus the area code.

"Holy shit," said Eugene, grinning. "How'd you do that?"

His lips loose, Lloyd Henry dialed another number by whistling in bursts, letting the air puff out his lips and blow them open. Somehow he was able to finesse the short little whistles into tones of varying pitches.

"Your dad is full of more goddamned surprises."

Eugene looked up into the rearview mirror.

Colm didn't respond.

Lloyd Henry was dialing another number, only this time it was with a rotary dial, a very different sound and remarkably accurate. His lips were slightly open, his teeth clenched, and he was doing something with his tongue in the back of his mouth.

"Don't hear *that* too often," he paused to say to Eugene. "Huh? A sound from the past."

He dialed some more using the rotary phone.

"Who you calling?" Eugene quipped.

"My bookie," Lloyd Henry joked, and then quickly corrected himself. "I mean, the president," he said, directing the remark at Colm. "The White House."

Eugene shook his head, tickled.

"Come on," Lloyd Henry said to Colm, still holding up the phone, his elbow bent back as if he'd stopped midway through a left-handed pitch. "Take it."

"I'll wait."

Colm didn't want Fiona's phone number to be somehow stored away in Lloyd Henry's cell phone, even if it was just her hotel number. He instinctively felt that his father shouldn't have that piece of information.

"I just signed up for a great service," Lloyd Henry said to Eugene in a convivial way, as if someone in the backseat wasn't rejecting him and everyone was getting along just fine. "Unlimited hours."

"Is that right?" Eugene said genially.

"There's a rest area six miles ahead," said Colm, his head turning at the passing sign. "They'll have a pay phone."

"Hokey-dokey," Lloyd Henry said with the tiniest hint of annoyance, smiling over at Eugene. "Privacy," he said quietly, accounting for his son's behavior. "He needs privacy." And then he mouthed the words to Eugene, "For his phone call."

"It's a beautiful thing," Eugene said after a muted burp.

"What's a beautiful thing, Eugene?"

"What you're doing here. Father-son relationship. Bonding. Road trip."

Colm was ignoring them both, studying the Rand McNally road atlas on his lap.

It was amazing. If they continued driving nonstop through the night, they would actually reach Las Vegas the next day. According to the tiny calculations on the map, the distance from Salina, Kansas, to Las Vegas was about sixteen hours of driving time, through Colorado, Utah, and into Nevada.

Colm didn't know where or how Lloyd Henry had acquired Eugene, but he wasn't going to ask. He himself had been pondering how to pick up a second driver, and now that Lloyd Henry had done so, Colm was just going to let things be.

"What's your game?" Eugene asked Lloyd Henry, taking sunglasses out of his shirt pocket and putting them on.

"Huh?"

"What do you like to play? The slots? Roulette? Blackjack?"

"Oh. I like the horses."

"They have horses in Vegas?"

"My gambling days are over anyway," Lloyd Henry said, motivated to change the subject. "Hey, Colm, notice anything different?"

"Your gambling days are over and you're going to Las Vegas?"

"Yeah. Colm? Notice anything?"

"I've heard that before." Eugene chuckled to himself. "Fifty bucks says tomorrow your gambling days are back."

"I got a new sling!" Lloyd Henry said loudly, directing his voice back at Colm.

"You can't go to Vegas and not bet."

"See?" He was glaring at Eugene to drop the subject.

"No one can go to Vegas and not bet. *I'm* gonna bet, tell you that much."

"Some lady in Ohio gave me a sling."

"She liked you," Eugene said. "Boy, did she like you."

"Nice lady."

"Missed opportunity there."

"Pulled it right out of her purse. See, Colm? My new sling?"

Colm didn't respond.

"Your towel is in the back. Folded up."

Eugene had voiced one of Colm's concerns. Here he was bringing a compulsive bettor to the gambling center of the universe, much like escorting an alcoholic into a bar. He didn't feel good about it. And there was no telling how being in Las Vegas would affect Lloyd Henry's behavior; it could bring out the worst in him. Colm wasn't worried about him gambling away the seventy thousand dollars because that wasn't in Lloyd Henry's possession yet, but maybe he'd suddenly jump ship and disappear.

"Here's the exit," Lloyd Henry said.

"I know." Eugene was already in the right lane.

Colm was thinking that the sooner he got Lloyd Henry out of Las Vegas, the better.

"We need to turn off here."

"I know."

"He needs a pay phone."

"*I know, I know,*" Eugene said, slowing down as he turned off onto the exit ramp.

"Needs to make a call," Lloyd Henry muttered to himself, slightly addled, as if the notion of Colm calling someone was disconcerting to him.

Eugene pulled up to a bank of pay phones in front of a small building with vending machines inside, connected by a long passageway to the restaurants.

"Need any change?" Lloyd Henry asked, as Colm opened the door and jumped out.

Ignoring the offer and closing the door, Colm was struck by the thought that he might actually see Fiona and Bunny the next day. His mind had been so swamped with trying to navigate this whole adventure that he hadn't really had room to look forward to seeing them, to daydream for a moment about what it would be like to be in the southwest with them.

Within twenty-four hours he'd be able to hold his baby sister, to have her wrap her pudgy arms around his neck and clutch him toward her. Within minutes of their reunion, she'd lie down on her back and put her feet up for him to grab so he could swing her back and forth upside down. Bunny loved that. It made her laugh hysterically.

"Desert Sands Hotel, can I help you?" It was the hotel operator with the hot pink neon voice.

"Room 423, please," Colm said.

"Oh, hi! Is this . . ." There was a pause. "C-o-l-m?"

She'd remembered not only how to spell his name, but also the fact that she hadn't been able to pronounce it. "I'll connect you."

More than anything, he was dying to see his mother sing in a Las Vegas hotel lounge. He smiled to himself, picturing her as he listened to the phone ring.

Facing the small building with the vending machines, he noticed a cupola up on the roof with a giant soda cup and straw inside, visible through large windows. Cameron had begged Colm many times to install a cupola on the roof of their house, mainly so they could put a Christmas tree with lights up there in the winter, but Colm thought it was a dumb idea.

She also wanted to have one of those little white octagonal gazebos, and the notion of that irked Colm even more. The gazebos were sold at a place that made fake country lawn structures like decorative wells and windmills and garages painted to look like barns, mostly assembled with staple guns and glue. The house already had a good-sized screened-in porch with molding hand carved by Colm McCarthy up on the ceiling and around the screens. Why put some dumb cookie-cutter fake bandstand in their backyard?

Colm stared at the giant soda cup and thought about the house. What would he do with it now that it was going to be his? Keep it the same, he thought. Keep it just the same.

"Hello?"

Colm was unprepared to hear Don's voice. It took him a second to realize who it was.

"Hello?" Don repeated.

"It's Colm," Colm said, still not quite comfortable saying Don's name.

"Colm," Don said, clearing his throat. "Hi. Sorry. I was asleep."

"Oh. Sorry."

"That's okay. I should get up."

"Is my mother there?"

"No. She's downstairs. She's rehearsing with the band."

"Oh." Colm was disappointed. He really wanted to talk to her.

"How you doing, sport?" Don asked.

"Okay."

There was a pause. Don cleared his throat again.

"I'm afraid we've got some bad news for you."

"Oh?" Colm said, his chest tightening up.

"Nothing serious, but . . ."

"What."

"Uh . . . well, Cameron . . ." He hesitated.

"*What.*"

"Chester is gone," he finally blurted out.

Colm didn't say anything.

"He's not there, Colm."

Silence.

"Cameron thinks . . . something . . . may have happened to him."

Hearing no response, Don struggled on. "Just . . . she went there, and . . . he wasn't there. Thought you should know."

Silence.

"*You're* there, right? Colm?"

"I'm here."

"Good. You probably know where Chester is. Right?"

"Yup."

"Good. Good. Cameron wants you to call her. She's pretty upset."

Colm was aware they were in different time zones, but this felt like different universe zones. *What was Cameron thinking? Did she wonder where he was? Might she not think that maybe Chester was with him since he wasn't there?*

How many times had she come by?

"So," Don said, trying to fill another silence.

Colm wanted to help him out. He appreciated the courage it must have taken Don to broach this subject, but Colm hadn't told anyone about Chester, and he wasn't about to tell Don now on a pay phone from Kansas. He was quickly trying to think through what message he would leave for his mother. Should he ask Don to tell her he might be there the next day? Or would it be better not to say anything and just show up; wait and see how things played out with Lloyd Henry?

The unexpected exchange about Chester had thrown him off.

"Okay," Colm finally said. "Well, tell my mom hi."

"Okay. Will do."

"'Bye."

"You take care, Colm."

"You take care too," Colm repeated, even though he intensely disliked that phrase. "Don." And he hung up.

He stood there a few moments, staring off, digesting and erasing the unsatisfying conversation.

Impulsively he picked up the phone again and dialed information.

"City and state, please," a recorded voice intoned.

"Pittsfield, Mass."

"What listing?"

"Kenneth Phelps."

After a few moments, a real operator got on and asked him for an address.

"Ellery Street," Colm answered promptly. He'd walked past Melanie Phelps's house many times, though how he knew her father's name he wasn't sure. Maybe it was on their mailbox.

As soon as the operator gave him the phone number, Colm had it memorized.

"Thank you."

He hung up.

The phone instantly rang. He wondered who could be calling him, and for a split second he thought it might be Melanie. He picked it up.

"Hello?" But no one was there. He hung up and went in to buy some food from the vending machines. The giant cup with the straw in it in the cupola had given him a craving for a milk shake, but the recent episode with Lloyd Henry passing out made him reluctant to go into the restaurant area.

There was a change machine for dollar bills. Armed with fistfuls of change, he was able to buy seven packets of orange cheese crackers with peanut butter, three small bags of barbecue-flavored potato chips, a small bag of pretzel sticks, four candy bars, some gum, and three cans of root beer.

After stuffing all the food into his backpack, he headed back out to the car, repeating Melanie Phelps's phone number over and over again like a mantra.

Colm wasn't sure where Eugene had ended up parking the SUV, but after looking around awhile, he realized that the two men playing catch beyond the last row of parked cars were probably Eugene and Lloyd Henry.

Unwrapping a Snickers bar, he forced himself to head over in that direction.

As he neared them he wondered . . . how could Lloyd Henry be playing catch with a cast on his right arm?

Badly, was the answer.

Watching Lloyd Henry anxiously looking up and shuffling back and forth to make a bare-handed catch, Colm was suddenly reminded of the yo-yo that Lloyd Henry had fumbled with outside church. And then, with growing unease, he thought of the bicycle. And the skateboard. In Lloyd Henry's hands these objects didn't seem so much like toys or items from a sporting goods store as tools from a toolbox. Lloyd Henry wasn't *playing* with them so much as *trying to make them work.* Trying to build something with them that involved Colm.

Frowning, Colm stopped, chewing on the chocolaty nut-filled caramel.

"Hey!" Eugene yelled out, irritated after Lloyd Henry had thrown the ball wildly all the way over to the gas station. *"Jesus, you're horrible."*

"Well," Lloyd Henry mumbled defensively.

"You throw like a girl."

"I don't throw like a girl."

"You throw like a girl."

Colm finished the Snickers bar and paused briefly to unwrap another one.

"I'm getting aerobic here," Eugene complained, "chasing after your balls."

"I'm right-handed, Eugene. Cut me some slack."

"If you're right-handed, why are we out here?"

"Don't be so cranky."

"Why are we out here?

"Lighten up. I've caught every one of your throws. Bare-handed."

"That's because I can throw. Unlike you."

"Bravo bravissimo. Get the ball."

"You catch the damn ball."

"Get the ball."

"I'm sick of getting the ball. Next you'll throw it out on the goddamn highway."

"Colm! Grab a glove!" Lloyd Henry called out, suddenly seeing Colm and flashing him a broad smile.

"We're playing catch!"

Eugene, winded and out of shape, trudged wearily off to retrieve the ball, muttering to himself. He was a large man, overweight by at least fifty pounds. He was wearing a bright-red Adidas jogging suit, the double white stripe running up his pant legs, but the sportswear failed to project a convincing aura of athleticism. It looked like the zipped jacket and pants had been sold together as a unit, which was unfortunate; he would have been better off with the pants at least one size smaller, because while his chest and stomach were packed snugly into the jacket, the pant legs were several inches too long.

"It's on the hood of the car! Waiting for you! The glove! It's got your name written on it!"

Colm had stopped about twenty feet away from Lloyd Henry.

He was noticing for the first time the bruise on Lloyd Henry's cheekbone from where he'd banged himself from his fall at the Roy Rogers. There was a sickly pale-green-and-pink discoloration emanating from the bruise and circling his eye.

"Make your phone call?" Lloyd Henry asked, smiling unconvincingly.

Colm just stood there, staring at him.

If the ghost of Christmas future had wanted to warn

Cameron how she might look in years to come if she went down the wrong path, he could show her this image of her father: a black eye, arm in a sling, worn knit hat pulled down over his forehead, shirt disheveled. He looked like a refugee, someone who had wandered by mistake out of a halfway house, possibly without his prescriptions.

The crazy thing was that women went nuts for Lloyd Henry. Colm couldn't figure it out.

"Heads up!"

Colm looked over to see the baseball that Eugene had thrown speeding toward them.

Lloyd Henry, unfortunately, was preoccupied, heading toward the car to retrieve the glove for Colm. When the ball nailed him hard squarely just below his left kneecap, he didn't take it well.

"What're you *doing*!!" he yelled, reaching down for his knee and looking up at Eugene with an anguished expression.

"I said 'Heads up.'"

"*Jesus!*" said Lloyd Henry, hopping around, trying to work out the pain.

"Are you all right?" Colm asked.

He couldn't help it. The question just popped out of his mouth.

Miraculously, Lloyd Henry stopped moving and stared at him. For a few moments he was all right. He was more than all right. Transported from pain by his son's first expression of concern for him, he was on the verge of smiling when Colm, sensing this unfortunate response, picked up the ball, tossed it to Eugene, and walked over to the Explorer.

"I'm sitting in front," he announced as he opened the passenger door and got in.

Immediately he busied himself with trying to open a package of crackers. The little black "open here" arrow was meaningless. Colm, suspecting that Lloyd Henry was still looking at him, bit into the packaging, managing finally to tear it open with his teeth. Just as the large grains of salt on the first cheese cracker touched his lips, there was a smashing sound so close to his ear, he wondered if a car had plowed into the Explorer. He looked to his right to see a fascinatingly fluid zigzagging of cracks in the window, streaming outward from a small central hole. Someone had nailed the window with the ball. Wild pitch, or no?

The driver's door opened. Eugene got in and tossed the glove into the back. He settled into his seat and started up the car.

The back door opened and Lloyd Henry got in.

Uncommunicative, he looked in the other direction.

Eugene did up his seat belt, adjusted his sunglasses, drove over to the entrance of the freeway, accelerated, and merged with the westward traffic.

Both men had neglected to retrieve the second baseball glove from off the hood. When it inched toward the edge, vibrating with speed, and finally dropped off onto the road, Colm felt a slight twinge. It had appeared to be brand-new, the price tag still attached. The glove with his name on it would stay in Kansas.

Ten minutes later Eugene found an oldies-but-goodies station on the radio. He turned the volume up just loud enough to mask Lloyd Henry's strangled snoring from the backseat.

Colm, chewing thoughtfully on cheese crackers, stretched his legs out and stared at the Kansas cornfields through the spiderweb maze of cracks in the side window.

They'd be in Colorado in less than four hours.

Chapter Fifteen

Seventy thousand dollars.

It was an inordinately large sum of money, Colm thought, peeling a grapefruit for Eugene. He was pondering some of the things he could do with that much money if he didn't use it as a down payment for the house. Invest it for Bunny's college education. Use it for his own, for that matter. Or he could skip college altogether (no one in his family had ever gone to college) and start a business straight out of high school. Maybe open up his own hardware store.

"How's that grapefruit coming?" Eugene asked, glancing over.

Colm dug his thumb into the peeled fruit, deftly opened it up, and handed him both halves.

"Mm-*mm*," Eugene said. "Thank *you*."

Of course there was no question but that he would

use the money for a down payment.

Still, it was fun to think about.

"To think that these grow on trees," Eugene said through a mouthful of grapefruit, spitting out a couple of seeds into his hand. "Just stop and think about it."

Colm unzipped his backpack and took out his last packet of crackers and peanut butter.

Over the past five hours, Eugene had displayed not only a propensity for philosophizing but also such a gifted ability to appreciate his own thoughts that Colm felt relieved of the burden of having to respond to them.

"Of all the places that God could have put grapefruit, and he put them *on trees*."

Colm stuffed a cracker into his mouth, thinking about a double cheeseburger.

"Genius. Sheer genius."

Colm looked over at Eugene. He was using his wristbands now as a kind of napkin, aggressively wiping the juice off his chin with them.

"Now let's just imagine He did it the other way around," Eugene mused, on a roll. "Let's imagine He put the vegetables up in the trees, and the fruit down in the earth. He could have done that. He could have. But, no. He chose not to."

Colm glanced over at the gas gauge. They had about an eighth of a tank left.

"He wanted us to reach up. Reach up. The fruits of our labor. Our sweetest reward."

Eugene had gotten two large coffees to go the last time they'd stopped for gas, and the caffeine was still at work. Politics, religion, geography, sports . . . Eugene didn't so much wander in and out of these subjects as talk about them all at once. His conversation worked like Windows software; all files were open at once.

"Intelligent design. I'll say."

Lloyd Henry (or *Lord* Henry, as Eugene referred to him) was still asleep.

Eugene rolled down his window, looked out at Colorado, and ceremoniously tossed a handful of grapefruit seeds out into the wind.

"Grow ye and multiply."

He brushed off the seeds that whipped back onto his chest and rolled the window back up.

After a moment he looked over at Colm, who was contemplating getting the clean pair of socks out of his duffel bag.

"I've got a son."

That seemed to cover all there was to say on the subject, because Eugene was silent for at least ten minutes.

Or maybe there was *so* much to say that he was daunted by the task. He stopped eating and brooded. His lips had disappeared, and he appeared to be chewing on them from the inside.

It was the prolonged silence that made Colm pay attention when Eugene finally broke it.

"I'm gonna tell you something about your father that you don't know," he said, in a burst of new energy.

Colm squinted his eyes, tempted to stop him.

"Your father . . ." Eugene began, dropping his voice for a weightier delivery.

Bracing himself, Colm flexed his toes, brought his arms up and rested his joined hands on top of his head.

"Your father turned his cell phone off on this trip with you, yes he did. He told me that. Said no one was going to steal time away from *your time together*."

Colm licked his dry lips.

The seventh packet of crackers and peanut butter had achieved little except to make him thirsty.

"Yes, he did. He said that."

Eugene looked out the window at a passing truck.

"Oh, I could get used to this," Eugene said, stretching as best he could. He drummed his fingers on the steering wheel and, happily settled, looked around the inside of the new SUV. "Yes, I could."

There was no telling how much more used to it Eugene could get, because just then the piercing wail of a police siren intervened.

Colm whipped around, alarmed to see a police car closing in behind them, the illuminated roof light flashing a revolving red and white.

"Westward expansion," Eugene said, ignoring the siren and returning to an earlier conversation he'd had with himself. "Now that's a concept, as American as it gets."

The police car pulled around in front and signaled them to pull over.

Colm gripped the door handle.

"Pioneers. Wagon trains."

"They want you to pull over," Colm said, his heart starting to race.

"Fine by me," Eugene said agreeably, pulling over and smoothly parking behind the police car.

Colm was imagining half a dozen crimes between the two men that could account for why they'd been stopped. Stealing an SUV. Transporting drugs. Escaping a penitentiary. He even flashed back to the day before, when he himself had driven illegally without a license.

"Go west young man. Go west." Eugene smiled to himself and finished off the last few segments of grapefruit.

Staring straight ahead out the windshield, he did not seem remotely focused on the cop who had gotten out of the police car and was now striding toward them.

Colm turned and shook Lloyd Henry.

"Wake up. *Wake up!*"

Lloyd Henry mumbled something unintelligible. His knit hat was pulled down over his eyes, blocking out the light. The visor jutted out from the middle of his nose. Colm shook him some more.

The cop rapped on Eugene's window with the back knuckle of his index finger. Eugene looked over and seemed almost surprised to see him. He turned the key momentarily to roll down the window.

"How might I assist you?"

"License and registration," the cop said, holding out his hand.

"Certainly," Eugene said, pushing up out of his seat, awkwardly thrusting his hand under his attached seat belt to dig deep into his pants pocket. "How're those Broncos looking?"

The cop either didn't know how the Broncos were looking or didn't want to share that information with Eugene.

Colm was scrambling to get the registration out of the glove compartment.

"What's going on, officer?" Lloyd Henry asked, now sitting up, bleary-eyed and trying to focus.

The cop stuck his head in and looked back at Lloyd Henry, who suddenly moaned, "Ow." Grimacing, he adjusted his sling. With the knit hat pulled down, the bruise on his cheek, the black eye, and the bewildered dopey expression hovering around his face, he did not present a respectable picture, Colm thought.

"What happened to your arm?"

"I was hit by a car, officer. Riding my bike."

The cop frowned. He looked at Eugene, who was busily rummaging through a thick collection of scraps of paper in his wallet as he hunted for his license. And then he looked at Colm and the smashed window behind.

"What happened to the window?"

"Baseball," said Colm, reaching over Eugene's imposing chest to hand the cop the registration. "They were playing catch."

"*They* were playing catch?"

The cop took off his sunglasses and looked back inside again at Lloyd Henry, as if Lloyd Henry might somehow look better not through dark-tinted lenses.

"Take a look at this, officer," said Eugene, chuckling, handing the cop a worn piece of paper he had carefully unfolded. "Very valuable. Ray Charles's autograph."

The cop looked at the penned signature. The last few letters of the "Charles" were missing, as if they'd been written off the edge of the paper.

"Get it?"

"Where's your license?"

Eugene handed it over.

The cop headed back to his car.

"So were you speeding?" Lloyd Henry asked, rubbing his eyes.

"Yes," said Colm, watching the cop up ahead get on his radio.

It was true they'd been speeding, but almost everyone else was going just as fast.

"Where are we?"

"We're exactly where it's your turn to start driving," said Eugene.

"We're in Colorado?"

"Orange Crush. Donner Pass."

"The Donner Pass isn't in Colorado," said Colm, in spite of himself.

"Ohhh, listen to the professor," said Eugene. "Do me a favor and peel me another one of those juicy grapefruits."

The professor didn't move.

"How fast were you going?"

"Eighty-five," said Colm flatly.

"Great," said Lloyd Henry disapprovingly.

"What do you mean great? You were the one in such a hurry. You were the one who said to step on it."

Lloyd Henry shrugged.

"Oh well. That's what happens when you're having an adventure," he said cheerfully.

"*What* happens when you're having an adventure?" Colm assailed him.

"This," Lloyd Henry said, vaguely waving his hand. "Stuff."

"Jail?"

"What, jail? No one's going to jail. For what? Speeding?"

"Stealing."

"Oh, here we go again. Here we go again. Stealing. Stealing what?"

"This car."

Lloyd Henry, taken aback, blinked as if someone had thrown a drink in his face.

"This car isn't stolen."

"It's not?"

"No."

"Are you sure?"

"Am I sure? Sure I'm sure. It's not stolen."

"Is it yours?"

Lloyd Henry paused.

"I have to get out," said Eugene.

"*Don't* get out," said Colm.

"I have to pee."

"Well . . . wait. You better wait."

"Till what? I have to shit?"

"Wait . . . till . . . the cop comes back."

"He doesn't care if I pee."

"Yes, he does. Don't get out." Colm was adamant.

"You think I stole this car. . . ." The plaintive, barely audible voice drifted forward from the backseat.

"*You stole this car?*" Eugene asked, surprised, lighting up.

"No. I didn't. I didn't steal this car."

Eugene seemed disappointed.

"I have to get out."

"He's back," said Colm.

"Mr. Pierce?" The officer was addressing Eugene through the open window.

"Yes?"

"Would you step out of the car, please?"

"Why certainly." Eugene looked at Colm, as if he had triumphed. "My pleasure."

Eugene undid his seat belt and got out of the car.

"I want *your* license," the cop said to Colm, "and I want *yours*," he said to Lloyd Henry.

"I don't have a license, sir. I'm only fifteen."

"*You're* fifteen?"

"Yes, sir."

"That's correct, officer," said Lloyd Henry, reaching forward to hand the cop his license. "I'm his father. He's fifteen. Big for his age."

"*Hey!*" the cop suddenly yelled. Colm jumped in his seat.

But the cop was yelling at Eugene, who had wandered around the other side of the SUV and was now peeing on the back tire. The cop quickly walked around and then awkwardly stood by, allowing Eugene to finish. It took a while. When he was done, Lloyd Henry very quietly made the sound of a toilet flushing as the two men strolled up to the patrol car.

Another cop who'd been sitting in the passenger seat got out and walked around to meet them.

"I can't believe you think I'd steal a car," Lloyd Henry mumbled.

Colm, his adrenalin still pumping, said nothing.

"Can't believe it." He seemed crushed.

Up ahead, Eugene was pointing out a flowering tree to the first cop.

"What else do you think I'd do?"

"Be quiet!" said Colm, watching the cop.

"Oh, that's nice."

Colm was trying to figure out what he would do if Lloyd Henry got arrested. Take a bus to Las Vegas? And then it struck him—*what if they thought he was an accomplice?* Maybe the cop thought he'd lied about his age, saying he was younger, just so they'd consider him a minor. He leaned back into the seat, feeling sick, as if he were on one of those carnival rides where you're strapped in to a giant spinning wheel and centrifugal force presses you back against the wall and the floor drops away.

Maybe in Colorado minors went to jail. The wheel was spinning faster and faster. He closed his eyes, feeling nauseous.

"Will you look at that."

Colm didn't.

"Will you look at that," Lloyd Henry repeated calmly.

Colm opened his eyes. Up ahead, the cops were putting handcuffs on Eugene, who was leaning, barrel chest first, up against the police car.

"They're *handcuffing* him?"

Eugene was looking back at them, sweat streaming down his face, yelling something. He yelled again, louder.

"You owe me five hundred dollars!!"

"Handcuffs?" Colm couldn't believe it.

"FIVE HUNDRED DOLLARS!!" Eugene was screaming at the top of his voice as the cops guided him into the backseat of the police car and closed the back door.

"Hunh," said Lloyd Henry, as if he'd just watched the mildly interesting conclusion to a weekly television drama.

The first cop got back into the car on the driver's side, and the second cop, a woman, adjusted her hat and started walking purposefully toward them.

"What'd he say?" Colm asked. His brain was scrambling to make sense of it. What had Eugene done? Had they put him in handcuffs *for speeding?*

Lloyd Henry opened the door and got out.

"Where are you going?"

Lloyd Henry pulled his wool hat back up off his forehead a little.

"I was told to be quiet," he said coldly.

He made a one-armed effort to tuck in his shirt, adjusted his sunglasses and sling, and sauntered forward to greet the woman cop.

Colm leaned forward in his seat, watching through the windshield.

The woman cop and Lloyd Henry approached each

other with the same slow measured speed, neither of them in a hurry. They walked toward each other the same way two people walk away from each other in a duel. Poised and at the ready.

Colm pulled the visor down to block the glare from the bright afternoon sun.

They met midway between the two cars, stopping at precisely the same moment. Her head was cocked to the right and his to the left.

Suddenly a crow swooped down between them and landed on a boulder a few yards away. Neither of them flinched or turned to look at it. Standing tall on the boulder, the crow flapped its wings hard a few times, as if shaking water off an umbrella, before folding them up and hunkering down to watch.

Lloyd Henry had his back to Colm, but it seemed that initially he was doing all the talking. She just stood there, arms crossed, listening to him, taking it in. After a while she handed Lloyd Henry what Colm assumed was his driver's license. Before long they were engaged in what appeared to be a convivial friendly conversation. The woman cop smiled; then she laughed. At first they'd glanced over at the police car a couple of times, but now it seemed as though they were discussing something totally unrelated to Eugene's arrest.

Lloyd Henry was illustrating something in the air with his left hand in broad sweeping gestures. She was captivated, her mouth slightly ajar as if she'd just had a little shot of novocaine; her whole bearing appeared mildly stunned and off-balance, like freshly stung prey.

Colm was enthralled; mystified.

When the woman cop took out a pack of cigarettes, offered one to Lloyd Henry, and then lit it for him, Colm stopped thinking. There was no point to it; his brain wasn't coming up with any answers. She lit a cigarette for herself, and the two of them smoked and joked around for another few minutes until the cop who was in the police car called something back to her.

Colm watched them all share a little laugh, and then the woman cop and Lloyd Henry dropped their cigarettes on the ground, extinguished them in tandem, and ambled over, chatting as if they were the best of friends.

"This is Colm," Lloyd Henry said, resting his arm up on the roof and smiling in at Colm, who stared up at them, transfixed. "Colm, this is Officer Loretta."

"Howdy," Officer Loretta said as Lloyd Henry opened the door and smoothly got into the driver's seat. She was about forty, and the braces on her teeth didn't diminish the power of her smile. She seemed healthy and outdoorsy, like someone who has just hiked down off the Rockies.

"Hello," Colm said.

"Sure you can drive with that hunk of plaster on your arm?"

"Oh yeah," said Lloyd Henry, reaching around the steering wheel and turning the key in the ignition. His new sling hugged his arm securely; if he was in pain, he was hiding it well.

"You boys have a grand time in the Grand Canyon," she said, rapping on the roof a couple of times, as if she were patting the horse they were about to ride off on. "Wish I could come with you."

"We-ell . . ." Lloyd Henry said invitingly, looking up at her.

She seemed sorely tempted.

Colm was frowning. The Grand Canyon?

"Oh boy, oh boy," she said, as if she were headed for trouble and had been there before. "I do get off in half an hour," she said, grinning, a glint of mischief in her eye.

"We can wait half an hour. Can't we, Colm?"

Colm didn't let on whether they could wait or not.

"Would I love to." She laughed to herself.

Officer Loretta removed her police hat, smoothed back her strawberry blond hair a few times, and stared contemplatively down at her boots, as if the answer lay in the stitching.

"I cain't," she said suddenly, decisively, raising up her head and putting the law-enforcement hat back on. "You ever been to the Grand Canyon, Colon?"

"No, ma'am."

"It is one of *the* wonders of the world. It'll blow your mind."

Colm didn't respond.

"Good place for a boy and his dad to hang out," she added approvingly, nodding at Lloyd Henry as if he were the best father in the world.

"We'll send you a postcard, Loretta," Lloyd Henry responded, confirming her compliment simply by modestly not acknowledging it.

"Speaking of which," she said, taking a pen out of her shirt pocket, "let's see that cast of yours."

Lloyd Henry gingerly twisted toward her, and she leaned in to write her name, e-mail address, phone number, and a short note on the cast.

"Sweet Loretta," Lloyd Henry managed to say. "Sweet Loretta Martin . . ."

Pleased silly, she looked away and shook her head, touched. And then, to Colm's horror, Lloyd Henry started singing.

At that point the crow took off.

"'All the girls around her say she's got it coming'" —

Lloyd Henry crooned the Beatles song straight at her—"'But she gets it while she can.'"

Now she was actually blushing.

"'Get in . . . '" Lloyd Henry bobbed his head up and down slightly to the beat, modifying the refrain. And now she was bobbing with him. "'Get in . . . Get in and see the wonder of the world. Get in Loretta.'"

The last line hung in the air, gathering poignancy.

"'Get in Loretta. . .'" Officer Loretta echoed in a whisper.

They stared at each other, lingering in the moment like a couple on the dance floor that continues holding each other after the band has quit playing.

Colm rubbed his eyes and squeezed the bridge of his nose.

"You take care now," she said, suddenly very serious.

"You too, Loretta."

She rapped on the car roof again, patting the horse one last time before stepping away and reluctantly strolling back up to the police car. Her walk was different now. Approaching them, she'd walked like a cop; this was more of a slow sashay.

"Nice lady," said Lloyd Henry, reaching under the seat for the lever to slide it back a little. "Mm. Big guy . . . short legs," he said of Eugene.

"Why did you tell her that?" Colm assailed him.

"What."

"That we're going to the Grand Canyon."

"Oh, you want to go?"

"No!"

"Could be fun."

"Now we *have* to go."

"Why?"

"You told her we were going."

"So."

"You told a police officer we're going to the Grand Canyon."

"We could go," Lloyd Henry said, adjusting the rearview mirror. "It's on the way. Check out the map." He turned and looked earnestly at Colm.

Colm shook his head, deeply disturbed.

Eugene was up ahead, handcuffed, in the backseat of the police car. The whole thing was too bizarre. Colm wondered if they'd taken his wristbands off to get the handcuffs on or if they'd just slid them up his arms. He tried to catch a glimpse of Eugene but couldn't through the tinted rear window. It was sad; he'd been in such a good mood.

Lloyd Henry reached over to shift into first and started to pull out.

"Wait," Colm said.

Lloyd Henry braked.

"Do you owe Eugene five hundred dollars?"

"Huh?"

"Do you owe him five hundred dollars?"

"Not anymore," Lloyd Henry said, starting to pull forward again.

"Stop!"

Lloyd Henry stepped on the brake.

"So you *did* owe him five hundred dollars."

Lloyd Henry rubbed his wool hat around a little, as if he were scratching his forehead with it.

"He didn't finish. The job."

"What job?"

"The job. We only got to Colorado."

"You were paying him to drive us?"

"To Las Vegas. We're in Colorado."

Colm thought for a second.

"But . . . he did half the job."

"No. No. No."

"You owe him for half the job."

Lloyd Henry took off his sunglasses and looked at Colm.

"How did you get to be like this?"

"You owe him two hundred and fifty dollars. Give

it to me. I'll go give it to him."

"How did you?"

Colm held out his hand.

"I don't believe this. I don't believe this. This is un-believable."

"Hurry up."

"He hit me on purpose," Lloyd Henry said, mustering some anger. "With that baseball. He hit me in the knee, hard, on purpose."

"Are you a man of your word or not?"

"What?"

"Are you a man of your word?" Colm asked, dead serious, heavily invested.

"What're you, a priest or something?"

A car door slammed shut and Colm glanced forward toward the police car. They were getting ready to go.

"A man of my word," Lloyd Henry muttered, shaking his head. "Jesus Christ."

"Hurry up!"

"He's a convicted felon! He's wanted in three states! For armed robbery!"

"He's going to jail?"

"Oh yeah, Eugene is going to jail. He's going bye-bye."

Colm opened his door to get out.

"What're you doing?"

"I'm going to go pay him myself."

"Wait. You're *what?*" Lloyd Henry threw his head back. "I can't . . . *Wait!*"

He reached for his wallet in his back pocket, flipped it open with his left hand, and stuck it between his knees. He took out five fifty-dollar bills from a thick stash of cash and handed them to Colm.

"Unbelievable," Lloyd Henry muttered.

Colm raced up toward the police car, suddenly stopped, and raced back.

Lloyd Henry watched Colm open the back door and reach in to grab a few grapefruit off the floor. "What're you doing? What're you . . . ? You're kidding. You're *kidding.*" Colm managed to pick up seven grapefruits, using the front of his T-shirt to carry them. "Oh, right, give the convicted felon some fruit. Tell *me* to be quiet; give *him* some fruit. That's great."

Colm kicked the door shut with his foot.

"Don't forget his pillow," Lloyd Henry added sardonically.

Colm stopped, thought, looked through the window at the pillow, and managed to open the door again. Grabbing the pillowcase with his fingertips, he turned and ran back up to the police car.

"You get all in a fit when you think *I* steal," Lloyd Henry yelled after him, awkwardly hoisting himself up and partly out the window. "Which I DON'T!!"

Lloyd Henry slid back down and landed on his seat.

"That's just great," Lloyd Henry mumbled to himself, shaking his head and sliding back down. "A man of my word."

Exhaling a long breath, Lloyd Henry leaned his head back against the headrest and watched Colm up ahead, carefully passing the grapefruit, the cash, and the pillow through the window to Officer Loretta's partner.

Chapter Sixteen

When Colm was little, Fiona went through a period of getting dressed up and taking her children to various cultural attractions in the Berkshires. She took them to the Norman Rockwell Museum; to Chesterwood, where the sculptor Daniel French had lived and worked; to Hancock Shaker Village; and on Wednesdays they sometimes drove up to Williamstown because the Clark Art Institute offered free admission that day.

Even as a young boy Colm was aware that Fiona was more interested in the people who were viewing the exhibits than the exhibits themselves. The men in particular. She had even expressed to six-year-old Colm and eight-year-old Cameron the possibility of her finding "a cultured intellectual" at these places. Colm wasn't quite sure what they were going to do with the cultured intellectual once they found him, but based on other remarks she made, his assumption was this person would have a lot of money and that could affect their lives in a positive way. For the longest time, he thought that intellectual meant rich.

Colm enjoyed these outings, if only because his mother always looked so beautiful and seemed particularly energized. He especially liked the Clark because it was out in the country and he could run around in the fields outside and wander the nearby trails. Sometimes they showed free movies. Also, there were two paintings upstairs in the gallery that he liked, both by an artist named Frederic Remington and both set in the Wild West.

One was enormous and brightly colored and depicted some cavalry up close on horseback trying to hold back a herd of horses that were galloping wildly, nostrils flaring, heads reared back. It looked so real. Colm would crouch down in front of it, gazing up wide-eyed and thrilled, sensing that the horses were about to charge off the wall.

The other was of a solitary Indian who was leaning forward slightly in his saddle on his horse, staring out from the edge of a high plateau way across a wide open valley down below, at tiny lights, campfires, off in the distance. It was set at night, and the canvas was filled with midnight blues that captured the vast night sky and the sweeping expanse below. Fiona used to hold Colm up so he could closely inspect the tiny flecks of yellow paint that were the stars. Up close the little brushstrokes of paint looked like messy little smears, but when you stood back away from the painting, they twinkled just like stars.

There was something restful in this image that appealed to him, and as he grew older, the appeal only deepened. The perspective was from behind the Indian, so looking at it, Colm felt as if he himself were the Indian, up on the horse, looking out over the vast expanse. It gave him a sense of well-being; even though the Indian was completely alone, he seemed safe and comfortable by himself out in the world.

They never found a cultured intellectual (though it seemed as if they'd come close a couple of times), and after a while the trips to the museums ceased. But Fiona did buy Colm two postcards of those paintings in the Clark gift shop. Originally he taped them up on the wall next to his bed, but when, at age twelve, he repaired and painted his room, he put them in a small frame and hung them between his poster of Lance Armstrong and his map of the world.

It was the image of the Indian on his horse that flashed through Colm's mind now, up on a plateau overlooking the distant town of Taos and a great swath of northern New Mexico. It was nighttime, and they'd stopped to change a flat tire.

Lloyd Henry had been on his best behavior ever since Denver, when Colm had finally acquiesced to going to the Grand Canyon.

Colm had agreed to go for several reasons, not all of which he thought through. It *was* on record with the Colorado police that they were going there, and it actually was on the way—just a slightly different route from the one he'd planned. Also, he wanted Lloyd Henry to be in as good and complacent a mood as possible once they got to Las Vegas. Colm was becoming increasingly apprehensive about taking him there, wary that his legendary gambling problem could cause trouble.

The plain and simple fact was that Lloyd Henry was *so* intent upon going to the Grand Canyon, and had for whatever reason repeatedly expressed a desire to stop there.

The good thing about agreeing to go was that it did shut him up. Once Colm had mapped out the new route—heading south from Denver to Albuquerque and then over to Flagstaff and up to the Grand Canyon—

Lloyd Henry was happy as a clam and quiet. He drove through the night without making inane observations, or sound affects with his mouth, or singing along with the radio (he stopped making castanet sounds to the Spanish music), and when they stopped for enchiladas at a local dive in Questa, New Mexico, he made no effort to start a conversation with Colm except to remark on the differences between the red and the green chili sauces.

Colm had ordered his burritos with the red sauce, just to be different from Lloyd Henry, but it was too spicy. Halfway through the first enchilada, he'd stopped and ordered a fried quesadilla with powdered sugar, which was enormous, messy, and delicious. He ordered three more while Lloyd Henry finished his enchiladas and three cups of coffee, and when they left, Colm took two more to go.

How they'd ended up in the tiny town of Questa was a mystery to Colm. Lloyd Henry had pulled off Route 25 to look for gas and had somehow wandered west onto a smaller road. Colm didn't say anything about it; he was the official navigator and he should have been pay-ing attention.

They were winding their way along a narrow two-lane road just south of Taos that headed to Santa Fe and

Albuquerque when the back right tire started thumping loudly. Lloyd Henry pulled over at the first opportunity, which wasn't until they were up on a plateau with a scenic overlook.

"Flat tire," he said in his quiet voice, turning off the engine. He looked over at Colm, who had already opened the door and gotten out.

The scent of sagebrush hit him straightaway, pungent and sweet. By the light of the waxing moon, Colm could see sagebrush everywhere, its small narrow leaves holding the moonlight in a bluish silvery glow.

He set to work and quickly located the spare tire, the jack, and tools.

Lloyd Henry got out and, sensing pretty quickly that his assistance wasn't needed, wandered over a ways toward the edge of the lookout. He lit up a cigarette.

After nimbly jacking up the Explorer, Colm was able to remove the lug nuts easily.

"Wow," he heard Lloyd Henry mutter.

Colm, neatly arranging the nuts in the overturned hubcap, glanced over at Lloyd Henry, whose back was to him as he stared out over the vast expanse.

"That's some view."

Colm followed his gaze out. He stood up and took a few steps forward to look. That was when the image of the Remington painting came to him. This was the same view, the same perspective. The difference was that whereas the night sky in the painting was a total surface area of maybe two or three square feet, this night sky was so big, Colm couldn't even take it in. He had to close his eyes and put his head down for a moment before he could open them and look up again.

Just like the Indian, Colm was up on a plateau looking out over a darkly blue and silent world, the distant lights of the town of Taos reminiscent of the distant campfires in the painting, stars shining brightly high overhead.

But there was another key difference. In the painting the Indian was alone; in this picture Colm wasn't.

If he *had* been alone, he would have crouched down near the edge and stared out, slowly assimilating the enormity of the landscape, taking in its epic scope and beauty. He would have been happy, content in the way he always was after he'd run up October Mountain, Mount Greylock, Pine Mountain, or any of a number of peaks where he ran in training for track. He enjoyed being alone on those summits, staring out at the rolling Berkshire Hills, the foothills of the Green Mountains of Vermont.

But the dark silhouette of the person with him now

intruded on his experience in an unexpected way. Standing twenty yards away like a shadowy cardboard cutout of a figure, Lloyd Henry provided not company, but the representation of something that had been cut out and missing for Colm his whole life. If Colm had yearned for a father as a young boy, and surely he had, he'd effectively blocked it out. But now a deep and wrenching loneliness swelled up from that place of yearning and was overtaking him, amplified in the sweeping empty space rolled out before them.

It was a pain his chest could barely contain.

The ember at the end of Lloyd Henry's cigarette glowed red in the night as he inhaled. Colm turned back to the car, knelt back down, and quickly finished changing the tire.

In the presence of the father he never had, Colm had never felt so lonely in his entire life.

The anger unearthed by Colm's feeling of loneliness didn't flare up at the Grand Canyon. Buried somewhere deep, it took a little while to surface. When the rage did erupt, suddenly and in a kind of seismic burst, it was at a far less opportune moment, over something insignificant.

They arrived at the southern rim of the Grand Canyon at daybreak, parking to the side of Hermit Road, where there was no view at all and where you had to cross the road over to Hopi Point in order to see the canyon.

It had been a long night.

The longest night of Colm's life.

Driving through New Mexico and parts of Arizona they had, at times, appeared to Colm to be moving across a moonscape, a foreign planet with unfamiliar dark

267

shifting shapes, massive geological formations he'd never seen before—distant mesas rising up steeply and leveling off, towering canyon walls, imposing mountain ranges that veered into other mountain ranges that theoretically shouldn't all be able to fit on the same horizon. In this scale of things, their black Ford Explorer felt like a tiny toy, a small beetle inching across the basement of night.

Lloyd Henry, wired with coffee and anticipation, hadn't pulled over once to take a nap. And Colm had remained fully awake though he would have liked to drift off to sleep. In that altered state beyond exhaustion, when a second wind picks you up and out of your body and you lose track of how tired you are, everything felt surreal, from the bizarre landscape to the loopy sense of time. Hours lost their shape in all this space; they went on forever.

Only two days and nights of nonstop driving, and it seemed to Colm they'd been on the road for months. They weren't traveling across America; they were navigating the world . . . traveling the way Lloyd Henry had traveled in Colm's mind when he was a kid, beyond time and space. This was the mythic Lloyd Henry here now in the dark beside him; the guy who'd left home to take a walk and had kept on going. And Colm was with him, ensnared in a journey without end; now he was part of the myth, and he would never escape.

When the first hint of daylight finally broke, it felt like a miracle.

Even the landscape appeared to have calmed down, reduced to gently rolling hills dotted with scrubby brush, piñon, and juniper on either side of the flat, unremark-able two-lane road that led to the Grand Canyon.

Colm let go of the door handle he'd been clutching for much of the night.

"Wow," said Lloyd Henry, glancing over at a herd of animals grazing off in the distance. "Those are some weird-looking donkeys."

In the predawn light it was impossible to gauge either what color or how far away the shadowy animals were.

"Those aren't donkeys."

"Yeah, they are."

"No. They're not."

Lloyd Henry took another quick glance, swallowing the slim remnant from a caffeine-loaded lozenge. He'd gone through half a box of them and had spilled several on his seat in the process.

"They're donkeys," Lloyd Henry reasserted.

"You just said they were weird looking."

"You don't think they're weird looking?"

"They're weird-looking donkeys, because they're not donkeys."

"Look at their ears."

"I *am* looking at their ears."

"Donkey ears."

Colm was trying to get a clear picture of a donkey in his mind so he could refute Lloyd Henry with specifics, but he had a hard time picturing one. His brain simply failed to conjure one up.

"Western donkeys," said Lloyd Henry. "You know, species can be different in different parts of the country."

"They're deer," Colm said, not at all sure that they were.

"*Deer?* They're not deer. Deer don't have ears like that. Deer have little ears; little twitchy ears."

"I don't know what they are," Colm said, annoyed and regretting he'd spoken at all.

"Maybe they're mules."

"They're not mules."

"Weird-looking mules."

Colm said nothing.

"Fun, huh?" said Lloyd Henry, upbeat and enjoying what, for them, could qualify as their first civil conversation. "Yup. We're having fun."

Colm looked away, disgusted.

"The Grand Canyon," said Lloyd Henry, digging for another spilled lozenge from under his thigh and popping it into his mouth. "The grand adventure!"

As the pinkish-white light began to reveal their surroundings in faint reassuring dabs of color, Colm dimly realized that their journey actually *was* getting close to coming to an end.

Not only would he see Fiona and Bunny later that day, but—and he was looking forward to this now a thousand times more—*the next day* he and Lloyd Henry would part ways. Forever. They'd arrive in Las Vegas that afternoon, but the next day they'd be in Bakersfield and Colm would deposit Lloyd Henry on Frank's doorstep, bidding him a permanent farewell.

He'd never have to listen to his stupid sound effects again. Ever.

And he'd have seventy thousand dollars: the down payment for the house.

They just had to get through the next twenty-four hours.

"No private vehicles allowed." Lloyd Henry had stopped the car and was reading a sign. "Hm. They want us to take a shuttle bus?" He frowned.

While Lloyd Henry parked and went into the Canyon View Center, Colm was preoccupied, studying the map and planning the day. They were less than three hundred miles away from Las Vegas. (Colm noted with interest they'd be going right past the Hoover Dam; under different circumstances Colm would have *loved* to stop there and take a tour. He'd read quite a bit about its construction and had watched an amazing documentary about it. The Air Museum Planes of Fame on Route 64 caught his eye as well.)

Colm calculated that Lloyd Henry had been awake now around thirteen hours. Prior to Eugene's arrest in the late afternoon the day before, he'd slept a good six or seven hours in the backseat; he ought to be up to driving the remaining five or six hours to Las Vegas. Once they arrived, Colm's plan was to get a motel room and leave Lloyd Henry, who should be exhausted by then, sleeping in the room while he went off to join his family.

He wondered whether he needed to say something to Lloyd Henry about not gambling.

"We're all set," said Lloyd Henry, smiling, energetically bounding back into the car. "Got a special permit; disabled person. Didn't take much."

He carefully placed a disposable camera he'd just bought up on the dashboard. *"Panoramic,"* he said, happy with the camera's features. "Thirty-six pictures. Here's some literature," and he started up the engine.

Colm took the brochures and pamphlets that Lloyd Henry gave him without looking at them or listening to a word he'd said. Through the smashed window, he was watching two teenage girls march by, laughing, dressed in hiking gear and carrying heavy backpacks, and now Melanie Phelps was back in his mind. She was like his screen saver; whenever his brain paused, she appeared.

"This place is *hoppin'* and the sun is barely up."

Following a shuttle bus that was half full of early-rising vacationing tourists, they proceeded along Hermit Road.

"I just want you to know, Colm, how much I appreciate this," said Lloyd Henry, leaning forward over the steering wheel. Lost in thought, Colm didn't even notice how excited he was. "This means a lot to me. It really does."

In Pittsfield, it was three hours later, Colm thought. Melanie Phelps was probably eating breakfast.

"Hopi Point. That's what the lady at the desk said. She said we should stop at Hopi Point. Some day, huh? Yeah. Beautiful."

Colm wondered what Melanie was going to do that Saturday morning and whether she was planning on going to church the next day.

"You coming?"

Lloyd Henry had pulled over to the side of the road.

"No."

"Aww, come on."

Colm remembered that two missionaries were speaking at church that Sunday, reporting on their recent experiences in Italy. Of all countries to do missionary work, Colm thought, Italy seemed an odd place to feel the call.

"No."

"Okay, I'll check it out. I'll be right back."

Lloyd Henry had parked, jumped out of the car, and been gone five minutes when it suddenly struck Colm that he could be back in Pittsfield the next night. He could hop on a plane in Bakersfield and *be within four miles of Melanie the very next night.*

"Colm, you have to see this."

He pictured her face poised in front of his, inches away.

"I'm not kidding. This is unbelievable."

Melanie Phelps had kissed him.

"Just walk across the road with me. Just . . . you have to look."

Kissed him? He'd played that tape in his mind so many times, it was frayed and it skipped and he didn't trust it anymore.

"You can't get this close and not take a look."

And then, out of the blue, Colm remembered those last words she'd said to him, as she'd backed away that day in the supermarket parking lot. "Call me."

"Come on."

Call me. What had she meant by that?

"Colm."

Why had she asked him to call her?

"Colm!!"

Colm looked blankly up at Lloyd Henry, who had come around and opened his door and was now leaning in, all keyed up.

"The light. The dawn. People are taking photographs, you gotta look."

Colm closed his eyes and opened them again. The oddest thing . . . Cameron? Was in Arizona? Cameron with a black eye and beside herself with excitement, beseeching Colm to do something, to go somewhere, to come look at something. It was classic Cameron drama: eyes popping, cockeyed grin conveying a sense of great urgency.

But it wasn't Cameron; it was, in fact, the person Cameron loathed more than anyone on the planet.

"Please," Lloyd Henry entreated, slightly embarrassed to be begging. It was this tinge of embarrassment that restored ownership of the face to Lloyd Henry. Cameron simply didn't get embarrassed. She got mad.

"No."

"You're at the Grand Canyon, for God's sake! You have to see it."

"No."

"You promised."

"I didn't promise."

Why had Melanie asked him to call her right after she'd kissed him?

"You did, you promised."

"No, I didn't."

Was it to explain something? What did she want to tell him?

"You said you'd go."

"I said *we'd* go."

"See!"

"No."

"*Please.* The last request of a dying man."

Colm jumped out of the car.

"Are you dying?"

"Well—" Lloyd Henry stammered, taking a few steps back.

"Are you?" Colm pressed, taking a few steps forward.

"No. Not really."

"Then why did you just say that? Why did you just say 'the last request of a dying man'?"

"Because . . ."

"Because why?"

Lloyd Henry cleared his throat and then appeared to get momentarily distracted by a small shrub.

"Because why?"

"We're all dying, Colm," he said finally, somewhat sheepishly. It was the best he could come up with. "Let's go."

"Are you terminally ill?"

"No. Not that I know of."

It was amazing; even after spending this much time with the man, Colm had absolutely no clue whether he was lying or not.

"You just have a swallowing thing."

"Come on."

Colm didn't budge.

Lloyd Henry bent his knees and then came back up, and then went down and up again a few times, as if someone were bouncing him. He was thinking hard.

"Colm, if you come look . . ." he said, quite desperate, "I'll show you the money."

"What money?"

"The seventy grand. I'll show it to you now."

Colm's entire body twitched. He shook his head, baffled.

"You want to see it?" Lloyd Henry asked.

"*You* have the seventy grand?"

"Yeah. I'll show it to you."

"Wait—"

"What."

"If you have the seventy grand, why are we going to Bakersfield?"

"To deliver me."

"That makes no sense."

"It's complicated. I told you."

"Frank doesn't have the money?"

"Frank has *lots* of money."

"Wait a minute . . . wait a minute . . ."

"Frank wants *me*. Not the money."

"So . . . you're paying me . . . to deliver you . . . to Frank?"

"Not exactly. It's complicated."

"But you have the money?"

"You want to see it?"

"No."

"I'll show it to you."

"No!"

"You don't want to see anything," Lloyd Henry

said, with mounting frustration. "You don't want to see the Grand Canyon. You don't want to see the money." He threw up his one good arm and paced around, upset.

Colm looked away, trying to figure it out. A jogger was coming up the road, dressed only in shorts and running shoes. When he passed them and continued on his way, Colm suppressed a strong urge to follow him. Nothing would have felt better right then than taking off on a long run.

"It's a small request," Lloyd Henry said, trying to compose himself and appear reasonable. "All you have to do is . . . walk across the road . . . look . . . at the canyon."

"We need to call Frank."

"Fine."

"Call him. Now."

"Now? Uh . . ." Lloyd Henry looked a little dubious. He glanced at his watch. "Frank's not exactly a morning person."

"What does that mean?"

"It's a lit-tle early to call Frank. Six in the morning? Gonna be a little grumpy." He shook his head as if it weren't a good idea.

Colm was thinking how strange it was that he didn't

want to see the money. That was his initial reaction, and it had been a strong one. It just didn't feel right; he hadn't earned it yet.

This new information about the money was disconcerting. The money was supposed to be in Bakersfield. Had they been driving all this time with seventy thousand dollars in the car? What would have happened to it if they'd been thrown in jail in Colorado with Eugene?

"Is the money in the Grand Canyon?" he asked suddenly.

"No," Lloyd Henry responded. "You mean like . . . buried? No. No. I mean . . . it's here. With us. At the canyon. But . . . not *in* the canyon."

Colm kept studying Lloyd Henry. The more he studied him, the less satisfied he became.

"I won't ask you to do anything else," Lloyd Henry said quietly.

Colm was starting to feel tired.

"Sunrise at the Grand Canyon," said Lloyd Henry, more than just a little fatigued himself. He sounded like he was beginning to lose some of his enthusiasm. "It'll be a memory." He seemed suddenly sad.

Colm reflected a moment, bent over to tie up a loose shoelace, and then started striding purposefully across the road. He paused as a National Parks truck passed by, then continued to Hopi Point, Lloyd Henry eagerly following at his heels.

There, beyond the lookout platform and a half a dozen tourists, was the Grand Canyon.

It took a moment for Colm to remember where they were, because what he was suddenly confronted with, by virtue of having simply walked across a road, didn't remotely resemble his notion of a canyon, grand or otherwise. He'd expected a single giant chasm in the earth. He'd expected to be able to look across to the other side. These were myriad canyons—an explosion of canyons that seemed to go on forever as if in an expanding hall of mirrors.

The geological formations laid out before him were simply incomprehensible; there was no place his eye could rest and make sense of the perspective. It was so perplexing, it made his brain hurt. In fact it occurred to him that he was looking into the brains of the earth, fold after fold after fold, on and on and on, the endless peaks and ridges and canyon walls now made more unreal by the spectacular dawn—the reds and pinks in the rock illuminated like spun gold.

Flummoxed, Colm's fatigued mind kicked back to its previous conundrum, the place where it had last gotten stuck: Melanie Phelps's words to him. "Call me." Why did she want him to call her? What did she expect from him? *More important, was she mad at him now that he hadn't called her?*

Someone was tapping on his shoulder.

"Excuse me, could you take our picture?"

Colm turned to see Lloyd Henry bent over, trying to open what looked like a tin of sardines. Stepping on the edge of the tin with one foot, he was peeling back the ringed tab of the lid with the index finger of his good hand.

"Could you?" Over Lloyd Henry's back, the mother of a young family was extending a camera to Colm. "You just press here."

Colm took the camera and aimed it at the parents with their three young children. He took their picture and handed the camera back.

"Thank you so much," she said.

"Sardine?" Lloyd Henry offered the opened tin to both parents.

"A little early for fish," said the man, who had made a hat for himself by tying a knot in each corner of a white handkerchief. The baby he was holding was fidgeting and beginning to cry.

"My father's favorite food," Lloyd Henry explained.

"Oh," said the woman, declining. "I'm Jeanne. This is Chip. We're from Toronto."

"How do you do. Yeah, my father loved sardines. Colm? Sardine?"

Colm was back staring at the incomprehensible view, ardently hoping that Melanie wasn't mad at him.

"Yeah, he passed away last winter," Lloyd Henry continued.

"I'm so sorry," said the woman. "Morris! Get down from there!" Her little boy had reached up to the rail and was alternately hanging from it and trying to hoist himself up.

"I want a sardine," Morris said, jumping down and pumping both fists in the air.

"No, you don't," said his mother.

"Great guy. One of a kind. Cheers," Lloyd Henry said, teary eyed, raising the sardine tin up in a toast and eating one. "Would you mind taking a picture of us?"

"Meg," the mother said to the eldest child, a girl of about nine. "Take the man's picture." And she relieved her husband of the crying baby.

Lloyd Henry put the sardine tin down on the ground to take out the camera, and Morris bounded over to it.

"Colm," Lloyd Henry said. *"Colm."*

When Colm finally turned around, Lloyd Henry stepped in next to him and smiled.

The little girl took the picture.

"Take another one," said Lloyd Henry brightly. "Take a bunch."

She took a little more time with the composition of the next picture, taking a step back, and then forward, and finally tilting the angle of the camera and her elbow until she was content. But after winding the film, she took a series of shots with fearsome rapidity. With each click, Lloyd Henry grew happier, secretly banking nuggets of gold with each picture.

Colm, his mind fully engaged with Melanie, stared straight ahead.

"Have you ever been to the capitol building in Harrisburg, Pennsylvania?" asked Lloyd Henry, ostensibly addressing the mother, who was trying to feed her baby a bottle, but actually aiming his voice at Colm.

"Beautiful fountain there at the capitol building. Magnificent. My father fitted the pipes for that fountain. Yup. The water sprays up in several directions. Very complicated. Best pipe fitter in Harrisburg. He got a plaque from the mayor."

After this short, heartfelt, and largely ignored eulogy, as the young photographer continued clicking with ferocious speed, Lloyd Henry took his wool hat off.

"I wish you could have met him, Colm," Lloyd Henry said to Colm. "I really do."

And then, with deep solemnity, Lloyd Henry kissed the hat, looking at the photographer with a sorrowful expression, and then turned to throw the hat ceremoniously over the railing.

"Amen," he said for lack of a better word. "So long, Pop."

Colm, reflexively whipping around and lunging with his arm extended over the rail, still in a bit of a stupor, failed to retrieve not only the airborne hat, but also the cheap little disposable camera that went whizzing past it a moment thereafter.

Evidently young Morris from Toronto had never experienced a mouthful of sardines before. Unattended and expecting something sweet, he'd rammed several into his mouth and had been so affronted by the onslaught of Portuguese brine that he not only kicked Lloyd Henry in the shin but grabbed the camera in a rage from his older sister and pitched it with great fury far, far out over the railing.

The four-year-old had the arm of a major leaguer.

"Noooo!" Lloyd Henry cried out, watching the camera continue its impressive trajectory out over the canyon and then finally down into the abyss. Only Meg the photographer would take home with her the priceless images of father and son at this momentous occasion, and these would soon disappear, fading in her subconscious like invisible ink.

"Morris! Apologize to the nice man right now!"

But Morris was too busy spitting out every remnant of silvery skin, fish scale, and tail that he possibly could, ramming all his fingers into his mouth and crying with unabated disgust. His father grabbed him by the arm. When a new busload of tourists arrived, sweeping down onto the overlook platform, the young family from Toronto made a beeline through it and vanished.

Lloyd Henry, holding the rail and gazing out into the canyon, was speechless. Bereft.

Colm, who had been preoccupied with Melanie, was now approaching an intolerable awareness of Lloyd Henry's emotional state.

"Let's go," he said, turning.

Colm walked briskly through the crowd of tourists back across Hermit Road. He got into the car, slammed the door shut, and did up his seat belt.

He had a throbbing headache, and when Lloyd Henry joined him some five or ten minutes later, finally getting into the car, he closed his eyes so Lloyd Henry would think he was asleep.

Colm was fully aware that something of major significance to Lloyd Henry had just transpired, and he wanted to get as far away from it as quickly as possible.

"Well," Lloyd Henry said finally.

Colm sneaked one eye open and saw that he was just sitting there, impassive, staring straight ahead out the windshield.

"Colm . . ." Lloyd Henry began. And he paused, as if he were summoning the right words, the right tone. "I know you don't want to know anything about me, and I don't blame you for that, but . . ."

"You're right. Let's go."

Still gazing forward, Lloyd Henry appeared to exhale his last breath and with it the fragile collection of words he'd been arranging in his mind with so much effort. He rested his head back as if he would keep it there forever. And then he sank back even more. The seat appeared to be swallowing him whole.

Colm took the keys out of Lloyd Henry's limp hand and put them in the ignition.

"Okay," said Lloyd Henry, biting on his upper lip with his lower teeth but otherwise not moving. "Okay."

He continued to sit and stare.

"Drive!" Colm commanded, feeling excruciatingly uncomfortable.

Lloyd Henry raised his head and emerged up out of the seat as if he were being partially, but not fully, inflated. He did up his seat belt, released the brake, had Colm shift into first, and proceeded to turn the car around, heading south to Williams and Route 40.

Colm didn't usually get headaches, but the one he had now was so strong, it was almost interesting. It started behind his left eye and arced around the top of his head and back down like a shepherd's crook to a point just above his neck. Somewhere he was grateful for it, because right now it offered him some relief; with the throbbing pain, he found it impossible to think.

After they had driven a little way, Colm picked up the slip of paper that had blown off the dashboard onto his lap. It had Lloyd Henry's name on it and it read, "Special Permit. Disabled Person."

Colm stared at it, failing to piece together the elements: the Canyon Park insignia . . . Lloyd Henry Drucker . . . special permit . . . disabled person.

He looked over at Lloyd Henry, whose lips were moving slightly but who wasn't saying anything audible. Special permit. Disabled person.

After a while Colm dropped the paper onto the floor and reached back into his duffel bag for his sweatshirt. He rolled it up and stuck it behind his head for a pillow, stretched out his legs, looked out the spiderweb window, and prayed, prayed for the next two days to be over.

Chapter Eighteen

In the outskirts of Kingman, Arizona, Lloyd Henry surprised Colm by suddenly swerving off the road and pulling up to a combination Laundromat and dry cleaner.

"What're you doing?" Colm asked.

Lloyd Henry turned off the engine, took out the car keys, and rested them on his thigh.

"I need a shower."

He gazed, not moving, through the large window at the backs of a dozen or so washing machines lined up against the window and the stacked double dryers on the far wall. Something about this cleaning operation had spoken to Lloyd Henry on an unconscious level and drawn him to it. They might just as easily have found themselves parked in front of a car wash.

When a Hispanic woman with two small children

exited, carrying a large plastic laundry basket with a towering pile of folded clean clothes, he stared at the basket longingly and followed its trajectory toward the backseat of a beat-up copper sedan.

Emotionally drained, his face appeared haggard and wan.

There'd been a noticeable change in Lloyd Henry's demeanor since the Grand Canyon. Gone were his playfulness and relentless buoyancy. He was serious and withdrawn; wistfully distant. Colm couldn't tell if he was angry, or sad, or disappointed, but clearly whatever had or hadn't transpired at the Grand Canyon was still affecting him.

"When we get to Las Vegas," Colm said cautiously, "we're getting a motel room."

Lloyd Henry frowned.

"Really?" he asked, still gazing at the Laundromat as if it were a mirage, some wonderful destination for privileged people on a cruise; a spa where lucky people who had won something were permitted to go.

"Yes. You can have a shower there. You can probably do some laundry. Sleep in a bed as long as you like."

Lloyd Henry appeared perplexed. His head toppled forward a tad, as if all the new information had settled into his forehead and was making it heavier. Colm still wasn't used to seeing him without his knit hat. There was no telling how long he'd been wearing it, but now that he wasn't, his thick hair was both matted and sticking up wildly in all directions.

"Why?" Lloyd Henry asked.

"Don't you want to clean up before you get to Frank's?"

Concentrating on a motel room, Colm was reluctant to even *think* about Fiona near Lloyd Henry, as if he might pick up the thought wave and trace it to its source.

"Can I ask another question?"

"What?"

"Why are we going to Las Vegas?"

This was just the kind of question Colm was hoping not to have to answer.

"It's on the way," said Colm. "It's only an hour, an hour and a half away."

Frowning again, Lloyd Henry appeared concerned.

"What I really need," he said, ruminating, his eyelids dropping slightly. "What I really need . . . is a drink."

"You don't need a drink."

"Yeah. I do. That's what I need."

"No drinks," Colm said sternly.

Unconvinced, Lloyd Henry wiped his nose with the back of his hand and reached around to insert the key back in the ignition.

"No drinks," repeated Colm, "And no betting."

Lloyd Henry's face suddenly came alive as he burst out laughing. He continued laughing in little uncontrolled outbursts, almost as if he were hiccupping, while he backed up the Ford Explorer, turned around, and pulled out onto the main road.

"I'm not kidding," said Colm, feeling stupid.

"Right."

Lloyd Henry nodded, but a little smile lingered, like a dab of color on his mouth.

An hour and a half later, they were in Las Vegas, Nevada. It was shortly after noon.

For the first time in his life, Colm found himself at the front desk of a hotel, checking in. Quickly scanning the registration card, it seemed he was going to be able to fill in all the blanks. As far as he could tell, there wasn't any age requirement for getting a hotel room.

"What's the license plate number?" Colm asked Lloyd Henry, who stood sullenly behind him.

"I don't know."

"Go look."

Lloyd Henry pivoted on his right heel and headed for the front door while Colm continued filling out the card. He paused a few moments before filling in the blank for his name. He was strongly tempted to write Colm McCarthy, but he needed to think about whether that would be illegal or dishonest. It wasn't as if he wouldn't be paying them the full eighty-nine dollars for the room, he thought.

When the man behind the desk came back toward him, Colm made a bold decision and tried out his great-grandfather's name for the first time. He had to write it twice; first printing it on one line, and then signing it on the line below. "Colm McCarthy" had such a different look to it from "Colm Drucker"; more peaks and valleys. He wished he could do the signature over, but resisted crossing it out and trying again.

"Smoking or nonsmoking?"

Colm looked up.

"Non. Smoking."

"How will you be paying for the room? Will you be using a credit card?"

"Uh . . . no. Cash."

"And how many room keys will you be needing?"

Colm pondered. He wasn't sure. "Two," he said finally. He could always pocket them both.

"Do you have any luggage?"

"Nope," said Colm, suddenly wondering about his appearance. It had been a long time since he'd combed his hair; or washed his face, for that matter. He'd changed T-shirts once so far on the trip but had worn the same pair of Army-green cargo pants; unfortunately, he now noticed, they had prominent ketchup and chocolate milk shake stains on them.

"The elevators are to your left and halfway up the hall, sir."

"Thank you, sir."

It was very peculiar, but when Colm entered the spacious Holiday Inn room with Lloyd Henry, neither of them carrying so much as a paper bag, somehow it felt smaller than the car. Something about sharing a hotel room with two king-size beds and a giant TV felt unpleasantly tight.

They both stood still for a few moments, each male occupying his own square foot of carpet, each taking in the matching floral bedspreads, the artwork with the Southwestern motif.

"Okay." Lloyd Henry examined the remote to the television and walked over to the bathroom. "What're you going to do?"

"Nothing," said Colm. And then he added, "I might go down to the lobby."

Lloyd Henry nodded.

"I'll be right back up."

Lloyd Henry nodded again and started to enter the bathroom.

"I don't suppose—" he said, stopping. But he didn't finish his thought.

"What."

"Never mind. I know the answer."

"What."

"I don't suppose you want to go see a show. Frankie Avalon and Bobby Rydell? They're playing tonight at Caesar's Palace."

Colm just looked at him.

"See? No. I know the answer is no," Lloyd Henry said stoically. He moved and paused again. "You don't have any nail clippers, do you?"

"No."

"No," Lloyd Henry echoed, disappearing into the bathroom. "No." A mumbled "Doctor No" drifted out as he closed the door. Colm heard the sound of the shower running.

He suddenly thought of something, glanced over at the small plastic dry-cleaning bags hanging by the front door, and went and got one. Then he went and knocked on the bathroom door. There was no response, so he knocked again, louder.

"Who is it?" Lloyd Henry called from within.

Colm rolled his eyes.

"Open the door."

The door opened a crack.

"This is for your cast," said Colm, sticking his hand with the bag through the crack. "You probably shouldn't get it wet.

There was an inexplicably long pause.

After hearing nothing from Lloyd Henry, Colm dropped the bag on the floor and pulled the door shut.

Even though there were two phones in the room, one between the two beds and one on the desk, he headed down to the lobby to call his mother.

The Desert Sands Hotel was about a mile away. After they'd driven past it earlier—Colm, of course, not saying anything—he had been on the lookout for a hotel close enough for him to walk back and forth between hotels. There'd been a sign out in front of the Desert Sands: WELCOME DAYTON, OHIO—CLASS OF '78, and FREE HBO and PIANO LOUNGE.

Fiona's piano lounge. Colm had smiled to himself.

Fiona and Bunny were possibly there, inside, right now. He'd started getting excited.

The hotel's name was up on the roof in giant curvy

script, just like in one of the postcards Fiona had sent him, but because it was daylight, the pink neon letters weren't lit up and the big ugly blocks supporting them were exposed. It didn't project the same allure. The whole city felt to Colm like its central switch was in the off position.

He imagined an extension cord with a giant plug leading from the edge of the city to an outlet in the desert; it was someone's job when it got dark to insert the plug and flood the city's monstrous circuit board with the electricity that was its lifeblood.

Now in the Holiday Inn, Colm had tucked in his T-shirt and located the telephones in a little anteroom off the lobby. As he dialed, he noticed a couple of slot machines near the phones.

"Desert Sands Hotel. May I help you?" The familiar voice didn't sound any closer, but it was, in fact, now 2,500 miles closer. Colm cleared his throat.

"Room 423, please."

"Just one moment, please."

As Colm listened to the phone ring, he tried to figure out what he was going to say. He wasn't at all sure if, or how, or when, he would broach the whole Lloyd Henry subject.

"Hello?"

Colm smiled. They were in.

"Mom."

"Colm!!" Fiona shrieked. "*Colm*, I've been so worried, you haven't called in three days, you haven't answered my messages."

"Well . . ."

"How *are* you, sweetie?"

"Okay."

"We're coming home tomorrow."

"I know."

"I can't wait to see you, sweetheart, I miss you *so much*."

"I miss you, too."

"What have you been doing? Wait a sec, wait, wait, I'm going to tell Cameron you're on the phone."

"*Cameron?*"

"Cameron! Cameron!!"

He could hear his mother moving out into the room and calling repeatedly for his sister. Completely undone by this turn of events, Colm grabbed hold of a lever on one of the slot machines; it moved down an inch and locked in place.

"She's in the shower," Fiona said, returning and picking up the receiver again. "She's going to be so glad you called."

"What is she doing there?"

"Just a sec."

"Mom, what is Cameron doing there?"

"She flew in yesterday. I left you a message, Todd's driving a U-Haul to Atlanta with his brother, and she was so upset about . . ." She paused. "Colm, sweetie. Don said he talked to you about Chester and you know where he is?"

Colm didn't say anything.

"It's just . . . She found his collar in the back hall, and she didn't see him anywhere, and she just . . . She assumed the worst, Colm, she was so upset."

"Why? Cameron doesn't even like Chester."

"No, no, she was upset about *you*, sweetie. She knows how much he means to *you*."

Colm released the slot machine lever. *That* thought had never occurred to him.

"But he's with you—wait a sec . . . she's getting out. She's coming. . . ."

"I have to go."

"Why?"

"I'll call you back."

"Why? When?"

"I'll call."

"Wait, Colm—?"

"'Bye." And he hung up.

"Excuse me." Someone was tapping him on the back of his shoulder. Colm spun around to see a short man in a three-piece gray flannel suit with a cane looking up at him through round spectacles.

"Would you happen to have the time?"

"Yes," said Colm, flustered. "It's . . . uh . . . it's Mountain Time. No, wait. It's Pacific Time. Yeah. Pacific."

Mildly puzzled, the man tipped his fedora and walked away.

Colm sat down on an oak bench across from the phone.

He had been expecting some unforeseen variables on this trip, but nothing like this. Cameron and Lloyd Henry. This was not good. If Cameron caught wind that Lloyd Henry was nearby, that Colm had hooked up with him, all hell would break loose. She would find Lloyd Henry, and she would destroy him. She would rip his cast off and pummel him with it.

He had to rethink everything.

Would he have to forgo seeing Fiona and Bunny? That would be disappointing, but he was going to see them at home the next night. What he wanted was to see his mother sing in a lounge in Las Vegas. Maybe he could see them and not mention Lloyd Henry. Maybe he'd never tell them about Lloyd Henry.

It occurred to him he'd been up all night.

Was Cameron planning to fly back on Sunday with them? He was flying back Sunday, too, but from Bakersfield, California. How could he slip away from them? It would be hard getting away from Cameron, especially if she was feeling sorry for him; she could get carried away when she was feeling altruistic and noble.

"Call me." He stared at the phone.

"Call me." Melanie Phelps's phone number started circulating his brain, around and around. Staring at the phone, he visually dialed her number, observing the pattern it made on the keypad.

"Call me." He shook his head.

He got up and wandered around the lobby, his hands in the pockets of his cargo pants, and eventually drifted into a gift shop that sold newspapers and toiletries. Studying the souvenirs and all the postcards, he tried to get some sense of the town; he had a strong feeling this would be his tour of Las Vegas. He looked through all the postcards of places he would never see: the Guinnness World of Records Museum, Excalibur, the Atomic Testing Museum, the MGM Grand, Cirque du Soleil, and all sorts of other fun-looking places.

The Hoover Dam would have been really interesting.

He bought three postcards, all of the Hoover Dam, and headed back upstairs to the room.

Lloyd Henry was passed out on one of the beds, his legs extended over the end as if he had barely made it from the bathroom and had flopped over, exhausted, a foot shy of the bed. He'd grabbed a corner of the bedspread on his way down and had twisted it around him. He was snoring loudly. His hair was wet, and he had an unopened miniature bottle of the hotel's complementary conditioner in the upturned hand sticking out of his cast.

Colm went and sat on the other bed.

He looked at the digital alarm clock. It was twelve forty.

He could take a short nap and figure things out when he woke up.

Chapter Nineteen

It was pitch-black in the room when Colm, barely awake, suddenly sat bolt upright.

The glowing red digital numbers of the clock were his only reference point, and it took all his concentration as he emerged from sleep to fathom the information they conveyed. There was a nine, a four, and a zero. It was nine forty. *Nine forty.*

In a heartbeat he turned on the light and looked over at the other bed. It was empty.

Lloyd Henry was gone.

Still fully dressed with his shoes on, Colm leapt out of bed.

After quickly glancing into the bathroom, he raced out of the room and down two long corridors past the elevators and the alcove with the ice and vending machines to the stairs. He flew down five flights of stairs and bolted through the ground-floor door out into the lobby, where he alarmed a few mingling guests as he came to a halt and spun around, searching.

"Oh dear," an elderly woman said in response to him, frightened, looking around and clutching at her necklace.

"Sorry. Excuse me," Colm apologized to another woman pulling a suitcase as he tried to get past her on his way out the front door. He ran out into the parking lot, dodging a minivan taxi, and raced around back.

The Ford Explorer was there, in the exact same spot where they'd parked it.

He paused a moment, slightly relieved, and caught his breath. Lloyd Henry couldn't have gone too far, although in Las Vegas maybe next door was far enough.

Colm ran back around to the front of the Holiday Inn and looked up and down the street, ablaze now with flashing neon lights and signs. It was the inverse universe of the dark, empty desert landscape they'd driven through the night before: a black hole had coughed up its innards, spangled celestial matter gone awry.

There were several fast food restaurants nearby, and Colm did a quick tour of them all, buying himself two double cheeseburgers and a milk shake at a Burger King en route. He scoured the area within a quarter-mile radius, wolfing down the cheeseburgers as he went, dropping bits of shredded lettuce and Bermuda onion as he searched for Lloyd Henry in a huge Blockbuster store, a Staples, a convenience store, a couple of bars, and a steak house. Everywhere he went there were slot machines and billboards advertising specials at casinos, nightclubs, and shows.

Colm wondered where Caesars Palace was and whether Lloyd Henry had gone there to see whatever lame group he had talked about.

Feeling in his pocket for the two room keys, he regretted not giving Lloyd Henry one; maybe he'd just stepped out and had wanted to come back. Maybe he'd gone to the front desk and had asked for another key and learned that Colm had registered under Colm McCarthy.

Maybe he was on a bus, heading out of town.

Slurping the last of his milk shake, Colm suddenly realized there were probably restaurants at the Holiday Inn. Dunking his cup and balled-up paper bag into a trash can, he ran back.

Lloyd Henry wasn't in either of the restaurants on the main floor. One of them had a panoramic raw seafood bar that took up the length of one wall, and Colm thought he saw Lloyd Henry in there, eating a lobster with two flight stewardesses, but it wasn't him. Downstairs on a lower level, at the end of a hallway of doors leading into conference rooms all thematically named after legendary outlaws (The Jesse James Room, The Billy the Kid Room), there was a dark lounge with a lone figure at the back sitting at the bar, hunched over.

Colm almost didn't see him.

It was hard to tell in the dim light whether it was Lloyd Henry, but as Colm drew closer, there could be no doubt. He was staring down into his drink, almost as if he were asleep, or closely inspecting something in his glass. A lit cigarette dangled precariously from his left hand, which rested, limp, on the counter.

Colm thought he heard Lloyd Henry mumble something, but the voice might have come from the movie playing on the bar's television overhead.

It wasn't until the bartender looked over at Colm that Lloyd Henry turned and noticed him.

"Hey!" he said, pleased to see him and rousing from his stupor. "Have a seat."

Colm stood behind the bar stool next to him.

"Did you see my note?"

"No."

"I left you a note."

Colm didn't say anything.

"You okay?"

Colm nodded. He was trying to figure out what to do now.

"I'm sorry," Lloyd Henry said, contritely, looking at his glass. "I'm having a drink," he acknowledged. He seemed genuinely ashamed. "Busted," he whispered to the bartender.

The bartender smiled as he filled a few small bowls with goldfish crackers.

"You want a beer? Something?" Lloyd Henry asked Colm. "We have to celebrate. Our last night together." He smiled through a morosely sad expression.

Colm couldn't quite tell if he was drunk, but it was clear this wasn't his first drink. He was slurring his words a little.

"I'll have a Coke," Colm said to the bartender.

"That's the spirit, that's the spirit. Have a seat."

Colm didn't sit down.

"You ever see this movie?" They both looked up at the television. "This is one helluva movie. *The African Queen*. Just started. Your mother used to love this movie."

He put his cigarette down on an ashtray, dropping an inch-long ash in the process, and raised his glass to his lips without looking at it. He took a long slow sip, savoring the movie and the scotch together, and kept the glass cradled against his chin.

"Yeah," he sighed. "Your mother loved this movie.

Humphrey Bogart. Katharine Hepburn. Bogie and Kate." He stared at Bogie and Kate nostalgically as if he were looking through a photo album from his own past.

"How long did you sleep?" Colm asked, collecting data.

"*Long* time. You slept good, huh?"

Colm didn't respond.

"His stomach is growling," Lloyd Henry said, looking at the movie and chuckling, filling Colm in on the plot.

Humphrey Bogart was sitting at a table with Katharine Hepburn and a preacher. Colm assumed they were in Africa. Humphrey Bogart's character, a river-boat captain, was embarrassed because his stomach was making noises. "Just listen to this stomach of mine," Lloyd Henry said the lines perfectly along with Humphrey Bogart. "The way it sounds, you'd think I had a hyena in me." Lloyd Henry laughed, tickled.

"You know, you're a lot like Rosie," he said, looking at Colm and taking a sip. "She's a missionary. She throws all his gin into the river." He shook his head as if he'd suffered the event himself and looked back up at the television. "All his gin."

He rubbed his hand back over his hair, which looked very different now, washed and combed and blow-dried. "So, Colm. What movies do you like?" He turned and fixed a doleful look on Colm that made him squirm.

One more day, Colm thought. One more day.

The bartender put a glass of Coke on the bar, and Colm drank it down quickly.

Not waiting for or expecting any response, Lloyd Henry observed his son swallowing, studying him, forlornly, as if from a great distance, and then he inched his empty glass forward toward the bartender.

"Just one more," he said quietly. "Just one. I promise." Whom he was promising was not clear.

The good thing, Colm was calculating, was that in all likelihood Lloyd Henry wasn't going to be straying far from here in his current state.

A couple of women dressed in strapless gowns and lots of jewelry at the far end of the bar were eyeing them both. Colm wondered if he could hire them to babysit Lloyd Henry; make sure he stayed there. He wanted so badly to run over to the Desert Sands Hotel and just catch a quick glimpse of Fiona singing with the band. Just one song.

"I have to tell you something, Colm." Lloyd Henry leaned toward Colm, who took a step back. "I think you may know this about me, but . . ." He put his head down, pausing to regroup. He was really struggling. "This is not a good place for me to be."

There was a fearful look in his eyes that Colm hadn't seen before.

"I know this town," Lloyd Henry continued, choosing his words carefully. "And this town knows me." He shook his head as if there were a major problem.

"We're leaving tonight," said Colm, deciding on the spot.

"That's good." Lloyd Henry pointed reflexively up at the ceiling for some reason. "That's excellent, because . . . That's very good."

"I have to go somewhere first."

"Where?"

"Very quickly. I'll be right back."

The bartender put a new drink down in front of Lloyd Henry.

"Maybe I should come."

"No."

"I could help you."

"No. I don't need any help."

"Are you sure?"

Lloyd Henry was visibly *dying* to know where Colm was going.

"Give me the car keys," said Colm.

"Okay."

Lloyd Henry stood to reach down into his front

pocket for the car keys. He fumbled them and then handed them to Colm.

"You're driving?" he asked, perplexed.

"No," Colm answered, wishing immediately that he hadn't. He'd just wanted to make sure Lloyd Henry didn't drive off.

"Oh."

"Maybe I should take your wallet."

"I think you should."

The bartender, washing glasses, watched discreetly as Lloyd Henry reached into his back pocket for his wallet and handed it over to Colm.

"No more drinks for him," Colm instructed the bartender while putting Lloyd Henry's bulging wallet in his pocket.

The bartender, who spent his nights witnessing dozens of human dramas, each original in its own way, studied first the solemn younger man and then the older one with the black eye and broken arm.

"He's driving," Colm explained.

"I'm driving," Lloyd Henry affirmed, not quite willing to sit back down yet and give up on the expedition.

"I'll be right back."

"Okay."

"Watch the movie."

"Okay." Lloyd Henry sat down and looked up at the television.

"You *promise*," Colm said sternly. "*No* betting."

"You bet. Just kidding."

Colm glared at him.

"Seriously," Lloyd Henry said, making his most serious face.

"We went to the Grand Canyon," Colm reminded him, as if positing that Lloyd Henry owed him. But that might have been the wrong thing to say.

"We did," Lloyd Henry agreed, but now he was looking sloppily sad again.

Colm stared at him intently, as if trying to glue him to his seat, and then took off.

It was a mild July evening, zero humidity, and stretching his legs as he jogged the mile to the Desert Sands Hotel felt good. Colm hadn't figured out all the details of his plan, but things were starting to take shape. He even felt relaxed enough to duck quickly into a souvenir store and buy a new T-shirt because, unlike Lloyd Henry, he hadn't taken a shower in three days and he felt the need to do some grooming. He picked out a black one with the embossed white head of a wolf on it, raised back and howling. It said NEVADA in small white letters next to the full moon.

On his way out of the store, he stopped to study a pink low-cut T-shirt hanging on the wall with lace around the edges that said LAS VEGAS in silver sparkles. After a few moments, he realized it was something Cameron might wear, not Melanie Phelps. He wouldn't even have any idea what size Melanie Phelps wore. Probably a small. Maybe a medium. The whole idea started to embarrass him and he left.

At a Mobil gas station across from the Desert Sands Hotel, Colm got the key to the men's room and washed his armpits with the Dial liquid soap from a dispenser, using wet paper towels to try to wash his upper body and face. He didn't have a comb, so he just wet down his hair, combing it back with his fingers.

His new T-shirt fit well, and he rammed the old one down into one of the big pockets in the front of his cargo pants.

"Thank you," Colm said, handing the key back to the garage attendant. "You probably know you have a running faucet in there," he added. The attendant, eating sunflower seeds out of a fifty-nine-cent bag, didn't indicate either way. "I tried to tighten it. Probably just needs a new washer." The attendant reached into his mouth to dig out a seed stuck in a back molar.

The parking lot was packed at the Desert Sands Hotel.

Taking a big risk and on the lookout for Fiona and Cameron, Colm slipped through the front door. It was after ten on a Saturday night, and even the lobby was filled with people milling about. The Stardusty Lounge wasn't far down the hall, and luckily, not only were there a lot of people everywhere, the lighting was advantageously dark.

An easel outside the lounge had a big poster resting on it advertising the evening's entertainment. Colm stared at it, grinning from the inside out, thrilled to see several glossy black-and-white photos of Fiona and her band glued at different angles on the poster amidst fancy lettering and a drawing of a spotlit piano.

"Last Night," it said in thick purple Magic Marker. "Fiona and the Desert Fireflies."

This was great. There was a close-up of Fiona in a black sequined dress with her blond shoulder-length hair brushed forward, partly covering her face as she looked over her shoulder seductively at the camera. Colm cracked up.

"Oh my God," he said out loud, unable to stop grinning, his voice lost in the din of the crowd.

Squeezing past people parked in the doorway, he made his way into the lounge and was finally able to hear the music inside. Way at the other end of the room, with keyboard, saxophone, drums, and guitar backing her up, his mother was singing Duke Ellington's "Do Nothing Till You Hear From Me." She sounded so great, Colm thought; her voice relaxed and rich.

Wearing a red lamé dress, she was sitting on a stool center stage, holding a cordless microphone, illuminated in a golden spotlight with purple light on the other musicians and the black velvet curtain behind.

Colm couldn't get over it.

The place was packed. All the tables and seats at the bar were filled and there was a lively crowd standing in the back of the room, talking over the music, drinking. Colm made his way toward the front. He needed to stay hidden but he also wanted a good view of his mother.

"But please do no-thing Till you hear it from me . . ." She was slowing down. The music came to a halt, and she smiled in a provocative, mischievous way before singing the last lyric a cappella, "And you . . . never will." The band jumped in with the last four chords and final snare drum roll, and the audience applauded enthusiastically, Colm among them. Fiona smiled radiantly, looking a little overwhelmed, a little less like a chanteuse and more like someone's mother, mouthing "Thank you, thank you so much," while the band kicked right away into the next song.

Colm grinned as they struck up a very laid-back intro

to Fats Waller's "Ain't Misbehavin'," a song he'd played on his guitar with his mother many times; also on the four-string ukulele she'd bought him for Christmas at Wal-Mart. She liked singing that song at a slower tempo than it was usually played, and he liked the way she fooled with it.

"Are you here alone?" An attractive young woman was peeking over her martini up at Colm, holding the stem of her glass with her fingertips.

It was an interesting question. He had to think about it.

"No," he said, after some reflection, shaking his head.

"Too bad." She shrugged and wandered off.

It was about halfway through the first chorus that Colm caught sight of Cameron sitting at a front table. To his surprise, she was holding Bunny on her lap. He was surprised they'd let her in, but maybe they were making an exception because it was Fiona's last night. Bunny was busy, sporadically waving and shredding a paper napkin; Colm had an overwhelming desire to hug her. Don, looking sporty in a cream-colored knit turtleneck, was sitting with them, staring up at Fiona, transfixed. He looked so smitten that he appeared almost to be in pain.

There was his family. For a moment Colm was overcome. They looked so nice, even Cameron, all sitting there together, all dressed up; a handsome family portrait.

He was even glad to see Don. It was peculiar; his response surprised him, as if he'd forgotten how much he loved them.

It was about halfway through the second chorus that Bunny caught sight of Colm.

For some reason someone had brought the lights partially up. Maybe the band was about to take a break, but as the room brightened, Bunny looked up at the sparkly crystal chandeliers, smiled, and softly crooned, "Light!"

From across the room, Colm heard her clearly.

Two chords later she bellowed, *"Colm!"* at the top of her lungs.

It was the first time Colm had ever heard his baby sister say his name.

Stunned and basking in the moment, Colm unwittingly became one of five people in that room forming a fateful five-star constellation.

Bunny was looking across the room with gleeful delight at Colm, whose gaze jumped tracks from Bunny to Cameron when her face flooded with horror at the sight of Lloyd Henry, making no attempt to hide himself in the crowd, looking like a love-struck teenager as he stared at Fiona.

Colm followed Cameron's gaze back to Lloyd Henry, who was standing near him and who had tears

317

streaking down his face, watching Fiona sing. "Ain't misbehaving . . . I'm savin' my love for you. . . ."

It was a revelation for Colm to witness such an outpouring of emotion from Lloyd Henry for Fiona. It had never occurred to Colm, his whole life long, to consider that his father had loved his mother. Once again he was momentarily frozen.

The time signature of the next series of events sped up exponentially as the constellation blew apart. Cameron deposited Bunny in Don's lap and started clawing her way through the crowd just as Colm dove for Lloyd Henry, grabbed him by his left arm, and yanked him out of the room, hauling him through the dense crowd, which added considerable drag to the task.

"Run!" he said succinctly to Lloyd Henry when he got him out into the hallway.

It was a command Lloyd Henry was familiar with. Drunk as he was, he followed Colm's lead and they both exploded out the front door of the Desert Sands Hotel and started running up the sidewalk, weaving in and out among pedestrians, running as fast as Colm had ever run in his life.

The amazing thing was that as fast as Colm was running, Lloyd Henry was running at least as fast, keeping pace with him. And then something truly remarkable happened. Lloyd Henry actually passed Colm. He was ahead of him, his one good arm pumping like the rod on the wheels of a locomotive. Colm couldn't believe it. Now he strained to run faster, not so much to elude his sister but to try to pass his father.

They ran past their hotel. They ran through and past a motorcycle gang hanging out in front of The Little Chapel of the Wedding Bells; past a film crew, past an arguing couple, a mime blowing bubbles, a young panhandler, and a few firemen assessing a smoking piano crate, the fire truck parked nearby. They continued running at least half a mile beyond the Holiday Inn, Lloyd Henry maintaining his lead, not slowing down a whit until he suddenly veered to the right down a side street and into the backyard of a duplex. Colm followed, and they both collapsed in the dark on the grass by a chain-link fence.

It was several minutes before either of them spoke.

"Did we lose them?" Lloyd Henry asked, half joking.

Colm was still trying to catch his breath.

"You're very fast," he said finally, trying not to show how astounded or winded he was.

"I used to run track," said Lloyd Henry, taking out a handkerchief and blowing his nose.

"In high school?"

"High school. College."

319

Colm didn't say anything.

After a little while Lloyd Henry moaned.

"What?"

"Nothing. Fiona." He moaned again. "She looked so good."

A light in the window of the second floor went on; Colm couldn't see anything through the pulled yellowed blind. He half expected someone to open the window and yell at them, but no one did.

He looked up at the moon through the trees. In a few days it would be full. It was hard to believe this was the same moon that cast shadowy branches on his bedroom wall at home.

"How's she doing? I know you probably don't want to answer."

"She just got married."

"Oh."

Colm leaned forward, unlaced one of his sneakers, and shook some grit out of it. Lloyd Henry, sniffling in the dark next to him, blew his nose again.

"Let's go," said Colm, tying his sneaker back up.

"Okay."

"We have to be careful."

"Okay. Why?"

Lloyd Henry got up and followed Colm, who moved

cautiously around to the front of the duplex, back up the side street, and out onto the main street. Fortunately there were a lot of pedestrians on the sidewalk, and they attached themselves discreetly to a group of Eastern European tourists.

"She's probably driving around looking for us," Colm finally answered.

"Who?"

"Cameron."

"Cameron?" Lloyd Henry stopped. "Cameron was there?" Colm yanked him forward, glancing out onto the street.

"Who did you think we were running away from?" he asked.

Lloyd Henry took so long to answer, apparently overwhelmed by the number of possible answers, that Colm forgot the question.

He was thinking that it was a good thing he hadn't registered under Drucker, because soon Cameron would be calling the front desk of every hotel, motel, and bed and breakfast in Las Vegas and the surrounding areas, searching for them.

When they got back to their room, Lloyd Henry went to his bed, hauled the covers up from off the floor, and fell down on his back.

"Here's our plan," said Colm, hanging out by the door.

Lloyd Henry, legs apart and one arm behind his head, stared up at the ceiling.

"We're leaving at four in the morning. That'll put us in Bakersfield around nine or so."

Lloyd Henry didn't say anything.

Colm kicked off his sneakers and went and sat down on the chair in front of the desk. He turned on the lamp and leafed through some brochures of local attractions and the hotel's notebook binder of information, pausing to read all the menus. There was a breakfast buffet, but it didn't open until six A.M. He studied the glossy pictures of omelets and pancakes.

"That hat you were wearing," he said, looking at a picture of glistening sunny-side-up fried eggs with a side of bacon and home fries. "That was your father's?"

"Yes."

"Why did you throw it into the canyon?"

Lloyd Henry didn't skip a beat.

"Because I didn't have his ashes."

Colm closed the notebook binder, stacked the brochures on top of it, turned off the desk light, and stood up.

He steadied himself for a moment on the back of the chair and then went over and squatted down in front of the mini bar, taking out a Coke and a Toblerone chocolate bar. His headache was back.

"If I watch TV," Colm asked, "will it keep you awake?"

He glanced over at Lloyd Henry, whose eyes were closed. "No," he mumbled.

Colm turned on the TV and put the volume down low. He sat on the foot of his bed and channel surfed.

"I'm sorry I followed you," said Lloyd Henry, drifting off to sleep.

"I'm sorry I brought you to Las Vegas," said Colm matter-of-factly.

Lloyd Henry actually snored a couple of times before muttering.

"Because I screwed up your night?"

"No. I just shouldn't have brought you here."

Colm watched a rerun of *Jeopardy* for a few minutes and then found the weather channel. He watched the local forecast—continuing hot and sunny—and found Turner Classic Movies. *The African Queen* was still on.

After looking unsuccessfully in the minibar and the bathroom for some aspirin, he pulled back the floral comforter, stacked all the pillows, and lay down on his bed, settling in to watch the remaining ten minutes of Bogie and Kate.

Chapter Twenty

Two hours later Colm was running water in the tub for a bath when the phone rang.

He was sitting in the bathroom on the toilet seat, eating minibar Pringles and watching the tub fill, when the first ring startled him so badly, he actually flung some Pringles out of the can. A few ricocheted off the wall and landed in the hot water, where they floated on the currents of the incoming water. Others scattered around the floor.

He grabbed both faucets and turned them off.

Out in the bedroom, Colm watched the phone ring, staring at the flashing red bulb.

After several rings he picked up.

"Hello," he said in a deep voice.

"Yes," a woman responded, "is Lloyd Drucker there, please?"

He had to pause a few seconds to reassure himself it wasn't Cameron.

"Who's this?" he asked, somewhat relieved.

"I'm calling on behalf of Frank Marcusi."

Frank.

"Is Mr. Drucker there?" she asked.

Colm looked over at Lloyd Henry, who was still lying flat on his back on the bed. He was so deeply asleep that, with his left arm flung out and his legs sprawled apart, he had the bearing of someone who has been dropped off the roof of a twenty-story building down onto the pavement.

"Mr. Drucker left a message for Mr. Marcusi to call him tonight," the woman continued. "He said he'd be up late."

"Oh." Colm pictured her working at a big desk in a fancy office somewhere, keeping unorthodox hours in an unorthodox, and possibly shady, business. He wondered if it was the right Frank.

"You're calling from Bakersfield?" he asked.

"We are."

"I'll get him."

"Just one moment please," she said, putting him on hold. The sound track from *The Sound of Music* kicked on.

Colm put the receiver down, went over, and shook

Lloyd Henry. After a while Lloyd Henry manufactured a noise in the back of his throat that a car tire might make slowly coming to a halt on a gravel lane.

"Frank wants to talk to you." Colm continued shaking him more aggressively.

"That's okay," said Lloyd Henry, limp as a rag doll.

Colm went to get the phone.

"You'd better talk to him," said Colm, bringing the phone over and holding the receiver against his ear.

"Huh?" Lloyd Henry said, evidently responding to someone in the phone. "Yeah, what?" His eyes were still closed, sealed like caskets. "Okay." After this short utterance, he remained immobile, passively receiving information as if intravenously. "Okay." Long pause. "Okay. Okay. 'Bye." A perceptible disengagement took place just beneath the surface of his face.

"Are you through?"

"Yeah." Lloyd Henry was rapidly catapulting back into sleep, a skydiver who has just fallen backward out the hatchway of a plane.

"So you talked to Frank?"

"Hmnr?"

"You talked to Frank?"

"Yeah."

"He knows we're coming?"

"Yeah. 'Bye." And he rolled over away from Colm onto his left side.

Colm returned the phone to the desk.

Well, at least there *was* a Frank.

He looked out the window, feeling in his pocket for the wooden apple top his great-grandfather had carved. He rolled it over in his hand, running his thumb over the crosshatching, the stem and raised leaves.

He studied the keypad on the phone a few moments, then picked up the receiver and dialed room service. He couldn't decide between a club sandwich and a Reuben (they'd both stuck in his mind since he'd studied the menus), so he ordered them both with a large side of french fries, a piece of pecan pie, and a brownie sundae with hot fudge sauce and vanilla ice cream.

And a pot of hot tea. In the colder months Fiona would sometimes bring him a pot of tea when he was doing his homework. Now the air conditioner was cranked up, and in his current situation he felt a yearning for tea with milk and sugar.

"Thank you, Mr. McCarthy." That took Colm a little by surprise. He'd given only the room number, not his name.

He sat in the chair by the desk, staring unflinchingly at the door with the focus of a dog waiting for its master to come home.

The most he could hope for, he realized, after the evening's commotion, was that everyone in his family was asleep. His mother; Cameron; even Bunny. If they were awake, they would be in various states of anxiety: confused, possibly worried, possibly angry. Definitely stunned.

This was going to be a hard one to explain.

He blinked his eyes rapidly a few times.

It was exactly two weeks ago, he realized, that he was standing in his yard, gazing down at Chester.

There was a knock, and Colm, initially startled, got up to let the waiter in.

After carefully signing the bill with his new signature, Colm took the tray into the bathroom and placed it on the floor by the tub. Then he closed the bathroom door. The water had cooled off significantly, so after he shed his clothes and got in, he let some run out the drain while adding a stream of pure hot.

When the temperature was comfortable, he lay back and plunged his head underwater. It felt extraordinary, being submerged, as if he were washing off the last three days. Normally he didn't like baths. He didn't have time for them, but now all he had was time. For a few moments he kept his head underwater with just his nose and mouth sticking up, his eyes closed beneath the surface.

He tried letting his eyelids flutter open just a tiny bit, getting a view of the world as a pale watery blur.

It was a restful landscape; consoling.

Remembering the food, he slowly sat up and poured some shampoo from a miniature bottle out onto the palm of his hand. He lathered up and then reached down for a portion of the hefty club sandwich, sinking back down in the water.

"Saturday night in Las Vegas," he thought, chewing on a mouthful of bacon, tomato, toast, and mayonnaise.

He wondered if, when he got back to school, any of his teachers would ask him to write an essay on what I did over my summer vacation. What a laugh that would be, he thought.

A soaked Pringles chip floated across his chest, like a lone lily pad.

After finishing off half the sandwich, he reached down for the piece of pecan pie and was able to cradle it all in one hand as he bit off large pieces. When he found himself eating the last bite, he was somewhat puzzled the pie was gone, because he barely remembered eating it.

Next he went for the brownie sundae. He rested the stem of the glass goblet on his submerged chest and dug into the gooey mess with a large spoon.

He wondered if Lloyd Henry was afraid.

What was Frank going to do with him? His assistant had sounded so cold on the phone; all business.

Spooning in a giant mouthful of melting vanilla ice cream mixed in with warm fudge sauce and a big thick chunk of brownie, Colm didn't savor the medley of rich sugary textures so much as sense that he was fueling up for the daunting task ahead of him.

It was like carbo-loading the night before a race.

An hour and a half later Colm was sipping the last dregs of cold tea when there was a knock on the bathroom door.

"Yeah?"

"You in there?"

Silence.

"Yeah."

Another silence.

"Everything okay?"

"I'll be right out." Colm sat up and prepared to get out.

"Don't hurry."

When they drove out of Las Vegas, it was still dark.

Lloyd Henry had lost one of his black-and-purple argyle socks, and they'd spent a fruitless fifteen minutes searching the room for it, virtually taking apart his bed.

"It's okay," he'd said finally, putting the mattress back on the box spring. "I don't need it."

"I have a pair in the car."

"That's all right. Thanks."

When Lloyd Henry had first looked into the bathroom after Colm had come out, he'd been perplexed and then impressed. "Wow," he said, looking around at the mostly empty dishes and other remnants of a banquet. "The last supper, huh?" He smiled halfheartedly.

Colm didn't think that was funny.

He left a five-dollar bill for the maid.

"Let me leave the tip," said Lloyd Henry, reaching in his back pocket for his wallet.

"No."

"C'mon. "

"No."

At this point, Colm wasn't even sure why he was saying no. What was wrong with Lloyd Henry leaving a tip?

"Uh-oh." Lloyd Henry suddenly spun around. Aiming for all the doors at once, he shifted from foot to foot to foot, in a panic.

Colm, remembering, reached into his pocket and handed Lloyd Henry his wallet.

"Onh." Lloyd Henry moaned with relief, shaking his head. "That would have been bad. That would have been *really* bad."

"You ready?"

"See the picture?"

"Huh?"

"Picture of you?"

"What." And then Colm, annoyed, realized what he was implying. "I didn't look through your wallet."

As Lloyd Henry opened up his wallet, ostensibly looking for a picture, Colm instinctively backed away.

"You and your puppy."

Colm paused for a second. That such a picture existed was a revelation, and that Lloyd Henry had been carrying it around with him all these years was too bizarre.

"Let's go," he said, and he was gone.

They stopped for gas in the outskirts of town, and while he was filling up, Colm looked over at a phone booth. He was going to call Fiona, but not until it was light out and they were a safe distance away. He still hadn't thought through what he was going to tell her.

"So," said Colm, now buckled in and looking at the map. "We want Route 15 south to Barstow."

"Route 15 south to Barstow," Lloyd Henry echoed

quietly. He started up the engine.

Colm continued studying the map. In less than an hour they'd be in California. Right over the border, the Mojave Desert began and extended out into the middle of the state, north of Los Angeles. They'd be passing through the Mojave National Preserve and an area called Devils Playground. Colm, his brow furrowed, examined the area up close near the ketchup stain on Nevada and wondered why it was named that.

Devils Playground made him think of Gammy, his God-fearing grandmother, and of the fact that it was Sunday and they should probably look for a church. Then it struck him. In all his planning, it had never occurred to Colm that he would be turning his father in on the Sabbath.

He took the mahogany top out of his pocket and, staring out the window, pressed the pointed tip of it into his forehead as he rested his elbow on the door.

For the whole trip, the closer they'd got to Bakersfield, the farther away it had felt, but now suddenly their final destination seemed to be charging toward them. Strangely, Colm wasn't sure he was ready.

The phone call at two in the morning had disturbed him. Why did they want Lloyd Henry? What had he done? What were they going to do with him?

The sun came up behind them. They were always driving away from the sunrise, heading west toward that section on the 360 degrees of horizon that swept around them where the sky was darkest, where night lifted off last.

"You don't have any gum, do you?" Lloyd Henry asked.

"No."

"Mint?"

"No."

"My mouth is dry." He pressed his lips together and ran his tongue around the inside of his mouth, trying to drum up some saliva.

There was a diner just outside Barstow where they stopped for breakfast. Lloyd Henry ordered a grilled corn muffin and a cup of coffee, and Colm stepped outside to call Fiona on a pay phone on the side of the building.

"Desert Sands Hotel!" It was her, the operator with the neon-pink script voice.

"Hello, this is C-o-l-m," said Colm, spelling out his name before she felt obliged to.

"Hi! I'll connect you to room 423!"

"No, no," he said. "I just want to leave them a message."

"Sure!"

"Do you have a pencil?"

"I have a pen."

Colm was still thinking through his message.

"Is pen all right?" she asked, after a while.

"Okay, this is the message. 'Hi, everybody. I'm fine. Have a great last day.'" He spoke slowly, pausing to give her time to catch up. "'See you soon in Massachusetts. Mom . . .'" He paused again. "'. . . You were awesome last night. Colm.'"

"C-o-l-m," she said eventually, giggling as if the spelling of his name were a running joke between them.

He worried how the message appeared on paper in her handwriting; she'd probably loaded it up with exclamation points and had dotted the i's with curlicues or little hearts.

"Could you deliver that to them right away?"

"I sure will, Callm."

"It's very important."

"You bet."

"Room 423."

"I'm all over it!"

"Thank you."

When he went back into the diner, Lloyd Henry hadn't touched his grilled corn muffin; each half had a large pool of butter collecting in the center.

"I'll be out in the car," Colm said, for once in his life not hungry.

Lloyd Henry just nodded. His face was washed out, pale behind the column of smoke rising from his cigarette parked in an ashtray.

Colm didn't feel great about not talking to Fiona, but he hadn't wanted to risk having Cameron answer. He just didn't feel up to explaining himself to his sister. Right now he was short on explanations.

"How would you feel about going to church?" Colm asked as they drove into Barstow.

Lloyd Henry flinched.

"You want to go to church?" he asked.

"It's Sunday."

"Hunh."

A few blocks later they passed a large church with a welcome sign out front.

"That was a church," said Colm.

Lloyd Henry let a car pass them and then backed up. He pulled into one of the few vacant spaces in the lot, turned off the engine, and looked at Colm as if he had done his part.

"You coming?" Colm asked.

"I'll wait in the car. I'm not big on church."

Colm thought for a few moments.

"Here," Lloyd Henry said, reading his mind and offering him the car keys. "Don't worry, I'm not going anywhere."

Colm took the keys and looked at the church.

"It might be good for you," he said.

Lloyd Henry shook his head. "Not my thing."

"Do you believe in God?"

"Mmnr," Lloyd Henry mumbled, wincing. He rolled his head around.

"Do you?" Colm asked again.

Lloyd Henry looked down at his lap, struggling for an answer. "Ohh . . . I'm into . . . what." He looked up. "Buddhist? Hindu . . . *karma* kind of thing."

"Karma?"

"You know, what goes around . . ."

Colm turned his gaze from the church to Lloyd Henry.

"I don't know."

Lloyd Henry licked his dry lips and thought hard for a little while.

"Well. Take me, for example."

"What about you?"

"Broken arm. Knee smashed up. Black eye. I'm a mess." Lloyd Henry looked out the side window, reflecting. "This whole trip . . . this whole trip has pretty much been a disaster."

Colm didn't say anything.

"Not that shit wasn't happening *before* this trip, but . . ." He gazed off at a family, all dressed up and late for the service, hurrying up the walkway to the church.

"Karma. Poetic justice," he mused, looking down at his broken arm. He flashed Colm a quick and feeble smile; almost apologetic. "God? I don't know. Jury's out on that one."

Colm stared at him. He was suddenly moved to ask him a barrage of questions: about where he was living, what he was doing, about track; about what distances he had run in high school and college and what his best times had been.

"Go on," said Lloyd Henry. "You go in. Don't worry. I've got plenty to do."

Colm opened the door and jumped out.

He turned toward the church building and hesitated. It took some effort for him to walk up the path.

The service was very different from the ones Pastor Steve gave. For starters the minister was a woman. And there were other differences: a call and response, hymns he didn't recognize, a big lavish pipe organ. This church clearly had more money than his church, and he felt a little uncomfortable being there even though the woman sitting next to him was friendly and tried to help him find his place in the book.

The minister was talking about tolerance in what seemed to be a positive way. Pastor Steve wasn't big on tolerance; he always said that the truth was more important than tolerance.

Colm wondered what counsel Pastor Steve would give him about his current situation. Was it a sin to turn your father in for a big cash reward? Were there any circumstances where it might be all right? What if your father didn't even believe in God and didn't know right from wrong and had abandoned his young family before his son was old enough to speak?

Restless, Colm looked out the window. He recalled two weeks ago looking out the window of his own church, watching a tall man in a knit wool hat out by the oak tree, eating a sandwich and doing tricks ineptly with a yo-yo.

That was before Lloyd Henry had broken his arm, riding a bicycle.

The yo-yo. The bicycle. The skateboard. The baseball and gloves. The unopened kite. Lloyd Henry had collected them all, like vocabulary of a language he'd never gotten to speak; for him they were all verbs, activities, and in the doing of them he'd hoped to create a noun, something concrete, a meeting place where he and his son could be together.

They were like the parts of a machine, the yo-yo and the rest; gears and wing nuts and belts and screws and bolts. With them Lloyd Henry had tried to construct something resembling a boyhood; Colm's boyhood and the sharing of it with him.

But Lloyd Henry was right, Colm thought; it had all been a mistake. Like the 112 men who died building the Hoover Dam, Lloyd Henry was getting maimed on the construction site, run over again and again. And it had nothing to do with karma, he thought. Lloyd Henry was being mangled by his own poorly designed time machine. You can't create the past in the present. It was too late.

It was simply too late.

Chapter Twenty-One

Frank wasn't home.

His house was Spanish-style pink adobe, with several balconies and ornate wrought-iron features. It was impressive from the street, with a well-manicured lawn, Colm noted; beautifully landscaped with all kinds of colorful exotic flowers. Birds of paradise, bougainvillea, palm trees.

Lloyd Henry had rung the doorbell on the gate twice, but no one had answered.

They'd already been waiting out on the sidewalk twenty minutes and Colm was growing increasingly skeptical.

"That's a funny-looking bird, huh?" Lloyd Henry was looking up at a little green bird in a magnolia tree on the other side of the wrought-iron fence. "What do you think that bird is? Never saw a bird like that flying around."

Colm pushed the doorbell again.

"He'll show up," said Lloyd Henry. "Don't worry. Frank always shows up."

Colm stuck his hands in his pockets and looked up the street.

"So what're you going to do with seventy thousand dollars?" Lloyd Henry asked, still looking at the bird. "Buy a car? Go around the world? Seventy grand. Lot of money."

He didn't really seem to be expecting an answer and he didn't get one.

"Bakersfield has an airport, right?" Colm asked after a while.

"Yeah, I'll give you a lift. You in a hurry? I could take you to the airport right now."

"No."

Lloyd Henry watched the bird fly across the front yard to the branch of a lemon tree.

"What, you want to meet Frank?"

Colm looked annoyed. Of course he wanted to meet Frank. Lloyd Henry had the money, but Frank was the one who was going to pay him. What joint enterprise had landed them the money Colm didn't even want to think about.

"See my fate? Check out the executioner?" He was still staring at the bird.

"What executioner?" Colm asked.

"Just kidding."

Lloyd Henry had left his sunglasses on the dashboard, so he squinted in the bright sunlight at Colm, who was staring across the street at a Jaguar parked in the driveway. He'd never seen one before, and if he hadn't been feeling so ill at ease, he would have crossed the street to look at it up close.

He was not feeling good about his current situation. And he was having a hard time gauging how Lloyd Henry was doing: whether he was anxious or scared to meet the man who had a reward out on him.

"You're a good kid, Colm. You're a good kid."

A car drove up the street but kept on going.

"Here."

Colm turned to look at Lloyd Henry, who was extending what looked like a check toward him.

"Take it. It's yours."

Colm, frozen, kept his hands in his pockets.

"Go on."

Hesitantly Colm stepped forward and took the check. It was a bank check made out to him in the amount of seventy thousand dollars.

"See?" said Lloyd Henry. "Man of my word."

Colm looked at his name typed out.

"How does this work?" he asked, momentarily confused.

"It's a bank check. You take it to a bank."

"I thought you said cash." Colm pursued the line of questioning not because he was being critical, or was disappointed. He'd just imagined a stash of large bills, hidden somewhere in the Explorer; maybe in the brown case in the back. He hadn't expected the entire amount to be contained in one small check. And he hadn't expected it to come from Lloyd Henry.

"Well," said Lloyd Henry. "That's a lot of cash to be carrying around. Gets bulky."

Colm barely heard him.

"It's good. It works. We could go to a bank now if you want."

"No. That's okay."

The words SEVENTY THOUSAND DOLLARS were actually typed out on the line below his name. He stared at the three words. It was hard, initially, to fathom that those three words on that piece of paper actually *were* seventy thousand dollars; different from the same words in Lloyd Henry's letter that described a cash reward.

"Yup. Man of my word."

Lloyd Henry looked up the road. Eyeing something, he sniffed and rubbed his nose with the back of his hand. Over Colm's shoulder, he saw a white Cadillac coming down the road.

"Well, well," he muttered. "Speaking of the devil."

Devil was one of very few words that could have penetrated Colm's concentration at that moment.

He turned, and together they watched a white Cadillac pull up to the curb and come to a smooth stop. The tinted window in the back rolled halfway down while up front the driver got out: an elegant young woman dressed in sleek pants with a peach silk vest and a buttoned-up ruffled white shirt. She came around to greet them.

"Hi. I'm Abigail," she said, sliding back her sunglasses and extending her hand to shake Lloyd Henry's. "Oh." She stopped, noticing his sling. "I see you've had some kind of mishap."

"You see right," said Lloyd Henry, smiling benignly.

"Hi." Abigail, not missing a beat, extended her hand to Colm.

But he was holding the check in his right hand, and at that moment it was immobilizing that arm. He didn't have the presence of mind to transfer it to his left hand.

"Hello," he said.

"I hope your trip was enjoyable." She addressed them both in a straightforward and pointedly pleasant manner.

"Well," said Lloyd Henry, shrugging noncommittally, "we made it."

"Mr. Marcusi is on the phone. He'll be with you shortly."

Lloyd Henry nodded.

They could hear Mr. Marcusi talking in low tones inside the car. At one point he stuck a hand out the window and waved. Then he held up an "I'll just be a moment" finger.

"And where is it again that you've come from?" The phrasing of her question combined with her quizzical look laid the groundwork for an exotic reply; as if they might have come from Ukraine, or maybe the Pleiades.

She was unquestionably the woman Colm had spoken with at the hotel who had called on Frank's behalf.

"You've heard of Massachusetts?" Lloyd Henry fell into a conversation with Abigail that, for Colm, was increasingly muffled by the widening gap between him and them.

They were grounded on the sidewalk somewhere in California while he was drifting away into new territory, riding the bumpy thermals of possibility. The small rectangular piece of paper he held up in front of his face was acting like a mainsail picking up wind, catching momentum; hoisted up the flagpole that was Colm, it had the makings of the flag of a new realm.

He was in a mild state of shock.

"Drucker-r-r-r-r!" It was a gravelly low voice, and it belonged to the short squat man emerging from the backseat of the Cadillac. He was wearing shorts and sandals and a short-sleeved gray silk shirt with colorful billiard balls silk-screened on it. For someone with a lot of money, he had skimped on his hairpiece; the dark and light shades of auburn were distributed throughout the coarse weave in ways that did not reflect the natural aging process. They might have been painted on with brushstrokes by a mildly enraged fashion designer whose supervisor has left for the afternoon.

"Fra-a-a-ncis," said Lloyd Henry, holding out his good arm.

Frank, clutching two large bags of what appeared to be birdseed against his chest, reached out and yanked Lloyd Henry toward him. He was at least a foot shorter, and his face wound up in Lloyd Henry's right armpit. He pulled back and thumped Lloyd Henry on his chest above the sling a few times.

"Look at you, what is this, domestic violence? Here." He handed Lloyd Henry one of the bags of bird-seed. "Abigail, get the ladder. Did you meet Abigail, my assistant? Oh . . . my . . . God. Look at this guy." Frank was looking at Colm with astonishment. "Look . . . at this guy. This your kid?"

"This is him," said Lloyd Henry quietly. Proudly.

"Can you believe it?"

"I know."

"Can you believe it?" Frank repeated, evidently having trouble believing it.

"Good-looking kid, huh? Smart as a whip."

"Does he look like Fiona, or what."

"Yeah, he does."

Frank reached up and slapped Colm affectionately on the face.

"Your mother liked me better."

"No, she didn't."

"I knew you when . . ." He sighed.

"He was one day old."

"That's right. One day old. My God. Time flies, doesn't it, Drucker?" He was studying Colm as if staring off at a view, a scenic overlook, so lost in thought that he stared right past Colm's bewildered expression.

"It does," affirmed Lloyd Henry.

"Whose money is behind this check? Yours or his?" Colm asked Lloyd Henry, completely mystified by their friendly rapport. He had been expecting animosity; conflict.

His interjection was so out of kilter with the warm nostalgia brewing that it passed on through without landing.

Lloyd Henry heard but pretended not to.

"Yup. Time flies," he reiterated and, with his tongue

fluttering behind his lips, he produced a quiet rendition of a helicopter taking off.

"Okay, we've got to save this bird," said Frank, through with his brief reflection on the properties of time. "You hungry? I've got some tiramisu thawing in the kitchen. It's excellent. From Trader Joe's, but first we've got to save the bird. Abigail, you have the ladder?"

Abigail had already toted the new eight-foot aluminum stepladder into the yard.

"I've got a two-million-dollar house, no stepladder. We just went and bought one. You were waiting out here? Why didn't you go in? Sit by the pool? You know your way around. "

"Aaa." Lloyd Henry shrugged.

"The gate was open. You look like shit."

"I know."

"What happened to you? Did you see the bird?"

"Little green bird?"

"Yeah."

"Chunky beak?" Lloyd Henry held his cupped hand up over his mouth area, demonstrating. "Like a parrot?"

"Yeah."

"He was just over there." Lloyd Henry looked around. "There he is. He's up on your balcony."

The bird was sitting on the wrought-iron railing

around a second-floor balcony. He was calm and appeared to be looking down at them.

"There he is," Frank said, pleased. "He's a lovebird."

"Hunh."

"This neighborhood is crawling with cats. Christ, there's one now," he muttered, suddenly charging a bush. "Get out of here! Go! Go on! Get out!!" An over-weight calico cat, hunkered down and seemingly ready to take on Frank, finally scampered away. Frank returned, put his hands on his hips, and looked up at the bird. "We've got to catch him."

"He's your bird?"

"No. He's a sign. My horoscope. This morning. Here, open up a bag. Throw up some seed."

Colm watched as the two men opened the bags of birdseed and threw handfuls of sunflower and mixed seed up into the air to attract the bird. He watched as Abigail moved the ladder hither and yon about the yard—back and forth, around and around—following the bird's move-ments until, fifteen minutes later, she had to leave on an errand. And then it was Frank who was moving and steadying the ladder as Lloyd Henry ascended with one arm, reaching up to places well beyond his reach.

If the scene were in a foreign film—Czech, or Italian—there might be an accordion playing in the background; tender thirty-second notes meandering in and out of a major and minor key, underscoring the frail complexity of human longing, and several near mishaps.

It wasn't the scene Colm had been preparing himself for these last few days.

He watched, increasingly detached.

At home *he* would have been the one who would have pursued and caught the bird, devising more effective strategies to catch him. But now it was the tall man with the bad karma, standing precariously on the top step of the ladder whisked to various spots around the yard by the short man wearing a lot of gold jewelry.

They didn't even ask him for his help; old friends from New Jersey, they felt complete as a team.

Colm didn't hear an accordion playing in his head. He heard a white rush of sound like surf breaking on a distant shore.

In a way it felt as if it were his own heart that was flitting around the yard, in the form of a bird. Maybe that was because his heart was pounding in his head, and he was trying to catch it, and hold it, and put it back in its cage.

Lloyd Henry's karma didn't cause him to fall off the ladder and break any more bones. After forty minutes of intense and free-form pursuit, he carefully and rather lovingly plucked the bird from the scarlet blooms of an azalea bush. The bird barely resisted, seemingly bored with the chase.

Its body fit snugly in Lloyd Henry's left hand, its tail feathers sticking out one end and its head calmly poking out the other.

When the men rushed the bird into the house, it was as if they'd forgotten Colm.

He remained alone in the yard, holding his check for seventy thousand dollars.

The sun's rays were hot on his face as he recalled standing in his own yard, so recently, holding Chester's dog dish. Now holding the check, he was transfixed in a similar way: tethered to an object in midair. Gripped by the torque of powerful and opposing forces.

He had traveled so far; so far, and yet here he was in the same place.

And it was the same person who found him now, calling him out of his momentary paralysis; only this time he wasn't calling by phone.

"Colm!" Lloyd Henry was on the adobe veranda, sans lovebird. "Come join us."

Slowly Colm looked over. From his waist up, Lloyd Henry was framed in an adobe archway, standing perfectly still, as if he'd been watching Colm.

Colm recalled the sound not of Lloyd Henry's voice, that first time his father had called, but the sound of his pauses on the phone; the sound, really, of the absence of his voice. It was in the photograph of Fiona and Cameron and him skating out on Pontoosuc Lake; Chester trotting over to the ice fisherman sitting on the overturned bucket. It was in the luminous gray sky, the voice's silence; up in the bitter-cold frosted air where snow squalls and other weather passed through. Up where people imagine their dead relatives to be, looking down on them, only he wasn't dead. He was just gone.

Colm remembered staring at the empty sky and listening to Lloyd Henry not talk.

Down below, he and his sister and mother and dog were as present as Lloyd Henry was absent; Cameron, nine years old, laughing and almost falling (almost crying), and Fiona, wearing not skates but big furry boots, watching her son busily clearing the ice with a snow shovel that was taller than he was. Looking at the photograph for the first time in years, Colm had been struck by how vulnerable they all looked out on the frozen lake, the bright colors of their parkas and scarves muted in the wintry landscape.

But the thing that had struck Colm the most was how small he was. Only seven years old and the man of the family; the one who had to watch out for them all.

Standing now in a yard in Bakersfield, California, he remembered that late-winter schoolday afternoon. He remembered how seriously he took the task of clearing the ice so that his sister would have more room to skate. How hard he had to work before it got dark. What he wondered now was how such a giant sense of responsibility could fit inside a person so small?

"You must be hungry." There was the voice.

After only four days, and this was terrible, the voice had already become familiar; in that short period of time Colm must have filed away hundreds of different inflections, tiny subtle shifts in tone and intention and mood. It contained the DNA of Lloyd Henry's character, and now it was embedded in him. How would he get rid of it?

And then Colm realized he must have already done exactly that—scrubbed that same voice from his memory, long ago.

In the very beginning of the family comprised of Fiona and Cameron and Colm and Chester, Lloyd Henry's voice had been present, had joined theirs in a daily chorus. For the first year of Colm's life, Lloyd Henry's voice had been one of the very first sounds to stream into his newborn mind; it must have come in like floodwater, coloring and staining the empty walls like a primary color.

"You okay?"

Colm would have to ask Fiona to put that photograph away. He would always think of Lloyd Henry now when he looked at it. Oddly enough, it had become for him a portrait of the one person who wasn't in it.

"Colm?"

"Okay," he mumbled to himself, aware that he needed to escape his current stance. His first impulses to move didn't work. He was all tangled up.

He tried again, willing the various circuits in his body to reconnect, and slowly he began to walk toward the door. As he held the check out in front of him, it occurred to him that the check was leading him by the hand.

He followed Lloyd Henry into the house and through the garishly decorated downstairs into the kitchen, where Frank was scooping out portions of thawed tiramisu into scalloped crystal bowls.

The lovebird was sitting on a swing in a pagoda-shaped birdhouse on a counter, examining the busy wallpaper design: magnified ivy that threatened to take over the kitchen. There was a cuttlebone near its seed dish and a chunk of mango handsomely presented on a dark-green lettuce leaf.

"Abigail turned me on to this stuff," said Frank. "Wait'll you taste it." And he sat down and promptly started tasting it.

"This isn't a reward."

"Huh?" Lloyd Henry had just bitten off half of a

chocolate wafer, prelude to the tiramisu.

"This money. It's not a reward. You guys are friends."

"What's he talking about?" asked Frank.

Lloyd Henry shook his head and waved it off, signifying it wasn't important. He popped the rest of the wafer into his mouth and sat down.

"Answer me."

Frank raised his eyebrows and kept eating.

"Excuse me?" said Lloyd Henry, though he had heard perfectly well.

"It's not a reward. What is it?"

Lloyd Henry moved the spoon on the table from one side of the crystal bowl to the other. And back.

"It's a payment," he said.

"Payment for what?"

Lloyd Henry took a breath and twitched his mouth around.

"For . . . companionship." He smiled.

"I didn't give you companionship."

"Okay," said Frank, standing up. "Anybody needs me, I'll be outside." He picked up his bowl and spoon and headed for the door. "No yelling. It'll upset the bird."

"We're not yelling," said Lloyd Henry. "Nobody's yelling."

Colm had been wrestling deeply with the whole notion of accepting a reward for turning his father in, but now that it was clear this enormous amount of money wasn't a reward, he had to start all over again.

"Where did this money come from?"

"What, you think I stole it?"

"I don't know if you stole it. Right now I don't know anything at all."

"Okay, okay. First of all, I didn't steal it. Second of all, why don't you sit down. You're starting to give me a headache."

"You told me that Frank wanted you for something you did."

"Frank wanted me . . . to come out. Visit. Okay, so I fudged a little."

"You lied."

"Oh, here we go again . . . the Ten Commandments patrol."

The enormous logjam in Colm was starting to give way.

"Where did this money come from?"

"Does it matter?"

"Yes. It matters."

"Why?"

"Are you serious? Are you *serious*?!"

Lloyd Henry looked over at the lovebird as if looking for support.

"You know, pardon me for saying this . . . but there

are times, and don't take this personally, when you get unnecessarily . . . heavy. You need to lighten up a little."

"You need to *grow* up."

"Oh really? Well, maybe you need to grow *down*. You are *way* too serious for a person of your age. You have a whole lifetime ahead of you to be this serious."

"How can I keep this money? I don't know where it came from, or why it was given to me."

"Just keep it. Enjoy it."

"I can't keep it."

"It was a windfall."

"Windfall?"

"I got lucky. Now you're lucky."

"No."

"You know, you should try saying 'yes' sometimes. Just for the hell of it. Saying 'no' so much . . . it's not good for you. 'Yes.' 'Yes!' Pulls your mouth back up, like a smile. Feels good. When you say 'no,' it makes you all . . . gaunt." He demonstrated. "Noo-o-o."

Colm just kept looking at him.

Lloyd Henry looked away and regrouped. "I wanted to give you something."

"Why?"

"Because." He sipped one of the little glasses of pineapple juice Frank had poured for them.

"Maybe you don't deserve to give me something."

"You are brutal. You know that? You are brutal."

"I'm sorry. I'm sorry I agreed to come on this trip."

Lloyd Henry wiped his brow with a cloth napkin and then snapped it lightly in the air a few times.

"A disaster," he said, echoing his previous pronouncement. "Before, you hated me. Now you *really* know what you hate."

"What you wanted was—" Colm paused, and then proceeded. "You wanted the person you think is your son—"

"*Think* is my son?" he interrupted Colm. "I've got news for you. . . ."

"To be with you when you scattered your father's . . . whatever . . . at the Grand Canyon."

Lloyd Henry leaned back in his chair. That, of course, was exactly what he'd wanted.

He wrapped the napkin around his hand by flipping it around, and then he wrapped it around the other way and gripped it. With the cloth around his fingers, he punched the edge of the table lightly, as though he had a boxing glove on. Feeling defensive, he went on the offense. "And what would be so terribly wrong with that, Mother Teresa?"

"You thought you could buy me."

"Oh, Jesus."

"How do I give this back to you?"

"You don't give it back to me."

"How do I?"

"Look. Why don't you think about it."

"Can I just sign it over to you? Or is it too much money?"

"Colm . . ."

"Do I take it to a bank and deposit it, and then write you a check?"

"Think about it. You're overreacting. Someday you might need some money."

Colm gripped the mahogany top in his pocket, hand carved by Colm McCarthy from the same hunk of wood as the masterfully carved mantelpiece at 43 Palmer Street, the house with the NO TRESPASSING sign out front that was currently up for sale.

"We need to go to a bank. And then I need to get to the airport."

"Okay, fine."

Lloyd Henry stood up. Colm walked out of the kitchen.

Chapter Twenty-Two

They drove in silence to the airport.

The banks were closed. It was Sunday.

"You have your ticket?" Lloyd Henry asked.

Colm didn't answer.

What he had was a ticket from Hartford, Connecticut, to Las Vegas, Nevada. He was hoping he could pay some kind of penalty fee and use it to travel in the other direction. He didn't even know if there were any flights leaving for Hartford that afternoon.

"That's good," Lloyd Henry said, as if Colm had answered him. "And what airline are you on?"

"Southwest."

"Southwest. Southwest," he mumbled, thinking about something else.

It was about twenty yards shy of the brand-new William M. Thomas air terminal at Meadows Field

Airport that the car faltered and came to a stop.

"Oh, great. That's just great."

Colm looked over at the gas gauge. It was on empty.

"Perfect." Lloyd Henry closed his eyes.

Colm couldn't remember seeing a gas container in the back. He had just bought a small one for Cameron for her birthday; it was a spillproof self-venting container that held one gallon and eight ounces.

"Do you have Triple A?"

"I have Triple F," Lloyd Henry quipped, without elaborating.

Colm got out and opened the back door. It took him a little while to collect all his stuff from the mess back there and jam it into his duffel bag. Lloyd Henry got out and stood on the sidewalk, watching him. He lit up a cigarette but only smoked a few puffs before dropping and extinguishing it with his foot.

"There're a few grapefruit left," said Colm, his head down near the floor.

"That's good," said Lloyd Henry, in a dark mood.

"You want me to clear them out of here?"

"No, no. Just leave them. I'll use them."

Colm closed the door, slung his backpack over one shoulder, and hoisted his duffel bag up over the other shoulder.

"Well," he said, looking Lloyd Henry squarely in the eye.

He was starting to feel better. More like himself. He had no doubt that he was doing the right thing by refusing the money, and with that certainty came an unexpected sense of relief. He didn't have to agonize over it anymore. Financing the purchase of the house was still a daunting problem, but for now he was just glad this trip was almost over. It had been a waste of precious time, but he had to move on.

"Yup," said Lloyd Henry, looking away, and back at Colm, and away again.

Colm extended his left hand toward Lloyd Henry's left hand. They shook briefly.

"So. You're going to mail me a check?"

"Tomorrow," said Colm.

"You don't have to send it tomorrow."

"I will."

Lloyd Henry seemed not to have heard him.

"You've got my address," he said.

"You gave me Donna's address."

"Yup. That'll work."

"I'll express mail it."

"Well . . . no need. I won't be back there for a while."

"I'll express mail it anyway."

Lloyd Henry nodded.

"You need anything? Cash?"

"No."

"No, of course. I can't give you anything, can I?"

Lloyd Henry suddenly got red in the face, and his bloodshot eyes started tearing up.

"I'm sorry," he said, looking pitifully sad. He seemed genuinely remorseful. "I didn't mean to lie to you. That wasn't my intention."

Colm was amazed by how grounded and clear he was feeling.

"I know," he said more softly.

He gave Lloyd Henry one last look.

"'Bye."

Lloyd Henry didn't risk speaking. He folded his lower lip under and nodded.

Colm waved with the fingers of the hand that was holding the strap of the duffel bag, turned, and took a few steps. Then he turned back.

"You know," he said against his better judgment. "You have given me something."

Lloyd Henry appeared oddly rooted in the sidewalk; as if he might spend the day and possibly the night there.

He'd run out of gas about the same time as the car.

"You were my role model."

"Yeah, right."

"My role model of who not to be."

Lloyd Henry, seemingly willing to hear anything at this point, leaned slightly toward him, listening.

"Everything you were I resolved not to be. Growing up, I heard all these stories about how you were a liar, how irresponsible you were. So I was going to tell the truth. Always. And be responsible. You were a compulsive gambler, so I will never, ever, gamble. You screwed up, so . . . I won't."

Lloyd Henry didn't respond right away, chewing on what Colm had said.

"Well." He finally spoke. "I guess that's something."

"It is," said Colm. "It's something."

Staring at Lloyd Henry now, Colm was able to start seeing him more clearly. He wasn't Satan, or even Satan's helpmate. He was just a worn-down middle-aged man with graying hair who had wanted to retrieve something he'd thrown away a long time ago.

He had left them, and they had made do without him, Colm thought. He and Fiona and Cameron had managed to fill in the hole of his absence; close it up like a hole in the ice that freezes over.

"I did give you something. Else. Once," said Lloyd Henry.

Colm adjusted his backpack.

"A puppy."

Now it was Colm who felt a flush in his face.

"The day I left. I don't know if you know—you probably do, but—I really screwed up. Before I left. That's *why* I left." He seemed about to launch into how he screwed up, how he'd bet their house away, but then he backed off. "You can ask Fiona—she's probably already told you, but . . . I let you all down. I had to leave. I had to remove myself before I did any more damage."

And here he stalled out.

"So . . . you got me a puppy?" Colm, his curiosity getting the better of him, gave Lloyd Henry a jump-start.

"I did," he said. "I went to the pound and got you a puppy. Named him Chester."

"*You* named him?"

"I named him after the horse I should have bet on. Baltimore Chester. The horse that beat me." He shrugged. "I wanted to leave you with a winner."

Now Colm was stalling out. It was time for him to go.

He gave Lloyd Henry one last furtive wave and took a few steps toward the terminal.

Once again he stopped and turned back. Lloyd Henry was continuing to sink into the sidewalk, as if standing in freshly poured concrete.

"There's someone you need to call," said Colm.

Lloyd Henry watched him come back.

"The man who hit you. On your bike."

Lloyd Henry was more focused on Colm's movements than on what he was saying. He had geared himself up so much to watch Colm walk away that when he returned, it was almost disorienting; as if he'd been surfing, board ready, and an anticipated wave had suddenly reversed direction.

"Let me have your cell phone."

After a few moments Lloyd Henry took out of his pocket first a folded-up postcard of the Grand Canyon and a small red rock from the canyon, then some gum wrappers, a half-eaten stick of beef jerky, and finally his cell phone.

"Why?"

"He wants to apologize to you."

"To me?"

Colm took the phone and started dialing the hospital, just in case Mr. Hafferty hadn't been released yet. His hope was that he was home. Fortunately, when Colm had visited him last, he'd made sure that Mr. Hafferty had his house key, because he wouldn't be able to let him in from here.

"He doesn't have to apologize."

Colm was calculating; it had been exactly a week

since Mr. Hafferty had mowed Lloyd Henry down.

"I wasn't riding very well. The last time I rode a bike was . . . I don't know . . . maybe thirty years ago."

"Hello. Yes, I'd like to talk to a patient." Colm waited while he was being transferred.

"I'm not used to hand brakes."

"Mr. Hafferty. I think he's in room 218."

"Foot brakes, that's what we had in Jersey. You backpedal and bingo, you stop."

"He is? Oh." Colm looked disturbed. "Yes. Please."

Colm put his duffel bag down on the sidewalk. "They put him in critical care," he said, as much to himself as to Lloyd Henry.

This was not good news.

"Hello?"

"Mr. Hafferty. It's Colm."

"Colm?" Mr. Hafferty's voice sounded frail. "I'm back."

"Back from where?"

"I was in a coma. But I'm back."

"How long were you in a coma?"

"I don't know." There was a pause. Colm assumed he was trying to remember. "You want me to ask someone?"

"No, you're feeling okay now?"

"I feel pretty good." He sounded cheerful.

"When can you go home?"

"I don't know." There was another pause. "You want me to ask someone?"

"That's okay. Mr. Hafferty, I found the man you hit."

"That wasn't you in Pennsylvania, Colm, was it?"

"It was me. I've been on a trip."

"I've been on a trip, too. But I'm back."

"I'm coming home today, or tomorrow."

"That's wonderful. I'll tell them to get us some éclairs."

"I'll bring some. And some Dunkin' Donuts coffee."

"Ohh," he sighed. "I could use a good cup of coffee."

"But first . . . I've got the man you hit."

There was a silence.

"I hit someone, Colm?"

"In your car. The man on the bicycle?"

"The bicycle? *Colm* . . . you found the man on the bicycle?"

"Here he is."

"Wait. Let me put my teeth in."

Colm waited a few moments.

"His name is Mr. Hafferty," he said to Lloyd Henry, covering the phone.

"Old guy, right?"

"He's a composer," said Colm, as if that would put him on his best behavior. "An obscure composer."

Lloyd Henry looked impressed.

"Hello, sir," said Lloyd Henry, taking the phone "How're they treating you? How's the grub?"

Lloyd Henry didn't say anything for a long time.

"Is that right?" he said, finally.

Fifteen minutes later, after listening to bits and snatches of a conversation about hospital food, pretty nurses, driving, old Schwinn bicycles, New Jersey, the weather, the California gold rush, lovebirds, the Smothers Brothers, and Lenny Bernstein, Colm signaled to Lloyd Henry to watch his duffel bag, and he headed up to the terminal to get some information.

The first thing he found out was that the nearest gas station was two miles away. The second thing he found out was that Southwest didn't fly out of Bakersfield.

"Really?" he asked the agent at the America West ticket counter.

She nodded sympathetically. "Burbank. LAX. Ontario."

"Are you sure?"

"I'm sure," she said, looking past him at the next customer in line.

He had expected to have some difficulty with the airline, but not that it wouldn't be there.

Finally moving aside, Colm went and stared despondently at the arrival and departure boards for a while. Then he went and called up Southwest.

Burbank and Los Angeles were the closest airports they operated out of. He was pleased to find out that at least he could use the ticket he had without any penalty; furthermore, it wouldn't cost him any more to fly from California than from Las Vegas.

Unfortunately flying *to* Los Angeles on any of the other airlines was going to cost four hundred dollars. That was way too much money, particularly since he didn't have seventy thousand dollars anymore. Staring up at the blue sky through the terminal's dazzling new skylight, Colm thought of Odysseus (they'd just read *The Odyssey* in sophomore English) and how the short trip he'd envisioned had morphed into an endless obstacle-filled journey.

He'd have to take a bus, or hitch.

But first he had to get his duffel bag.

As he walked along the sidewalk toward Lloyd Henry, he wondered how much it would cost to take a taxi to the bus station.

Lloyd Henry, standing way over near the SUV that was out of gas, was off the phone and appeared to be busily guarding Colm's duffel bag, staring down at it as if it might sprout legs and walk away. In point of fact he was deeply lost in thought.

So lost in thought that when Colm came up and stopped two feet away, he didn't notice. Colm stood by, realizing he'd never called Lloyd Henry by his name. He'd never called him anything, largely because he hadn't ever really wanted to address him. But now he did, and he didn't know how to address him.

When Colm picked up the duffel bag, Lloyd Henry continued staring down at the space where it had been.

"I'm going," said Colm.

Lloyd Henry finally raised his head and fixed his gaze on Colm. There was a discernible change in his expression. In his whole bearing. It was as if something had lifted him up out of the concrete.

"You're all set?" he asked.

Colm nodded.

"You want me to call Triple A?" Colm asked reluctantly. They had a card.

"No," said Lloyd Henry. "Thanks. Some lady stopped. She's bringing gas."

So that was why his mood was brighter, Colm thought. But it wasn't why.

"Listen," Lloyd Henry said, as Colm started to leave. "There's something I want you to do with that money."

Colm turned to listen.

"Deposit it, but don't send me a check. I want you to go to Berkshire Medical Center in Pittsfield and pay for Irwin's bills."

"Irwin's bills?"

"Mr. Hafferty, your buddy. His medical bills. He's got no health insurance."

Colm looked perplexed.

"Gonna cost him a fortune. Forty grand, easy. All those tests."

Colm looked more perplexed.

"Then I want you to take the rest of the money and get him set up in a good health insurance policy. There should be enough to cover him four, five more years."

He seemed to be serious.

"Why?" It was the one word Colm could get out.

"Why? Because he won't take the money from me. You guys from Pittsfield, you're all weirdos. You won't take money."

He didn't exactly smile, but a lack of tension in his face made him look relaxed in a way that Colm had never seen.

Colm was flummoxed.

"Are you rich?"

Lloyd Henry's brief chortle conveyed that he was not.

"Where did that money come from?" Colm asked, trying to fathom this turn of events.

The last time Colm had asked that question, Lloyd

Henry had resisted answering. Now he responded with only a little difficulty.

"It was an inheritance. From my father," he answered. "Who I hadn't seen in twenty years." He shrugged. "I didn't want to piss it away."

A plane flew overhead, and the noise was momentarily distracting. Colm, reconnoitering, confirmed to himself that he was at an airport, but it was the wrong airport, and he needed somehow to get to the right airport, he wasn't sure by when.

"I'm good at pissing away money."

"You want to pay for Mr. Hafferty's medical bills?" Colm phrased the statement as a question, but he could have served it up in any of a number of ways. He was still in the early stages of trying to assimilate the information. It was going to take a while to wrap his brain around this one.

"What," said Lloyd Henry, "you don't think I deserve to?"

He looked as if he half expected to be reprimanded.

"No, it's not—" Colm didn't finish the sentence.

It was Lloyd Henry's seeming unawareness of the scope of his generosity that was getting to Colm. For a moment Colm thought Lloyd Henry might be insane. It was bizarre. How could someone who was so clearly a loser, a shiftless liar, and a gambler, someone who amused himself by stealing candy bars and making sound effects with his face, have it in him to do something so selfless and, well . . . charitable?

And it was for his dear friend and neighbor, Mr. Hafferty.

"That guy thinks the world of you," Lloyd Henry stated simply, without any overt sentimentality. "Says you've rescued him more than once."

Another plane took off, roaring overhead.

Lloyd Henry looked up. Then he looked over at the new airport terminal.

"They did a good job on this building," he observed. "Good job."

As Lloyd Henry scrutinized the building with his full attention, Colm felt as if he'd been unhitched, like a trailer from the back of a truck. He'd been released.

"You better get going," said Lloyd Henry, looking back at Colm. "You don't want to miss your flight."

Colm didn't budge.

After a full two silent minutes Colm finally spoke.

"Could you wait here?"

"Huh?"

"Could you wait here awhile?"

"Okay."

Colm, thinking hard and ineffectively, nodded. "It might take a while," he reiterated, making sure he'd expressed himself clearly.

"Okay. Yeah, sure. I might have to park the car. I could put it in short-term parking."

"Put it in short-term parking," repeated Colm, barely listening.

"Okay."

"I'll be back," said Colm as he started to leave.

Lloyd Henry nodded, displaying no curiosity about this arrangement. "Take as long as you want."

A white BMW pulled up behind the Explorer, and after a woman wearing a pink-and-white baseball cap sprang out and opened her back door to retrieve a red gas container, Colm headed for the terminal.

He had to eat something. That's all he knew.

He ordered a large barbecue chicken pizza at a California Pizza, and a grande iced coffee with cream and four packets of sugar at a Starbucks counter. Setting his duffel bag and backpack down, he cleared off a small table, threw away the trash, and sat down to eat. When he was done, he ordered another large pizza, chicken chipotle, and a grande vanilla Frappuccino. He ate slowly, chewing each piece carefully, as if a nutritionist had advised him to chew each mouthful thirty times.

Then he called Southwest again and found out that the last flight for Hartford from Los Angeles was departing at 1:30. It was now 12:10. There was no way he could make it to Los Angeles, which was easily two hours away by car.

He went back to the Starbucks counter and bought a large square piece of coffee crumb cake, which he washed down with another Frappuccino. (He wasn't nuts about the Frappuccino, but it was the closest thing he could find to a milk shake in the terminal.) He also got an Odzwalla strawberry mango juice and an expensive chocolate bar with third-world references on the gold foil wrapping.

Then he went back outside.

From a distance Colm could see that Lloyd Henry was there but the Ford Explorer was not.

He noticed something different about Lloyd Henry, and as he got closer he realized that now he was wearing the pink-and-white Dodgers baseball cap. It was hot, especially out on the sidewalk, and the gas lady must have offered it as protection from the sun. He could have found shade nearby, but maybe he was afraid Colm wouldn't see him.

"Hey," he said affably. He didn't seem in a hurry to go anywhere, content with his post. Having finally found a comfortable place inside, apparently it didn't matter where he was.

The two of them looked at each other a few moments, on new turf.

Whether or not Lloyd Henry deserved to give Irwin Hafferty seventy thousand dollars to pay for his medical bills and a health insurance policy was debatable (a jury would likely conclude they were equally at fault in their traffic collision), but the fact that he was *going to* had engineered a major shift. The magnetic field between Colm and Lloyd Henry had been repolarized.

And it wasn't the cataclysmic quality of the change that was initially so peculiar to both of them, as much as the fact that it had happened so suddenly and unexpectedly. It had come out of the blue.

If a small green lovebird had found itself one moment perched on the windowsill of a window carelessly left open in a Bakersfield condo, and the next moment out in the world, it might experience a similar adjustment.

They stood facing each other now, in repose, as if a referee had called a time-out.

"What's up?"

"I have to get to Los Angeles," Colm said, asking for help. "I need a ride."

* * *

According to Lloyd Henry's loosely Buddhist/Hindu worldview, whose karma was it when Gammy said she wouldn't allow Fiona to sell the family home at 43 Palmer Street? Was it Fiona's? Colm's? Gammy's husband Lou's? Bunny DeCavalho's? Don Schroeder's?

Maybe it wasn't karma. Maybe it was Jesus who stepped in on young Colm's behalf. Jesus, the living God.

Or maybe the undoing of Fiona's plan was the result of an unusual alignment of stars over Mount Carrington on New Zealand's south island. Or the harmonic overtones of a ringing noise in the eardrum of a grazing mule deer up on a plateau by the Grand Canyon.

Or good luck; or bad luck.

Maybe Fiona, after her initial love affair with Las Vegas, would have come to feel guilty anyway and realize her mistake in contemplating a move that would have so disrupted the lives of her children.

Maybe it was Colm himself, tuned in as he was in complex ways to his God-fearing Bible-toting grandmother, who unwittingly affected the course of events. Through some action of his own: a thought; a gesture; perhaps simply by virtue of having told her he loved her.

Whatever the cause, it came to light that not only was the house still in Gammy's name, she did not want it sold.

Fiona's parents had given it to her and her young

children after Fiona's husband Lloyd Henry had gambled away their small ranch house at the racetrack on a horse named Quantum Leap, and disappeared soon thereafter. She had not put the house in Fiona's name for fear Lloyd Henry might return and charm his diabolical self into their lives again, in a position to gamble away the house that her father, Colm McCarthy, had built with his own two hands when she was just a toddler.

It was Cameron, in need of borrowing money and unable to locate her brother, who had called Gammy and innocently mentioned in the process of shmoozing her up that Fiona had gotten married again and was thinking of selling the house.

"Over my dead body," Gammy, never one to mince words, had replied.

This was the news that Cameron was so eager to share with Colm, particularly after she'd found Chester's collar and had assumed the worst. But Colm never returned her phone call.

It wasn't until he flew home from California that he learned the details, minutes after walking into the house: that Fiona and Don weren't moving to Las Vegas (though they were planning to invest in a two-week time-share there), and their house was not up for sale. (At least not, per Gammy's instructions, until Bunny had graduated from high school, at which time it might indeed be over her dead body.)

They were all up past midnight waiting for him in the kitchen—Fiona, Don, Angie, Walter, and Cameron. Angie, wearing a turquoise version of the frilly Nevada T-shirt Colm had eyed for Melanie, had made a welcome-home lasagna, and Fiona had just emerged yet again from her beautiful new laundry room, speechless and teary eyed.

When the front door opened, she raced down the hall to embrace Colm, followed by Angie and the others, except for Cameron, who trotted up the stairs to get Bunny, sound asleep in the little secret room off the landing. Bunny had spent her first day home roaming the house and the yard in search of her brother and the big brown dog, and had finally dragged her worn blanket into that hidden cubbyhole and gone to sleep, her new Las Vegas Beanie Baby armadillo with her.

They kept assuring her that Colm was coming home soon, but no one could tell her when.

Colm hadn't called again to tell them. And he didn't need a ride home from the Hartford Airport, because someone was waiting for him there.

When Lloyd Henry dropped Colm off at a Holiday Inn in Burbank, not far from the Bob Hope Airport on

Hollywood Way, he took a room for himself, too. He hadn't planned to; he was just exhausted. Colm hadn't protested and in fact had actually let him pay for both rooms. They were both so tired that they slept through the afternoon and evening well past midnight.

They woke up within half an hour of each other and both watched television all night long, separately in their own rooms on different floors.

Around six in the morning Lloyd Henry knocked on Colm's door after reading the breakfast menu that Colm had filled in and hung on his outside doorknob.

It was Colm's idea to go see the Pacific Ocean before his flight.

At seven thirty in the morning, there was a surprising number of joggers and vacationers out on the beach near the Santa Monica Pier. It was an overcast day, and that particular morning a solitary blue whale was hanging out not far beyond where surfers paddled, waiting for waves.

"Chester died," Colm told Lloyd Henry after he had run along the beach by himself and joined his father, who was sitting on a bench overlooking the ocean.

"*Really?* I'm sorry to hear that. Sorry to hear that."

Colm took a swig from the half-gallon carton of orange juice they'd picked up at a convenience store and put it back under the bench.

"He was a great puppy," Lloyd Henry said sadly, looking out at the water.

Colm stared straight ahead too.

Sitting side by side, Lloyd Henry on the left and Colm on the right, it was as if they were still driving and someone had lifted the car up over their heads and taken it away, leaving them exposed out on the grassy overlook. Still facing west.

A young boy in baggy shorts, wearing an iPod, elbow pads, and knee pads, skated by on his Rollerblades on the paved path behind, but they didn't see him.

Colm thought about asking Lloyd Henry about his father, but it was all he could do to tell someone for the first time that Chester had died. And who better to break the news to than the person who had picked him out of all the puppies at the animal rescue shelter and adopted him.

So they didn't talk about Lloyd Henry's father, about how he had died of liver cancer in a VA hospital that winter. How Lloyd Henry's aunt had insisted he not be cremated, even though he'd told Lloyd Henry (who'd showed up at the last moment, as soon as he'd heard) that he wanted his ashes scattered in the Grand Canyon.

They didn't talk about track, or the New Jersey state record that Lloyd Henry set in the 10,000-meter event when he was sixteen.

For the most part they just sat there quietly, watching the freighters on southerly routes out near the horizon; the sailboats, the pelicans, the surfers, the beachcombers.

"We should have brought the kite," Lloyd Henry said at one point.

Colm nodded, absently.

But they had brought the kite. It was in the backseat of the Ford Explorer parked not more than thirty yards away.

They were busy flying a contrivance of their own making, stitched out of the cloth of their new shared past, the line invisible like the fishing line of the ice fisherman sitting on the overturned bucket in the skating photograph. Perhaps he was flying *them* now, down below the ice, reflected up in the luminous gray sky; and that's why Chester had trotted over to take a look, pulled by the lure of the two most important men in his life sitting side by side, mourning his passing.

Maybe the line was the rope that Lloyd Henry had come to the end of.

And now he was doubling back, having found his way.

Colm drank some more orange juice, thinking alternately about Melanie Phelps and the house; they lived next to each other in his mind. He was thinking maybe the next day he'd go talk to Mr. Frangione, his lawyer, and he'd certainly stop in and see Audrey at her Century 21 office to make sure she wasn't showing the house. He wondered if his family had taken down the NO TRESPASSING sign.

It had occurred to him to start buying lottery tickets, but he was concerned they might be a form of gambling.

"We should go," said Lloyd Henry, not moving.

They sat another ten minutes before getting up.

Up the coast to their right, the low cloud cover was burning off and the distant curving view of the coastal towns and the hills rising away from the ocean was quite magnificent, but neither of them looked that way. Nor did they look down to the left, where the big Ferris wheel at the end of the pier was idle, it being too early for the rides to be operating.

They both stared straight ahead; after all, they had come to see the Pacific.

Whether they realized it or not, they had shared a similar journey to this overlook. They both had recently suffered the loss of a member of their family — in fact, the same family. (Lloyd Henry's father never got to meet Chester, but they would have gotten along well; Colm's paternal grandfather could be ill-tempered, but he was at his sweetest with his dogs.) Both Colm and Lloyd Henry had been putting their best efforts into trying either to hold the family together or to reclaim it. In a house. In a snapshot. Both pretty much wanted the same thing.

Colm took the wooden top out of his pocket and spun it on the bench next to him. When he noticed Lloyd Henry looking down at it, he decided to give it to him.

"Here," he said, picking up the top by its stem and handing it over to Lloyd Henry. "Keep it."

"Keep it?"

He could add it to his collection of toys, Colm thought.

Lloyd Henry looked at the mahogany apple, a genuine article from Colm's boyhood, in the open palm of his left hand. For a moment or two he didn't move, didn't breathe, as if a dragonfly had miraculously landed on his hand. His face became flushed, but Colm, staring back out at the ocean, didn't notice. After a while, Lloyd Henry very slowly closed his fingers around the top.

When they got back into the car, Colm picked up the Rand McNally road atlas that had lived under his feet the past few days and tossed it into the back.

Lloyd Henry pulled out of the parking lot, and after taking a left onto Santa Monica Boulevard, they began heading east.

Chapter Twenty-Three

"**I**'m making you my official role model," said Lloyd Henry. "I'm done lying."

Colm bent over to straighten up his bags and backpack because a man carrying a cup of coffee and his open laptop had just tripped over them. They were sitting at the gate, and even though the plane wasn't leaving for another hour, there were already quite a few people there.

Colm had checked his duffel bag, but Lloyd Henry had stopped at a news store in the terminal and bought him a few things for his flight: a couple of magazines, some Good & Plenty, a box of chocolate-covered macadamia nuts, a horseshoe-shaped Bucky pillow, and a postcard of Santa Monica. There was a bench in the picture of the palm tree–lined walk overlooking the ocean; it wasn't *their* bench but it was close enough.

Lloyd Henry had bought the same postcard for himself; it was the closest they came to having a photograph of the two of them from their trip.

Colm didn't really like licorice or read *Rolling Stone* or *People* magazine, but he let him buy those things. It was giving him such pleasure.

"I have to say, though," continued Lloyd Henry, "sometimes what one person might call a lie is really just . . . conversation. Talk. You're fleshing out the story."

"You just have to ask yourself," said Colm, "'Am I being truthful?'"

"Easy for you to say."

"No. It's not easy. Sometimes it's very difficult."

"Excuse me, are these yours?" a voice asked.

They both turned around. Lloyd Henry's car keys had slipped out of his pocket, and the tanned blond woman sitting behind them had spotted them when she'd put her book down on the floor.

"Thank you so much," Lloyd Henry said, taking the keys from her.

"You're so welcome," she responded, tossing him a smile and an opportunity to say more before she reluctantly turned back around.

"Nice lady," Lloyd Henry said to Colm.

"You think all ladies are nice."

Lloyd Henry thought a moment.

"All ladies *are* nice."

"No, they're not."

"Well." He thought some more. "I like to assume they're nice, until they prove me wrong. That way I get to enjoy a little honeymoon with all of them."

An announcement regarding a departing flight came on.

"Let me ask you a question," Colm said tentatively, now that they were on a subject that seemed to be in Lloyd Henry's wheelhouse.

Lloyd Henry was looking down at a very small child who had set up a wooden puzzle of a big red barn and barnyard animals on the floor in front of him.

"What does it mean, when someone asks you to call them?"

"What does this have to do with lying?"

"It doesn't."

"Oh. Okay. Can you repeat the question?"

"So . . ." Colm struggled. "A woman, a girl, is saying good-bye to you, and she says, 'Call me.'"

"Yes?"

"What do you do?"

Lloyd Henry looked puzzled.

"I'm not following you."

"I *know* what 'call me' means," Colm blurted out. "I just don't know what the expectations are."

Lloyd Henry tilted his head.

"Especially if I've waited too long."

"How long?"

"A week."

"A week? You've waited a week? What's taking you so long?"

Colm shook his head and looked away.

"It's not that simple."

"No, of course not. It never is. So . . ." He gestured for Colm to elaborate.

"First, she kisses you—"

"Wait, wait, wait. She kisses you?"

Colm didn't say anything. He'd wanted to lay out the full picture.

"Kisses you how? Nice little peck? On the cheek?"

"No."

"No?"

"No." Colm was starting to get a little red.

"Colm." Lloyd Henry shook his head at this glaring deficit in a young man's education. "Oh boy. Okay. First of all, do you like this person?"

"She's amazing."

"Pretty?"

"Pretty. Unbelievably smart."

"Hmm. Okay. Here's my advice."

Colm listened intently.

"See that pay phone over there? Go over there, pick up the phone, and dial her number. You know her number?"

Colm nodded.

"Of course you do, okay. When she answers, you say, 'Hello . . .' What's her name?"

"Melanie."

"Melanie. Pretty name. I knew a Melanie once." He started to drift off into a pleasant memory.

"Okay." Colm's voice yanked him back. "And then she says, 'Hello,' and then what do I say? She's probably completely forgotten she asked me to call, and I'll have nothing to say, no reason for calling."

"This is what you say. . . ." Lloyd Henry was on solid ground. "This is what you say. 'Melanie. I'm in California, and I'm looking at the Pacific Ocean, and it's a beautiful day—'"

"It's not a beautiful day."

Lloyd Henry looked at him.

"You want to tell her it's a gray shitty day? This is what I mean about fleshing out—"

"Okay, okay," said Colm, briefly cracking a smile. "Keep going."

"So. 'I'm in California, and I'm looking at the Pacific

Ocean, and it's so peaceful and beautiful, and I'm think-ing of you.' That's it. Keep it simple."

"And then what do I say?"

"That's it."

Colm looked dubious.

"Suppose she asked me to call because her father wants me to mow the lawn or something. And then I've put her in this awkward position."

"She kissed you?"

"Yes."

"Colm." Lloyd Henry paused. "Trust me. She will pick up the ball and take it from there. Your work will be done."

"I don't want her to think I'm an idiot." He was remembering, as he had so many times, that Sunday morning at church when he'd seized up and imploded.

"You want her to think you don't like her? Because that's what she'll think if she asked you to call her and you don't."

Why was this so difficult?

"Okay. Go over there, pick up the phone, and tell her what I told you."

Colm, chewing on the tip of his tongue, looked at the phones.

"Tell you what . . . this is better, this is better," Lloyd Henry said. "Tell her you're at the Grand Canyon. Women *love* the Grand Canyon—they find it very romantic."

"I'm not at the Grand Canyon!"

"But you were."

A few heads turned toward them.

"Look," said Lloyd Henry, more quietly. "If you wait till you get home, it won't mean as much. If you call her when you're this far away . . . she's got to appreciate it."

That sounded like a good point.

"You've overthinking this, pal. You're thinking way too hard."

Colm stood up.

He hoisted his backpack over his shoulder and then took it off and put it down on the chair.

"Watch this for me."

"Yup."

Colm stepped over the small child on the floor, who, failing to make much progress with his barnyard puzzle, was becoming increasingly frustrated. As Colm headed, resolute, toward the phone, Lloyd Henry bent over and put in the duck.

Colm walked down the carpeted terminal with the stride of a tradesman newly arrived on the scene, tool belt around his waist. He grabbed the receiver and without hesitation quickly dialed the number he had dialed so many times in his head the past few days. It rang three times, and then she picked up.

"Hello?"

"Hello, Melanie?"

"Colm?"

"This is Colm. I'm in California."

"Really?"

"But I was at the Grand Canyon." He closed his eyes and then rocked back slightly, as if he were teetering on the edge of a great abyss.

"Oh, I *love* the Grand Canyon." Her voice got all soft and warm.

"You do?"

"Colm. I'm so glad you called. When are you coming home?"